The chorus of   there, distinct, firm.   cking and bushes being pushed aside. There was no question that he was still coming. Carrying out the commands of Death and completely under its firm control, his pursuer was determined, definite, undeterred.

Al looked up. Birds sprang out of the trees, their wings flapping frantically. Field mice, squirrels, rabbits passed each other in fright. Something very ominous was upon them. Raw instinct sounded alarm in every living thing and he heard them clearly. His senses were heightened now. Al could almost hear his pursuer's heavy breathing along with his own.

"Why?" he screamed, throwing his voice behind him without pausing to turn. "Why the hell are you doing this? Why now? Why me?"

Publishers Weekly praises Andrew Neiderman's
THE BABY SQUAD:
"[A] nightmarish novel . . . fast-moving . . . intriguing."

. . . and DEFICIENCY:
"Neiderman unleashes a remorseless monster . . . in this
fast-paced medical murder mystery."

The Hunted is also available as an eBook

ALSO BY ANDREW NEIDERMAN

ANDREW NEIDERMAN

THE HUNTED

POCKET STAR BOOKS

New York   London   Toronto   Sydney

This book is a work of fiction. Names, characters, places and incidents are products of the author's imagination or are used fictitiously. Any resemblance to actual events or locales or persons living or dead is entirely coincidental.

An *Original* Publication of POCKET BOOKS

 A Pocket Star Book published by
POCKET BOOKS, a division of Simon & Schuster, Inc.
1230 Avenue of the Americas, New York, NY 10020

Copyright © 2005 by Andrew Neiderman

ISBN-13: 978-0-7434-8320-9
ISBN-10:   0-7434-8320-0

First Pocket Books printing August 2005

10 9 8 7 6 5 4 3 2 1

POCKET STAR BOOKS and colophon are registered trademarks of Simon & Schuster, Inc.

Cover design by John Vairo Jr.; photo of Forest © Steve Casimiro/ GettyImages; photo of Silhouette of Woman © Alain Daussin/GettyImages

Manufactured in the United States of America

For information regarding special discounts for bulk purchases, please contact Simon & Schuster Special Sales at 1-800-456-6798 or business@simonandschuster.com.

For our daughter, Melissa, and our son, Erik,
the crowning jewels of our lives

THE HUNTED

Prologue

AL JONES PUT HIS HEAD DOWN, folded his arms over his nose, and charged right through the bushes. Normally, he would have circumvented this vegetation, but he had no time. Tiny branches found openings in the defensive wall he tried to create with his arms. It was truly as if the woods itself had turned against him. These branches scratched, tore, and poked at his chin, cheeks, and forehead. Thorns from blackberry bushes easily punctured his uncovered and unprotected thighs, but he didn't hesitate. There was no time to worry about any of the wounds. He had to go forward.

Naked, he was freezing. Fall was more like winter in the upstate New York Catskills this year. There were a few inches of frost in the ground and they had already had their first snow in mid-October. It had been weeks since the trees lost their leaves. That gray brush of Mother Nature had been wiped across the forest. Except for the pine, there was no green, and with the foliage gone, no orange, red, or yellow, but just the dismal charcoal frown everywhere he or anyone else gazed outside the small hamlet of Centerville, one of the oldest communities in Sullivan County.

Vaguely Al realized the cuts he was suffering were becoming serious because of how deep they were going and how fast they were accumulating. Blood streaked down his forehead. It got into his eyes and made him blink. There was a constant buzz in his head. About a hundred or so yards back, he had caught himself on a low-hanging maple tree branch. It had nearly taken his head off and dropped him on his rear, but he didn't take the time to evaluate any head injuries even though he had felt the sharp sting across his scalp and was dizzy for more than just a moment.

He had barely waited for his blurred vision to clear before he charged ahead again. Jut like now, there wasn't even a second's pause available. Stopping to catch his breath had become a luxury. One step followed another, his bare feet pounding down and the soles of them getting punctured repeatedly by sharp small stones and broken twigs. He could see the little blood trail he was leaving behind.

Besides all that, his knees were complaining vociferously, and his lungs were threatening to explode. However, he was afraid to think too long about any of it. If he did, his entire body might mutiny and just stop performing. Utter abject terror had already gripped him and was moving quickly up his legs, around his waist, squeezing toward his heart. It was one thing to be threatened with death, but another to be tormented, to be forced to strip and then be told to run for your life.

"Go on. Run like a frightened deer," Al's pursuer had said. "Run like you made him run, like he's still running."

"Who?" he wanted to ask, but he could see from the look in his eyes that there was not going to be any discussion, just a struggle to live.

Now, because of the great fear building in his chest, everything Al did and everything that happened around him reached his consciousness after a good ten-second delay. It was as though he was already out of his body. He was so far from what it did and what happened to it that like an echo, everything reached him well after the fact. This intensified his terror. Death was already racing side by side with him and working its way into him. He flayed about like a madman who could actually see the Phantom dark spirit and was trying to drive it away. One watching might think he was being attacked by angry bees.

The overcast afternoon sky seemed to be descending, crashing down upon him. It was as if the whole world was closing in, cutting off his every avenue of escape. When he was a young boy, he thought of the forests here as endless. As he grew up, the world shrunk around him. And now, now he felt he might just run off the edge of the earth. He was that close to the end.

Finally, unable to take another step, he paused and leaned against an old maple tree. The bark smelled fresh, good, giving memory to a stack of pancakes. He rested there, breathing hard, listening to the thumping his own pounding heart made as it reverberated through every bone in his body. Then he took a breath and turned to tune into the sounds behind him, hoping to hear nothing.

But the chorus of his own impending doom was there, distinct, firm. He could hear the branches cracking and the bushes being pushed aside. There was no question that he was still coming. Carrying out the commands of Death and completely under its firm control, his pursuer was determined, definite, undeterred.

Al looked up. Birds sprang out of trees, their wings flapping frantically. Field mice, squirrels, rabbits passed each other in flight. Something very ominous was upon them. Raw instinct sounded alarms in every living thing and he heard them clearly. In fact, in a strange way his senses were heightened now. Al could almost hear his pursuer's heavy breathing along with his own.

"Why?" he screamed, throwing his voice behind him without pausing to turn. "Why the hell are you doing this? Why now? Why me?"

There was no response except for the sounds of his pursuer's footsteps, relentlessly drawing closer.

Al Jones moaned to himself and pushed off from the tree. He thought a moment and then went down the slope to his right. He knew there was a brook that ran off Silver Lake. Maybe he could get far enough ahead to lose him in the water. Few men he knew could track someone through the water. The current would carry away his blood trail. He could escape.

His new direction took him up a small hill. On the way down, he caught his toe in some exposed birch tree roots and lost his footing. He tumbled, hitting the ground hard with his right shoulder. The blow nearly knocked the wind out of him, and it took all his strength to get himself back on his feet. His ankle felt strained, but the pain was endurable, had to be tolerated, even though it did cause him to limp and slowed his flight.

He hit the water, welcoming the icy splash on his face. And then he jogged down the brook, taking as good care as he could not to stumble on the small, slippery polished rocks. When he rounded the turn, he paused and then ran toward the field of dry grass off to his left.

There, he paused again, lowering himself to his knees, and waited. The silence restored his confidence and his hope. It resurrected his courage and along with it, his embarrassment. He was, after all, naked.

"You're going to pay for this, you bastard, you sick bastard," he muttered and rocked himself. He looked down right when something moved and caught his eye. It was a buck and with quite a good rack, maybe a ten-pointer!

Damn, he thought. You would have been mine for sure.

He rubbed his ankle, and then he rubbed his chin and his cheeks where the branches had scratched him. He felt the bump on his forehead. It was like a small apple embedded under his skin. Rage tightened his jaw, and he pressed his hands on his face as if to hold it together. The stubble of his two-day beard didn't bother his callused palms. He had been working for Cornfield Gas for nearly thirty-five years, delivering and installing tanks. It had given him heavy shoulders and put ropes of muscle in his back, but he was nearly sixty now, soft in the stomach and with nowhere near the wind endurance he used to have.

Old man Cornfield had been a hard man to work for, frugal, demanding, but his son Charlie was softer, more easygoing, lackadaisical about the business he had inherited. Everything came easy to him and he was easier to intimidate. Since he had taken over the business, he had permitted Al to use the company truck to go back and forth from work, and didn't keep track of the miles Al put on it. Al could get away with using it for something personal occasionally, as he had done this morning when he left the house early to hunt deer before the season actually had begun. It was illegal, but he had his reasons.

First, he couldn't afford to take off work on the day it started, and second, he wasn't going to be in this forest when all those idiots from the city, men who rarely held a rifle all year, much less all their lives, came up here equipped with radar scopes and all sorts of electronic paraphernalia and invaded the Catskills' big game season. If they didn't get the best kills, they drove them so far and so deep, a hunter like himself would have to trek days to get a decent rack.

But this, what was happening to him now, was unexpected. Hell, who would have ever anticipated . . . ? Why now? After all this time, why now?

A loud snap brought his head around.

"Can't be," he muttered looking in the direction

of the brook. "How would he know where I got out?"

Maybe the blood at the bottom of his feet left some sign where he had stepped out, but still, the water should have washed away enough of it, at least enough to make it very, very difficult. This was too much, too much. It was as if he had known exactly where Al would go, anticipated his every thought.

He could do that, Al thought sadly. He could.

He waited, squinted and saw a shadow moving through two tall hickory trees. He swallowed back his fear and stood up. Then he backed away from the tree he was at and turned to head across the clearing. If he made it, he could go through the little gully and head east toward the Glen Wild road. Once he broke out where there were traffic and people, he would be safe, he thought.

He walked fast, broke into a jog, and then, started to trot again when suddenly, he heard his name.

"Al!"

He shouldn't have stopped. He should have kept running. Maybe . . . maybe he wasn't a good target. A man on the run is not an easy shot.

"Hey, Al," he heard.

It sounded almost friendly, like someone he knew would sound when he had spotted him and wanted to get his attention. It was all so confusing, yet it made him turn to look back, and he lost his balance.

He fell, braking his fall with his right palm. Then he stood up, intending to continue, but the bullet came crashing through his chest, tearing into his heart.

The impact was like a small punch. It surprised him and for a moment, he tottered, confused, a stupid smile on his lips. Then he looked down, saw the blood streaming and raised his eyes toward the gray sky.

"Oh Mother, no," he said as his legs gave out and he fell forward like a man about to vomit up breakfast. He was on all fours a good few seconds before he turned and fell over on his back.

He died with his eyes open, watching the swoop of a chicken hawk making its way toward Meyer Bienstock's coops just on the other side of the ridge, where there were safety and longer life if he had made it.

But he didn't.

And so . . . it had started.

One

WILLIE BRAND HEARD THE PHONE RINGING in his sleep. He actually dreamed about picking up the receiver and beginning a conversation. It was the same conversation he had dreamed himself having so many times in his life. The state bureau of criminal investigation was calling. They had changed their minds. They needed him; they actually needed and wanted him. He wasn't going to be stuck in this one-horse town after all. He fantasized running over to tell the old man. He expected as always to find him there still in his prison correction officer's uniform, but just as always, when he got there, the rocking chair on the front porch was rocking, but there was no one in it.

It was too late . . . too late to make him proud. Why was it always so important to do that anyway?

Was it because the old man never expected he would amount to anything? When did he first decide that? When does a father look at a son and feel a deep sense of disappointment? Hadn't he built himself up, became athletic and determined at an early age he would go into law enforcement? Other boys his age weren't thinking past the upcoming weekend or what new toy they would get. Why wasn't his attitude something in which his father could take pride?

He remembered the first time he wore his Cub Scouts uniform. How proud he felt strutting about the house in the blue and gold. He had already won a medal for his mastery of tying knots and making a fire on a camping outing. His comfort and expertise in the forest brought him compliment after compliment from his den mother. When he brought all that home, his father glanced at it with vague interest barely uttering a grunt of pride. Why did he always see a stranger in his father's eyes, like something detestable that had been left on the doorstep?

He opened his own eyes because the phone was still ringing and keeping them closed didn't stop it. The numbers on the pad glowed back through the darkness at him, resembling a small creature with green neon orbs. It went in and out of focus, something that was happening to him more and more these days, making it harder to conclude about the reality of what he saw, what he heard. Was he awake? Or was the glowing phone in his dream, too?

His mother had heard the phone ringing one tragic afternoon. He could envision it all: the way she looked up from what she was reading, her hesitation, and then her slow, but resolved walk to the table in the hallway where the phone rested, in this case like a sleeping black snake. His mother was truly amazing. Sometimes, the phone would ring and she would say, "There's trouble," and sure enough there was. How could she do that? A ring was a ring to him.

Maybe it was that ability that finally drove her into the deep depression, a dark hole of sadness from which she could not emerge, a hole which finally determined she had to be institutionalized. Was he responsible for that, too? Too bad he never had a brother or a sister. An only child has to bear the burden of his parents' troubles and their guilt as well as his own. It was too heavy a load. The shadows in the corners of his mind were growing like a cancer.

His phone continued to ring and the cold numbness that had seeped in under his face retreated. The phone became clear in his vision. Like it or not, this wasn't a dream. This was the crusty world of reality in which he resided.

He thrust out his arm and seized the receiver

violently, slicing the next ring just as it had begun. Most of the local people, the old-timers, had never gotten used to the idea of calling the police station, especially this early in the morning. They either knew his number or found it out and called him directly. It didn't matter how early it was or how late it was. He knew people believed they could call him any time they wanted. He theorized that just because he wasn't married, they thought they could abuse him continually. How many times had he been jerked out of a well sought after sleep because someone had a dog barking too closely to his home or someone saw a strange automobile cruising his street? People were becoming more and more paranoid, even in the small Catskill hamlets and villages, miles away from big city life with all its urban headaches.

But country people watched television too, and, to some extent, he had to admit, it was creeping in ... the evil was oozing up and down the New York State Thruway. There were more burglaries, more stolen cars, more of everything despite the flat growth in the year-round population. For the last few years, he had been pleading with the village board to expand the police force, but those arrogant bastards had ridiculed his requests.

"To do what," they asked, "enforce parking meter violations during the summer months?"

"The sheriff or the state police handle the big stuff," they said.

To him it was like rubbing salt in a wound, the wound being how little they all really respected him. He was here only for the nickel and dime crimes and problems, a discount law enforcement officer with little more importance than a school janitor scraping used chewing gum out from under desks and chairs.

"Brand," he snapped into the mouthpiece. In Centerville, his name had become synonymous with police. Small town or no small town, he was at least proud of that.

"Willie, this is Flo Jones. I . . . I'm sorry to bother you."

Then why do it? He wanted to say, but he didn't. Instead, he sat up and flicked on the table lamp. The dusty orange-yellow shade dropped a small pool of sickly white light over his thick muscular thighs and hairy lower legs as he rose. He seemed to rise out of his body and float above himself for a moment and then settle back into it. These crazy sensations were growing more frequent and more intense.

Got to lay off the brandy, he thought, but he knew he wouldn't. It was what got him to sleep most nights these days. The habitual insomnia had grown more intense and when he did sleep, he was tormented by a myriad of horrible images, some from the past, some so unfamiliar, he conjectured they might be from the future.

"It's all right, Flo. This is why they pay me those terrific wages," he said dryly. "What's up? The Benson kid shooting out windows with his air rifle this late at night?" Willie had great memory for complaints. Flo Jones had made that one nearly a year ago.

"No, it's nothin' like that. It's . . . I think I better report my husband's missin'. I was sittin' up all night thinkin' about it. Actually, all of us is up now."

"Missin'? Who? Al?"

He flipped open the small pad he kept on the table next to the lamp and turned himself toward it. Then he wrote the time and after that he wrote: *Flo Jones reported her husband missing.* He would do things by the book. No one was ever going to accuse him of being shoddy when it came to his work. Any other local policeman would do nothing, figuring this would probably prove to be no more than a wife reporting a husband who was on some drunken bender.

"Yes. He . . . well, he went out late in the afternoon, day before yesterday and hasn't returned. Went by himself."

"Went out? Out where, Flo?" he asked. There was so long a pause before she replied that he actually thought the phone had gone dead.

"Flo? Where did he go?" He would make her say it.

"He . . . went deer huntin'."

"Day before yesterday? Gun or bow?" he asked quickly, already knowing the reason for her reluctant answer. Hunting deer with a bow and arrow was legal day before yesterday, but Al Jones wasn't one to use a bow and arrow. He knew him well. Al was nearly fifteen years older than Willie, but in a small town like this, fifteen years one way or another didn't stop you from knowing each other pretty well. Also, Al's father and Willie's had been good friends who had hunted often together. Memories of their smiling, younger faces haunted him. Why did his father always have a better time with his friends than he had with him? Sometimes, Willie wished that he was nothing more than his father's friend.

"Gun," she said softly.

"But that was . . . that was before the season opened," he moaned.

Indignation and pride rose to the surface of his confused pool of thoughts. Why did everyone take advantage of him, break and bend laws expecting him to look the other way all the time? What sort of a policeman did they expect him to be? Above board only when it came to strangers, tourists, but bending for the locals? It made him feel more like a hypocrite than a cop, than someone trusted with a gun and a badge and the lives and welfare of the people he served.

He would make her feel bad.

"That's a serious violation of the hunting ordinances, Flo," he chastised.

"I know. I told him not to do it, but he carried on. Said the city slickers get up here and fill the woods, drivin' the deer to kingdom come. Said they made it more dangerous than anything, shootin' at whatever moves first, and then lookin' to see. Remember what happened to Tom Singleman last year?" She spoke quickly, trying to convince through the intensity of her words.

"I remember Al blowing off about this in Sam's Luncheonette, but I didn't think he was that serious."

He paused for a moment. It was as if he lost track of what he was saying. Similar memories of his father exploded like flashbulbs. The long diatribes against tourists, the complaints about the highway department, a shopping list of moans and groans that made him, a young boy, wonder whether they did live in the greatest country in the world after all. He was tempted to ask what the highway department was like in Egypt, but he had no more courage to be satirical than he did to be contradictory. His father still believed a young boy's place was off in the corner, all eyes and ears and no tongue. It was the way his father had been brought up, and maybe to treat Willie any differently was to deny that his own father had done it right.

"Willie?"

"Yeah, well," he said looking at his pad again. "Are you sure he's missing? Did he go far out, camping maybe?"

"He didn't take anythin' to camp with, Willie. I waited, thinkin' he mighta stopped at someone's place—Ted McNeill maybe, but Ted ain't seen him. He woulda called me if he a done that anyhow. They boys wanna go off lookin' for him as soon as it's light, but I don't want them lost too."

"You keep the boys home. It's my job now, Flo. Any idea what area he staked out?"

"Usually goes over to Dairyland, cuttin' in behind the Lake House, ya know, but I ain't sure."

"I think I remember him talking about that area. Okay, I'll see about getting up a party to sift through the woods. If you hear anything from him, call the station. I'll be there by seven."

"Thank you. I'm sorta on pins and needles up here. Maybe he's gone and shot himself in the leg or . . ."

"Don't start figuring on the worst things, Flo. You'll only get yourself sick with worry. Give me a chance to organize a search party."

"Thank you. I'm sorry about . . . about his goin' out before the season and all," she said.

"Me too." He paused a moment anticipating more, but she didn't reply. "So long," he added and waited until he heard the click. He shook his head and then called Bruce Sussman, the patrolman on duty. It took nearly six full rings before he lifted the receiver.

"What the hell you doing?" he demanded.

"I was in the bathroom, Chief."

Willie grunted. He knew the his patrolman had been sleeping in his chair, probably with his feet up on his desk. He related Flo Jones's phone call.

"He's out drunk or shacked up somewhere, ten to one."

"Yeah, we'll save your predictions for the lottery. You pick up Jerry and have him stay in the office," he said. "I'll go right over to the luncheonette to work up a search party."

"These guys ain't going to like losing hunting time to look for a damn poacher, Chief."

"Tell me about it, Sherlock Holmes."

Willie had little respect for either of his patrolmen, but with the kind of wages the village was paying, he was lucky to have any help at all the way he saw it.

"Get the Kuhns. They both got their deer the first day as usual, Chief," Bruce said, a note of bitter envy in his voice.

"You just pick up Jerry and let me worry about who to get," Willie said and hung up the receiver so sharply he imagined the echo punching Sussman's ear. Then he lay back in bed and groaned. "Fucking deer season," he said as if he was rehearsing his lines for the public. "I wish it was different," he muttered. It was such a simple wish, but he said it again.

He said it as if there were someone in the bed with him, but there wasn't. There had never been.

And the way he felt, there never would be.

The odor of raw deer meat lingered in the misty air despite the brisk cold breeze that scurried leaves and sent small pebbles rolling along the walks in Centerville. Two bucks dangled over the garage door at Kuhn's Body Shop. Their glassy eyes were stuck in a death stare. Both had long, dull red seams the lengths of their stomachs. Blood that had dropped beneath them had become dark purple stains lost in the hue of the tar driveway. Their hind legs were bent slightly and protruded at nearly identical angles, frozen in rigor mortis. Their forelegs were sloping back against their stomachs, but the hooves were bent upward. They looked as though they had been shot in midair and their bodies had locked all joints instantly.

Nothing stirred in the streets of the small Catskill mountain hamlet. The hum of a tractor trailer moving across the nearest major highway could be heard in the distance. Heavy metal signs advertising hardware stores, department stores, and bus stops were nudged by the breeze. The resulting metallic chorus of groans added a dismal note. It was as if the dead were performing a symphony written in graves.

There was a look of hibernation in everything. The summer resort season had long since ended for the upstate New York community. Most of the stores were closed for the remainder of the year. Windows were empty or soaped. The sole movie theater in town had *Heckman's Hardware Store* advertised on its marquee.

The first rays of the sun revealed a dark gray sky bruised with angry clouds pasted from one horizon to the other. Suddenly the front door of the Dew Drop Inn cracked open, its echo ricocheting through the village with the rapport of a gunshot. Two men in red and black checkered hats, jackets, and pants stepped out. Each man carried a Winchester 308 rifle mounted with a five-power scope.

The men spoke in subdued voices out of deference for the early morning. The stillness made them aware of all sound. Their short laughter reverberated so quickly that it made them think there were men of similar voices simultaneously preparing for a hunt. They paused for a moment and listened. Neither would admit to the other that something, for some unfathomable reason, gave him the jitters. They each shook off their nervous feelings and continued walking into the morning sunlight.

Down at the T where Main Street crossed Old Bowery Road, the lights snapped on in the front windows of Sam's Luncheonette. A small neon sign spelled SAM'S in a faded pink, but the frost on the window made it look out of focus to any passerby. A moment later two cars moved in funeral fashion through the village. The bodies of four men were silhouetted in each. A short while after, these cars were followed by the car carrying the two men from the Dew Drop Inn. Their car paused as they looked across the street to admire the two bucks hanging over the front door of Kuhn's Body Shop. Then, the two men looked away, looked toward the advent of their own kills, and headed toward the luncheonette, just as Aaron Kuhn opened the front door of his home and stepped out into the cold, gray day.

He stood on the front steps of his house and took a deep breath, enjoying the sharp, crisp morning. He pitied people who lost it, remaining in bed, cloistered and submerged in stale, heated air. He swept back the loose, long strands of light brown hair that had fallen over his forehead, and then he walked toward the body shop. At six feet two, he carried a well-proportioned one hundred and eighty-five pounds. He had worked with metal hammers, anvils, and crowbars from the very day he could wrap his fingers around handles. This early apprenticeship had helped form his hard, thick forearms and wide shoulders. He had a narrow waist and the rippling muscles that crossed his back gave him a correct, almost arrogant posture.

He stopped at the door of the body shop and unlocked the handle without so much as a glance at the two deer that dangled. It was as if they had always been there. He jerked the door upward and the springs carried it the rest of the way.

Aaron stood for a moment, gazing into his garage. He contemplated the bashed in door of Rose Fern's '99 Ford Mustang before him. It was an otherwise sporty model, as clean and shiny as the day it had been purchased.

The doctor's wife had been drinking again and she had lost control around a turn and slapped the side of the car against a parked village water department truck. Fortunately, no one was in it at the time, and Rose was so loose behind the wheel that she suffered no injuries. Aaron was quickly summoned to get the battered Mustang off the highway and hidden in his body shop. He would do the cosmetic metal surgery as soon as possible, helping to make it seem as if the event never had occurred. But before he took another step in, he heard his brother Walker's voice.

The twenty-seven-year-old man stepped out of the garage and shielded his eyes to look back at the house. Walker stood at the top of the porch steps. Aaron's twenty-four-year-old brother was naked from the waist up.

"You crazy? Put a shirt on, Walker. It's about twenty-two degrees."

"Our fearless chief of police just called. He's getting up a search party. Seems Al Jones has been missing for two days. Went hunting and never came back."

"Two days? Two days?" He held up his fingers to be sure he had heard right. His brother smiled that wry smile of his that made girls giggle and then he shrugged.

"Going or not?"

Aaron turned and looked back at Rose Fern's car.

"Yeah," he said. "I guess we gotta go. It's more important than this. Mom up yet?"

"Phone woke her. She's fixing some breakfast and carrying on about your not waking her. Chief says they're going to leave from Sam's in about an hour."

"Okay, okay. Go back inside before you come down with pneumonia and Mom blames me."

Being the older, Aaron had been blamed for his brother's indiscretions for as long as he could remember. It wasn't just his age. His parents, especially his mother, recognized he had a more mature and responsible manner. He was always on time. He always fulfilled his obligations, and for the most part, he always obeyed rules and laws, whereas Walker was always the one placed in the corner of the classroom or sitting outside the principal's office. He was Huck Finn who got away with most infractions simply on the strength of his good looks and cute impish smile.

Walker waved off the chastisement nonchalantly and then reentered the house. Aaron looked after him, trying not to pay attention to that pang of envy that occasionally stirred in his heart. There were times when he really wished he could be as light-hearted. Walker would be forever young, forever cute, and maybe forever happier.

He turned and looked at the battered Mustang for a moment and then brought the garage door down. The vibrations shook the dangling deer, who looked like they had begun to resurrect themselves. The action caught Aaron's eye. He shook his head and started back toward the house. Halfway there, he stopped and turned to look back at the empty streets just brightening with the rising sun. There was something . . . something. He had felt it almost as soon as he had woken this morning and even had sat up in his bed, staring at the window with some expectation.

He saw nothing in the street now to justify his feelings, nothing except shadows retreating with the growing flow of sunlight, but the feeling that had begun at the base of his stomach continued to spiral upward until it gripped his heart. A surge of instinctive fear cut through him. He was a woodsman, a hunter's hunter. He respected instinct.

He narrowed his eyes and panned the street again. It was as if . . . as if he were being watched. He had felt the feeling before, especially that time the bobcat stalked him.

What was stalking him in the streets of his hometown? he wondered and then drove away the thought with a shake of his head, just as though he were shaking off raindrops.

❧

Marilyn Kuhn stood in the kitchen doorway, her hands on her hips. Aaron's mother was a tall woman, standing nearly five feet eleven. She didn't look her fifty-two years, even though her hair, the color of a dark pecan, had become inundated with light gray strands. She never added color and rarely wore it down, despite it being shoulder length.

Marilyn was still a very attractive woman. She

was practically without wrinkles. Her forehead looked as smooth as it had when she was a teenager. And she had a full, svelte figure. Many older men sought her attention, but she gave none the time of day. Her interest in men waned the day her husband Grant had died, yet she still dressed and prepared herself as if he were there, ready to admire her at the dinner table.

Sometimes, Aaron caught a slight smile on his mother's face at dinner. It was eerie because it was as though she had just heard one of his father's compliments, as if he still spoke to her.

Were the words between them, the vows and expressions of love so deep and strong that they lingered long after her husband's death?

"What's this all about?" she demanded, pursing her lips, just as she always had when she reprimanded him or Walker. "And how many times have I told you to wake me when you get up so you don't go working without a decent breakfast? Your father always had a good breakfast," she chastised.

"No sense getting everyone up because I don't sleep late," Aaron said taking off his jacket. "After a while I work up an appetite. I told you."

"Many a morning you would forget about breakfast altogether, Aaron William Kuhn."

"Ma," he pleaded. He imagined himself fifty with her still treating him like a twelve-year-old. When his father was alive, they would complain about it together, try to gang up on her, but they were no match. She had the eyes. She could stare them into submission.

"Well, what's this all about, phone calls from the police, banging and busting all over the house?"

"Walker got the call. I was set to work on the Fern car. Where is that idiot?"

"Shaven'. He wants to look good for the animals in the forest. I got buckwheat pancakes. Sit down," she ordered with a layer of love under her feigned annoyance.

"I heard that, Ma," his brother called as he bounced down the stairs.

The Kuhns' house was one of the oldest in Centerville, a two-story wood building once serving as a rooming house. There were ten rooms upstairs, although they only heated three now. The downstairs consisted of the living room, the kitchen, a bathroom, and a small sitting room that his mother called the Courting Room.

"Grandma Kuhn told me half the marriages in Centerville began in that room," she had told them dozens of times.

Walker popped into the kitchen doorway. He was only a few inches shorter than Aaron, but he had softer features. He was leaner in build, yet muscular and strong. He wore his dark brown hair long, usually taking a good deal of razzing when some of the older men came to the garage to pass the time and watch him and Aaron work.

"I didn't exactly whisper it, Walker," Marilyn Kuhn said, her hands on her hips. "The day I worry about what my sons think about what I say in my own house . . ."

"Okay, Ma. Okay," Walker said raising his hands in surrender.

"What's the 308 out for?" Aaron asked, seeing the rifle against the wall in the hall.

"Yes," Marilyn said jumping on his question. "Why is that gun there?"

"Well, seeing as we got doe permits this year because of the overpopulation, I thought . . . maybe. Since we're going to be out there anyway."

"To look for a man, not to hunt doe, for crissakes."

"Never know. One might just pop out and join the search party." He smiled and rubbed his hands together as he went to sit at the table.

"Jesus, you smell like a French whore," Aaron remarked.

"Just a little aftershave."

Marilyn Kuhn slapped the pancakes so hard on Walker's plate, he jumped back in his seat.

"Ma!"

"I don't like you cuttin' out the doe. Let the department of conservation do it."

"Woman's lib, Ma."

"Woman's lib? What's that got to do with it, I'd like to know?" She looked at Aaron, but he shook his head and jabbed his fork into the pile of pancakes.

"Equal rights for male and female," Walker said. "If you can shoot one, you can shoot the other."

"Nonsense. Your father never shot a doe and you shouldn't start. Now what's this about a search party?"

"Al Jones got lost hunting. Been gone two days."

"Probably off drunk somewhere and his wife doesn't know about it," Aaron mumbled.

"Then why you givin' up your work to go look for him?" Marilyn Kuhn asked.

"I said probably, Ma."

Marilyn Kuhn smiled to herself and sat down to enjoy her own pancakes.

Her boys were good; her boys were decent people. They were tough as nails on the outside, just like their father, but they had compassion and they had her softness when it came to beautiful things. A child should be a combination of his parents. Too many she knew weren't. They were influenced more by one or the other, especially in a world where single parent families was becoming the rule and not the exception.

Why were the good things, the substantial things, the things that matter the most so much harder to hold on to these days?

Don't get me started, she told the voices within her.

❧

Willie Brand heard the phone ringing in the police station as he was getting out of his patrol car. He figured it was Bruce Sussman coming up with some reason why Jerry Hartman couldn't get down to the station this early. He cursed both of them as he stepped through the doorway.

The Centerville Police Station was part of the municipal building, a building that housed the mayor's office, the fire department, and the community center. It was the newest and largest construction in town. Willie had wanted his office to be larger than the fourteen by fourteen cubbyhole they planned out, but he couldn't convince the town fathers of his need for that either. Prisoners were never held over there, they reasoned. All the serious cases were taken to the county jail in Monticello, the county seat.

Most of the local people sided with him when he made his case at the town meeting, but afterward, they forgot about it. Just like most things around here, he thought, especially when it came to community action or involved tax dollars. Talk, talk, talk, but rarely do. There was never a shortage of wind here, just no sails to catch it and move anything along. His father used to say that, too, only, Willie thought, his father contributed to wind. Even as a ten-year-old, he realized that.

Of course, Willie would never dare say that even behind his back. His father could just look at him and know he had thought something mean about him or something he wouldn't like. Maybe it was a skill he had to develop as a prison guard, especially at a maximum security prison. "Know what they're thinking even before they think it," was his motto.

Willie lifted the receiver.

"Brand," he said.

"Willie, this is Andy Martin. You know, up to the Gray poultry farm?"

"I know who you are, Andy."

I should, he thought, I've known you all my life. Another one losing it.

"What's up?" What was this going to be, one of those days? he wondered.

"There's a truck been parked off the lower field here. Been parked for nearly two days, I believe. Looks like it belongs to the gas company. No reason for a delivery of gas tanks to the woods or to me. I don't use gas. I have the wood stove and . . ."

"All right Andy. What about the truck?"

"Nothing, except no one's in it or come for it. Maybe you saw it when you drove by yesterday."

Willie sighed and rolled his eyes.

"I wasn't up your way yesterday, Andy."

"Oh. Thought you were."

"You said it's a gas truck? You sure?"

Maybe there wasn't even a vehicle there. Andy Martin was close to eighty, he thought, and had been living alone for nearly twenty-five years.

"Cornfield's, I think. Blue."

"All right, we'll be up to check it out," Willie said.

"I don't mean to bother you none. I just don't like somethin' parked out here that long," Andy Martin said.

"Okay, Andy."

"Doesn't seem right to me."

"I gotcha. Thanks," he said and hung up before the old man could add another word.

How many elderly people were there out there like that? Willie wondered and thought about his grandfather. He remembered him only vaguely, but he remembered him being stubborn and alone and always grumbling. His father was truly an apple that didn't fall far from that tree, but when it came to me, Willie thought, they used to say the tree was at the top of a hill and the apple just rolled on and on.

Cornfield's truck? he realized. Al worked for Cornfield. This thing was coming together very fast, but he'd still have to search through the woods, maybe a lot of it. He would need help. Everyone expected that he would ask for it.

A few moments later, he heard Hartman pull up. The six-foot, two-hundred-pound, blonde, and blue-eyed twenty-three-year-old took his time getting out of his car and coming into the office. He yawned as he opened the door.

Willie shook his head. Like him, Hartman was an athletic man, a former local high school football hero who had enlisted in the army right after high school and gotten into the military police. A popular hometown boy, he naturally had an easy time being hired by the village. Willie knew Hartman didn't have all that much ambition, but if he did, he would eventually become police chief. If he wanted to take the state exam, he could probably become a state policeman, too. He looked the part. Willie was still as firm and bull-necked, still dedicated to exercise, weight-lifting especially, but he couldn't help being jealous of the younger man. He had promise. He had a future if he only cared enough.

Youth was sure just wasted on the young, he thought. If he were my son, he mused, he would be different.

Hartman lived with his father, Ronnie Hartman, a plumber. Jerry was his only child and he had lost his wife to cancer a little more than four years ago. He was a plain-looking, dull man, a direct contrast to his handsome, easygoing son who often resembled a younger Harrison Ford.

"You look ambitious this morning," Willie quipped.

"Sat up watchin' a late show with my father," Jerry

said. "Bruce told me to tell you he'll meet you at Sam's. He's havin' breakfast there."

"All right. Mind the store," Willie said. "If Flo Jones calls, raise me on the two-way."

"Right, Chief."

Willie grunted and hurried out. When he stepped through the doorway of Sam's Luncheonette, he felt like Gary Cooper in *High Noon* going to the bar to ask for volunteers to help fight the Miller gang.

The small luncheonette was already smoke filled and crowded with hunters. The restaurant itself was small, with hard wooden floors and paneled walls. Two deer racks were mounted at the far end, on both sides of the large luminous electric clock. At night, when the lights were out in the restaurant, the clock radiated the time in neon blue. Very mediocre paintings of country scenes were hung on the left wall. The front of the restaurant consisted of a large picture window, now quite misty and clouded by the smoke and condensation. Beside the neon light that spelled SAM'S, there was an etching of Sam and his wife that Bob Longo, the local high school art teacher, had done for a month's worth of free dinners.

Bruce was sitting at the counter, shoving scrambled eggs into his mouth and gulping coffee. Willie didn't move from the doorway. For a moment it was as if he had completely forgotten why he had come.

Sam, a short, bald-headed fifty-four-year-old man with a round pudgy face and puffed Popeye arms, turned from the grill and raised his eyebrows. He had known Willie all his life and had been friends with his father. Sam and he didn't need a whole lot of words between them. A look, a gesture delivered paragraphs.

"Somethin' wrong, Chief?" Sam asked in a loud voice. Some of the conversations stopped; voices lowered, heads turned.

Willie blinked and snapped to attention.

"Got a man missing two days in the woods," he announced. "I need some volunteers to help form a search party."

"Who's missin'?" someone shouted.

"Al Jones."

"Good riddance," someone said and there was laughter.

"Wife's worried," Willie said. The luncheonette became somber again. "The man's got a family."

"He went out two days ago?" Sam asked from behind the counter. Willie nodded and Sam shook his head. "Thought he was just blowin' off about it like he does about most everything."

"Head Start Jones," someone quipped.

There was more laughter.

"Sure he's still in the woods, Chief?" another man asked.

"It's looking that way and it's looking like something's not right. His truck's been parked on the road for days. Andy Martin just called and told me so."

There was a low murmur.

"All right, I'll go," someone said. That was followed by only three or four more "me too's," but Willie figured he had enough to make a decent attempt at locating the man.

"Let's get started then," Willie said.

Willie smiled at the sight of the Kuhn brothers waiting outside, leaning against their car. He had almost forgotten about them. He tilted his hat back. Behind him stood his pathetic search party: a half dozen men.

"Morning, Aaron," Willie said.

"Chief." Aaron nodded. "Any ideas where to begin?"

"Well, yeah. I got a call from Andy Martin a little while ago, telling me about a Cornfield truck parked in the field by the poultry farm. You all know Al works for Cornfield, so I guess we'll start with the truck and then go into the woods at the Lake House road . . . drop two off, go in a hundred yards or so and drop two off, do it again and again and all head directly northeast. There's a stream that cuts across up there."

"Catfish Creek," Aaron said.

"Yeah, anyway, Toby here remembers Al talking about going up there."

"You heard him too, chief," Toby said.

Willie blinked and stared at him. His eyes were steel.

"Or maybe you didn't," Toby added. After all, it wasn't too cool to reveal that the chief law enforcement officer overheard someone say he was going to break the law.

"Okay, let's mount up," Willie said. "Ralph and Toby can come with us. Aaron, you and Walker take Carl and Ted. These two want to go in their own car," Willie said indicating two strangers.

"This all you could get?" Walker asked.

Willie shrugged. "Everyone thinks he's sucking on a bottle somewhere. No sense wasting any more time trying to recruit any more. Besides, we can cover the territory pretty quickly, don'tcha think?"

"Let's get going. I got work to do," Aaron replied without commenting on Willie's prediction.

Willie led the search party out of Centerville and up a secondary road to Dairyland. They located the Cornfield truck quickly, and Willie checked it out.

"It's Al Jones's truck all right," he announced holding up an envelope. "Some of his mail here. Let's get started. Anyone finds anything, we shoot off two sets of three rounds, okay?"

"Where you figure on stopping?" Aaron asked.

"Route 52. It's only about a mile past the creek, right?"

"More like two, but that's fine."

They followed the chief's plan, spreading out every hundred yards or so and then heading northeast. The clouds had parted and streaks of sunshine sliced through the forest of naked trees. Only the pine threw off long, deep shadows, running over the rocky earth. With the rest of the forest leafless and barren and only the brush with which to contend, they had good visibility.

It was Aaron and Walker who found him. Aaron spotted the coat first and then the flannel shirt. When he located the pair of pants, he checked the pockets and found Al Jones's wallet.

"What the fuck . . ." Walker looked around, spooked by the sight of the discarded garments. "What's he doing, getting laid somewhere?"

"Don't think so," Aaron said. A few moments later, he located the second shoe and one of the heavy woolen socks. When they found the underwear, they stared at each other for a moment before going on.

"This is too weird," Walker said. Aaron nodded and listened to the forest. Spooked, Walker added, "Maybe we should signal the others."

"Let's just go a little farther," Aaron suggested. "Maybe we shouldn't wait another minute."

Aaron paused when they approached Catfish Creek and touched Walker's arm.

"What?"

"Sounds like someone else. Behind us. The others should be down or up a hundred yards."

"Maybe those city slickers ain't walking a straight line, Aaron," Walker said, but he couldn't hide his nervousness. This was all too weird. If there was someone else right behind them, he had stopped too.

After a moment Aaron went on, Walker keeping an eye on their back end. Aaron followed the tracks just the way his father had taught him and his father's father had taught him. They crossed the creek and located the signs.

"This is some distance for a man to travel naked in this weather," Aaron muttered.

Walker was speechless and hesitant but Aaron plodded on.

Not a hundred yards in, they came upon him.

Aaron told his brother to signal, but Walker just stared at the corpse. Then he turned and brought up some of that fine breakfast their mother had made.

So Aaron fired off the rounds.

TWO

GARY LESTER HAD WORKED for the Department
of Conservation all his adult life. However, even
though he spent most of his working hours outdoors, there was nothing ruddy and vigorous about
his complexion or his build. There was almost
always an absence of color in his face. When he was
outside for long periods of time in cold weather,
the skin around his nose would redden and his
eyes would become teary. The lower ends of his
earlobes would blanch, but the rest of him would
remain remarkably unchanged. It was as if he lacked
blood.

At thirty-five he had the appearance of a man in
his late fifties. He was at least twenty pounds over-
weight for a height of five feet eleven. There was a
softness in his face, exaggerated by the heavy reced-

ing hairline and the thin black hair that he wore swept back with no style. His small, beady eyes were lost beneath his wide, slightly protruding forehead. He had rather large nostrils and smooth, almost feminine lips.

He was not a wholly unpopular boy in high school, but his interest in things that required solitude earned him the reputation of being a loner. Early on he indicated his ambition to become a forest ranger. His classmates found that somehow odd and nicknamed him "Smokey the Bear." He accepted it and even won the respect of some of his teachers and fellow students with his independent work in forestry. After high school, he did go to school for forestry, but instead of becoming a ranger and going off to the wilderness of the Northwest, he returned to his hometown and secured a job with the state department of conservation.

He married a small, comely girl, Denise Coontz, from Big Indian, a tiny outlying community that consisted of a post office, a general store, a lumber company, and a bar and grill simply called Big Indian Saloon. They had two children, both boys and both quite unlike their father in temperament. They were healthy, athletic types, mixers who often got into trouble for horseplay at school. To Gary, his boys were confusing, impossible to understand natural forces at work in the universe. He made superficial attempts to control them and then, more or less, left the responsibility to his wife.

Big game season always overwhelmed him. As a conservation officer, his chief responsibility was enforcing the game laws. It meant going out there, being in the din, inspecting kills, checking licenses. During the season he was often out day and night accompanying state police who searched for night jacklighters, hunters who used search lights and often shot deer from vehicles along the road at night. The fines were stiff and the penalties heavy, yet every season it seemed to get worse.

Often when he returned home, almost before he opened the front door of his house, his wife was there to greet him, which annoyed him. He hated the sense of being pounced upon or scouted, hated it the way a man who talked aloud to himself was sensitive to anyone eavesdropping. Besides, his wife's melancholy was a source of irritation. These days Denise seemed to have habitually tired, sad eyes. She was fragile looking, thin with a complexion almost as pale as Gary's. When she fixed her hair, put on some lipstick and wore a dress than wasn't faded, she looked cute enough, but those were rare occasions. The weight of her lot in life was beginning to darken the circles under her eyes and deepen the lines around her mouth.

He didn't need reminders about the dreariness of

his life, the small home that had become claustro-
phobic with the boys growing older, more active, his
and Denise's lack of real friends and a social life, not
to mention the glass ceiling he saw hovering over
him and his career ambitions at work.

But that was what his wife's face was: a constant
reminder, a mirror catching his dark moments and
reflecting them back at him.

When Gary greeted her this morning, she had
been up early, getting their children ready for
school.

"What?" he demanded without so much as saying, "Good morning."

"I didn't hear you get up," she said.

"So? I didn't want to wake you."

"Where have you been so early in the morning? I
went up to look for you."

"I've been out getting my rig ready," he explained.
"You think I just get up and drive off. There's lots of
preparation involved in my work."

"I know, Gary."

"Well, what did you want?"

"Brian Donald just called," she replied. "I didn't
know where you were and he sounded upset."

"Figures," he said.

Lately, Gary had been finding it more and more
difficult to get along with his immediate supervisor.
He suspected the man had fears he might be creep-

ing up on him. He was constantly complaining about Gary exceeding his authority. Everyone wants to keep you confined within boundaries, he thought. Just like wild animals, people cherished their territorial rights. They pretend to be generous, to be civilized, but in the end, primitive instincts won out. They always will, he thought.

He marched past her without further comment and went to the phone in the kitchen to call.

"There's a change," Donald said without so much as a hello, how you doing? "You're in the Monticello area today."

"Why?"

"Because we need you there, that's why. Meet me at the sheriff's office in about an hour."

"Sheriff's office?"

"First fatal accident occurred in Centerville. Just got word," Donald said, softening his tone of voice.

"Oh?"

"Don't know all about it yet, but something's fishy."

"What'dya mean?"

"Just meet me," his supervisor repeated with impatience and hung up.

"What is it, Gary?" Denise asked as soon as he turned from the phone.

"First fatality," he said. He said it as though it proved everything he had always believed.

"Oh dear. I just hate to hear about that."

"So don't ask. I got to get going."

"What about breakfast?"

"I'll get something on the way," he said starting for the front door.

"Be careful," she shouted. He spun around angrily.

"I've told you at least a hundred times. With those idiots out there, being careful is practically impossible. What good is it if you follow the rules, but others don't? Every victim of a drunk driver screams that back at us."

She didn't reply. It would have been so much easier for her if he had simply said, "Sure," as most husbands would have said. She always found his lack of the simple compassion curious. Even if it was a result of his frustration with his job, it wasn't right to take it out on her.

She went to the front window and watched him get into his truck.

"Something's eating at him," she muttered as if there were someone at her side. "It happens every big game season, only it seems worse than ever this time."

She shook her head. Whatever it was, it was beyond her. Her husband kept too much to himself. She wondered whatever happened to that softness, that gentleness she had been attracted to when they had first met? He was quieter then. There was a vulnerability she liked, something she could put her arms around. A woman should be able to comfort the man she loves. That was something so basic. He shouldn't resist it; he should welcome it, cherish it.

Did he change she wondered or just become who he really had been all the time? Either answer left her despondent. If he changed, it was because of their marriage. If he didn't, he had fooled her. Why did he want her if he didn't like her, didn't long for her to be part of his life and have her to share everything with, including his fears and disappointments? What was the point?

What's the point of any of it? she wondered.

She buried herself in her household chores so she wouldn't dote on this and other troubling questions.

❧

Steve Dickson, the youngest man to serve as district attorney in Sullivan County, tapped his long, rather bony fingers on the desk. There was a western flavor to his style of dress, reinforced by the black leather boots that ran up over his calves he had bought in Jackson, Wyoming, during his vacation. With his other hand, he brushed back the long, straight ebony black hair. He wore a thick but well-trimmed mustache turned down just a little on each side, framing the corners of his mouth. His strong but narrow chin, gave his face a lean, serious expression. The intensity of his gaze was amplified by the high cheekbones and the manner in which a small fold of skin formed at the bottom of his brow.

Willie Brand stood by the window, his gaze fixed on a young woman trying to park an S-class Mercedes in a spot for compact cars. She worked very hard at it rather than simply seek out a proper space. Her stubborn determination irritated him. Some people were like that. They treated everything with equal significance, no matter how small it really was. It was as if God was keeping track of every failure or if they diminished their individual worth if they failed. Willie kept his back to Dickson and waited.

Dickson's office was another minor annoyance to Willie. Instead of pictures of state and national politicians, the man had autographed blowups of football and basketball stars. There was even a poster of John Lennon giving the peace sign. How did that belong in the chief prosecutor's office? Everything was changing. All the old stable values were being tossed off like too much weight on a sinking ship. The creeping crud of the new, permissive generation, the spoiled Yuppie crowd, was seeping in everywhere, even here, once a bastion of stability, family values. Why, there were people in the stands during high school basketball games who didn't bother to stand at the beginning of the national anthem.

Dickson continued to peruse the report and the pictures a moment.

"Why naked?" he asked aloud.

Willie's eyebrows lifted and he turned.

"I have no idea," he replied. "Maybe the killer belongs to a nudist colony."

Dickson stared at him a moment, his mustache twitching with his thoughts and his vision of this killing.

"Seriously, Willie, any of it make sense to you, clothes scattered all over . . . ?"

Willie shrugged.

"I'm not a high-priced investigator, but it looked to me like he was forced to undress and then given a chance to run, just so the killer could pursue him, hunt him down, track him the way they're out there tracking deer as we speak," he said.

"This is one sick fuck."

"Another in a line of them, yes," Willie said. "Or, maybe someone more calculating, someone with another agenda."

"What other agenda?"

Willie shook his head.

"Like I said, I'm not one of these high-priced investigators, but maybe it's one of those fanatic environmentalists or something. Didn't they blow up the tire factory in Liberty Falls last year?"

"That's still to be determined," Dickson said and looked at the pictures again. "A thing like this . . . if it was in the hands of a sensationalist newspaper . . ."

"Yep," Willie said, nodding. He took a toothpick out of his top pocket and worked in between his back molars. He glanced out the window and saw the woman had squeezed her car into the space. She got out and looked as if she had just successfully done delicate brain surgery. "Everyone is a little sick. For one reason or another," he muttered under his breath so low it seemed to come from someone else.

"What about your search party?" Dickson asked. "I mean, the others besides the Kuhn brothers?"

Willie shook his head.

"What about them?"

"I don't want someone running to the press, to television and radio people."

"I asked them to keep their mouths glued shut until we figured out how we're gonna go about this. They promised, but you know that saying about two can keep a secret if one is dead."

"Yes," Dickson said sadly.

"I did manage to keep it out of any news program or paper for a while. It don't take long for news of a death to be spread in our community. The damn reporter from the local bureau of the *Post* was calling my office almost before we returned from the woods! I did my best to make it sound like a simple hunting accident, one in a long line. We'll be okay for a little while," he said and paused to hear the district attorney's expression of approval, but the young man was silent.

Brand smirked. He didn't see how a thirty-one-year-old kid could run the county's prosecution office anyway, even if he did run a brilliant campaign to win the office away from a four-term incumbent. Maybe he just didn't get it, didn't understand what they had going on here. He looked too relaxed, that tanned face from a recent Florida vacation making him look even more out of place in the cold, wintry Catskill world.

"Look, a thing like this could cause panic in the woods—hunters panicking, shooting each other. Who knows?" Willie punched out.

"Yeah," Dickson said, but not with as much concern as the woman who worked her ass off to park her car did, Willie thought. Frustrated, he blew air between his lips and lowered his shoulders.

"What do you want me to do?"

"Let's see what the investigator from the State Bureau of Criminal Investigation comes up with after speaking with the Kuhn brothers."

"Right, the expert," Willie said with disdain.

Dickson thought a moment, looked at Willie who he noticed was staring at him, and nodded. "Of course, you did the right thing, Willie. We'll keep a lid on this as long as we can. Besides this whole nudity thing, it's a weird killing. There were two wounds and the one in the forehead was close up?"

"Had to be standing right over him," Willie replied. Straddled him, maybe and just shot off one round."

He wiped his hands over his face as if to wash the imagery out of his mind.

"Just like a professional hit man style, putting his stamp of approval on it," Dickson said. "His signature so to speak. A different sort of hunter, but a hunter."

Willie looked up and smiled.

"Professional hit man after someone like Al Jones? What's he gettin' him for, cheating at cards at Sam's Luncheonette or somethin'?"

Dickson smirked and shook his head.

"Of course," Willie continued, enjoying mocking Dickson's idea, "maybe a professional hit man likes to hunt big game. Maybe he's tired of just killing the easy prey and then came up with this when he got bored or something. That's it. This is a sick game run by hit men from New York. There could be a dozen of them out there as we speak. It's a contest or something and hunters are the targets."

"Ridiculous," Dickson said as if Willie had started the discussion about a professional hit. "A little bit too much movie of the week in that." He shook his head. "No. It's either someone who really hated this guy or a complete lunatic. But you're right about all the danger, the paranoia that could develop out there," Dickson concluded.

Willie nodded and gazed out the window again, this time losing himself in the memory of his father the day before he was shot. They had been gathering firewood together, working quietly, communicating in the rhythm of their labor. It had been one of the rare times he had felt close to him. He had almost given him a compliment for the graceful way he split wood. He was big for his age and very strong.

Dickson seemed to sense his thoughts.

"Must be hard for you confronting a death in the woods, Willie, with what happened to your father and all."

Willie nodded, a little surprised that Dickson knew his personal history.

"It was a long time ago. He took his time to teach me all the safety rules, and he goes struttin' through the forest with the safety off, trips over a log . . ."

"How old were you?"

"Not quite twelve. A good twenty yards behind. He wasn't one to wait up for the rest of us. Too anxious. He was always ahead of the pack one way or another."

"God." Dickson shook his head. "You shouldn't have been out there in the first place."

"Those days, rules, laws had even less of an influence on people, especially people like my father."

"You never hunted since, did you?"

"Got enough to hunt just doin' my job."

"I hear ya."

Willie held his gaze so intently, Dickson raised his eyebrows.

"What?"

"I was just thinkin' about what you said. What if it is a raving lunatic loose in the woods?" Willie asked. "It's the age of serial killers, isn't it?"

"I don't want to go there. We could have quite a problem on our hands. Everyone's expecting a big crowd this hunting season and from what I hear, we have a great number of them here already."

"Don't you think it might be best to put a stop to hunting in my immediate area at least?"

Dickson shrugged and shook his head.

"Best? Maybe. Easy to do? No way."

Willie turned to look out the window again, a half smile on his face.

"Maybe this lunatic will make it easier for you," he said.

❧

Aaron drove back in silence from district attorney's office. He and Walker had given all their information to the BCI investigator, and the retelling of their discovery left them both emotionally drained.

Walker was still a little embarrassed at his getting sick at the sight of Al Jones. He surprised himself. He had seen death many times in the woods, but always wild animals. There was something deep about seeing another human being like that, left like that, looking like hunted game, the blood dried on his skin, his eyes glassy, the smell of death spiraling up at him. Maybe it brought home his own mortality or maybe he was just a wimp after all. Aaron didn't so much as hiccup. Where did he get all that inner strength? If it was inherited, why hadn't he inherited it as well?

"What are you going to tell Ma?" Walker asked as they pulled into Centerville.

"No details. We'll just say we found him shot."

"You think those other guys are gonna keep their mouths shut like they promised Willie?"

"No. Maybe they'll wrap this up before the stories get too wild," Aaron said, but he didn't believe it. Actually, aside from the fact that whoever had killed Al Jones had made him strip first, he had nightmares of something similar happening to him. Often, he had paused miles out in the woods and thought to himself how vulnerable he was. And it wasn't the first time he had sensed someone else there, someone walking in his footprints.

It was one of the reasons why his father never liked to go out alone.

"A man alone in nature takes risks," he had said. "You break your leg and you can die out here, Aaron. Never be arrogant about your ability to take care of yourself in the woods or anywhere else in nature for that matter. Never think you're too good to ever need help."

Of course, in his wildest imagination, his father would never have come up with this.

"Who the hell would want to kill the bastard like that?" Walker mused aloud.

"Someone getting even with him for something," Aaron replied. "That's vengeance piled on vengeance."

"You think so?"

"Actually," Aaron said as they drove into their driveway, "I hope that was all it was."

"What'dya mean?" Walker asked.

"It's like everyone who looked at Jones was thinking. I could see it on their faces when they looked around and into the woods behind us. What if someone's out there just doing that to hunters?" Aaron replied. He shut off the car engine, but Walker sat staring for a moment after Aaron got out.

"Jeez, you think that's possible?" he asked, catching up with him at the steps to the front porch. Aaron paused at the door.

"Why not? If psychotic bastards can kill all sorts

of people in city streets, why can't they do it back in the woods where it's even easier?"

Walker thought a moment and then shook his head.

"Naw, it's got to be just someone after Jones. I could probably come up with a list arm's length myself if I thought about it."

Marilyn Kuhn stepped out of the sitting room as they entered.

"You don't hafta tell me," she said staring at Aaron. "I see it on your face, son. Not a good finish to this story, is there?"

Aaron described Al Jones, less the gruesome details and without mentioning his being naked.

"Shot in the chest? Still, couldn't it have been a huntin' accident? Maybe some city fella did it and ran off," she said. "Or maybe whoever did it, didn't even know he had."

"There's just no way that could have been an accident, Ma," Aaron replied. He lowered his eyes too quickly to avoid hers.

"That bad, huh?" she asked. He nodded. She looked at Walker. He didn't just shift his eyes. He turned completely around and pretended interest in his rifle. "There's somethin' you two ain't sayin', ain't there? Well?"

"Any calls?" Aaron said in reply instead. She nodded, her hands on her hips.

"Dr. Fern's wife. Seems a doctor oughta be able to do somethin' about an alcoholic, doesn't it?"

"You know what you always tell me about the shoemaker and his shoes. What did she want?"

"Her car, what'dya think? Said you told her she'd have it by late this afternoon."

"What?"

"I told her you went to get some parts."

"Why Mom," Walker said turning back to her. "You told a white lie." He smiled from ear to ear.

Marilyn Kuhn bit her lower lip and lowered her head to scowl at him. Walker laughed.

"It's not deceitful when you're trying to avoid troubling someone who's already troubled," she said. "And besides, who are you to stand there and judge someone? I heard the way you got that Lester girl to go out with you."

"What? Ma! I can't believe . . ."

"So it was true then. You lost a bet?"

"Who told you that?"

"Not me," Aaron said lifting his hand and laughing.

"Bunch of gossips come around here," Walker said. "You oughta have more important things to do than listen to those women gossip, Ma."

"You telling me about wasting time?" she asked, raising her eyebrows. "How many times I tell you judge not that ye be not judged, Walker? How many times have I told you about people in glass houses throwing stones?"

"All right, Ma. All right," Walker said putting up his hands.

Aaron laughed and then returned to the body shop. Walker joined him a few minutes later and they began their work on Rose Fern's car. Sometimes, they could walk side by side for hours and barely say a word to each other. It was as if they spoke through their actions, working with a coordination that came from doing it all for years and years alongside their father.

Finally, Walker turned to Aaron and said, "I don't know why I threw up like that."

Aaron peered up at him from where he was kneeling beside the automobile.

"Are you kidding? I don't know why I didn't," he said.

Walker smiled at Aaron's generosity and returned to what he was doing.

During the course of the day, Kuhn's Body Shop often became a village hangout. Men would stand by and watch Aaron and his brother work and chew up topics that ranged from national issues to local sewer problems.

Now, because of the two bucks hanging out front, they were a special attraction. Gradually, as the day wore on, the talk about Al Jones's death became the chief topic. Few men knew Aaron and Walker had been the ones to find the body. When that was learned, they were bombarded with questions. Aaron kept his answers vague and pretended a great need to concentrate on his work. Just before they were about to close up for the day, he got a call from Willie Brand.

"I know you've had half the town in your shop today, Aaron. You two keeping your lips tight?"

"Fought off a day's worth of pumping. I don't know how much longer it'll keep, Chief."

"Yeah I know. Expect another visit from the BCI. They want to keep going over what you found and how you found it. They might ask you to take them back into the woods and trace how you discovered each piece of clothing. Forensics says from the marks on his chest and legs, it looks like he'd been running naked for quite a while. I can't make any sense of it and neither can our brilliant young district attorney."

"Maybe whoever did it wanted him as naked as a deer," Aaron said. Willie was silent a moment.

"I sorta told the district attorney the same thing, but I don't think he gets it. Drugs and car thieves. That's more up his alley than something like this."

"Great minds think alike, Chief."

"Right. It's good to know I have someone in this village who can understand me."

"I wouldn't go that far," Aaron said, and Brand laughed.

"Me neither," he said.

After Aaron cradled the phone, he wiped his hands and started out. Walker was standing near the door staring out the side window. He looked concerned.

"What is it?" Aaron asked.

"Someone's inspecting our deer."

"Who?" Aaron squinted against the late afternoon sun and then shaded his eyes with his hand.

"Smokey the Bear. Maybe we'll get some sort of department of conservation award."

"Let's go before we get some more curiosity seekers," Aaron said and pulled the garage door down. Gary Lester sauntered across the street to greet them.

"Two beauties," he said. "Amazing."

"That we got 'em or that they're so good?" Walker asked.

"That you two got two like that so quickly. Yeah," Lester said wiping his forehead with the back end of his coat sleeve. "Woods are packed with doe this year and you guys come up with these two bucks. Just like that." He snapped his fingers.

"When you know what you're doing, it ain't hard," Aaron said. "Rough day?"

"Can't even begin to describe it. I had to go to Monticello first and hear about this killing of Al

Jones. They could have told me it all over the phone. I have a lot to do and I have to sit in an office and listen to speeches. Finally, I'm turned loose and I'm right in it all."

"In it all?" Aaron asked. "What's that mean?"

"You guys don't know the half of what goes on around here. First, there's this business about Al Jones, and then I catch this idiot with a twenty-two pistol. A twenty-two pistol! He thought it would be less cruel to use a small caliber gun and when I tried to explain to him that he'd probably only wound a deer and cause it great suffering with a twenty-two, he thought I was pulling his leg because he was from the city."

Gary shook his head.

"Over at Cranberry Lake," he continued, "the state police stopped a guy who had a goat tied to the front of his car."

"You're bullshittin' us," Walker said.

"Honest. A goat. Tommy Budd's prize goat. He's fit to be tied himself."

"Anything else?" Aaron asked dryly.

"One more beaut. Someone shot the head off Mac Bernstein's lawn deer. Kept shootin' and shootin' until he hit it. Imagine shootin' and not realizin' it couldn't be alive if it just stood there while you shot and shot? And how do you go hunting around someone's home?"

"I guess you earn your salary," Aaron said. He started away.

"So you two found Al Jones," Lester said. Aaron stopped and turned. There was something in the way he had said that.

"Yeah."

"What'dya think?"

"We're not cops. It doesn't make a difference what we think," Walker said.

"Difference is, he's still out there. Just lucky you two don't hafta go back out. You got yours," he said looking up at the bucks.

Aaron gazed at him a moment and then nodded at Walker.

"Let's go. Momma's got dinner ready," he said.

"Hearty appetite," Lester cried after them. "After what you guys been through, it's amazing you can eat."

Aaron didn't turn back. When Walker came up beside him, he grimaced.

"Can't stand that guy. Never could," he muttered. "He's the sort that would make Dad's temples beat. When I would see the muscles tighten in his neck, I knew better not do anything to get him mad today."

Walker agreed and then looked back once to watch Smokey the Bear get into his vehicle.

Aaron couldn't shake off the feeling he and Walker were retreating into their house.

He was in the woods many times before all this was to begin. He stalked through the woods like a hungry deer, stopping often to listen. Vaguely, he understood he was reenacting something. Whenever he stopped, he was so still he was indistinguishable from the trunks of trees. As if to challenge fate this time, he deliberately dressed in a brown jacket, the jacket made of deer hides. There was sweet irony in that, almost as if he was carrying out some poetic revenge. There would be no red and black checkered hunting outfits for him. He hated the pattern. The design came to him in nightmares. At times he dreamed his bedroom had walls of red and black checkers.

He felt he had the patience of a deer. Standing quietly for the longest time, waiting and listening, he didn't grow tired or bored. Most of the hunters were different. They couldn't take the silence and the lack of movement. Their nervous systems clamored. They had to talk or move about. But not him. He could move about in his mind and that was enough. That had always been enough. He knew that and he knew how good he was even though he was never appreciated properly. Hell, he was never appreciated period.

Just look at me, he thought. Just look at what I

can do. He held his head so still that it was amazing his neck didn't ache from being in the same position for so long. His entire body looked frozen—his legs bent, his arms up, holding his rifle against his body. Not a finger moved. Only the pupils in his eyes went slightly from one side to another.

And his sense of smell was uniquely developed. He could smell them before he could see them. It got so he knew every natural odor in the forest and could distinguish something alien simply by the scent of it captured in a breeze. Just like a deer, he knew how to read the breeze. It was part of his cunning now because of the training that had been imposed on him. He was literate in the forest where so many illiterates plundered.

When he did move, he moved on a carpet of air. There was a way to walk through the bushes, a way to cross a bed of leaves, a way to traverse streams. There were very few loud noises in the forest; it was a home for subdued sounds, a place of cool silence. The sound of a gunshot was like an earthquake. It drove madness into the animals and shattered their sense of natural calm. He didn't like doing it, but now, he had to, didn't he? It was only a vague idea at first and then it grew stronger and stronger until he was a man possessed with a mission.

"They deserve it," he muttered. "Look what they did to us."

And he hated their eyes, their all-knowing, arrogant eyes. Who liked to live with those eyes turning on him day after day, followed by that smile? They all had the same wry smile and as long as they did, they owned him. He could feel it and he hated them for it.

It was dusk now. They should have been well on their way out of the woods, but he heard them off right. They were walking deeper into the forest, not heading out of it. They had always been night shooters, he thought. The lowest of the low anyway. Of all of them, these two were probably the easiest to understand. It was simple: They were greedy, bloodthirsty. It wasn't enough for them to hunt all day, to come out here and rape the land, tear its animals to bits. They had to be at it at night too, going into the woods carrying powerful flashlights as well as powerful rifles to find the unsuspecting deer, and then blind them with the bright beams. That was hunting to these vermin. As long as he had known them, that was how they were. They even cheated at cards.

He clenched his teeth and pressed his rifle harder against his body to quiet his building anger.

When he knew they had gone past him, he moved to his right. This part of the forest was very wet. There were swampy areas ahead which brought the sweet scent of soaked weeds and earth. Only a half a mile to the left was Loon Lake, a duck sanctuary. When he was a young boy, he had come here often to watch their incredible formations as they stopped on their way north or south, depending on the season. Nature was beautiful when it was caught unaware, when you were as much a part of it as anything else, when you weren't here to kill.

He heard them step into water and curse. This encouraged him. As always, the forest was cooperating, actually helping him. He believed Nature had a consciousness and that consciousness was in tune with his own. Nature knew he was different and that he wasn't guilty of anything, nothing deliberate.

They would move to the right now, seeking drier land, he thought. He crossed quickly so he would be on their left and moved up to flank them. Their voices grew louder. He crouched and listened. When they came into view, he took the safety off.

Not more than twenty yards to his immediate right, a buck stood, its ears perched. His trained eye caught sight of it immediately. He knew it wasn't listening to him; it was listening to them. He cursed the animal for its innocence. They all waited too long. During the last few years, he thought he could detect a growing stupidity. Perhaps the pollution of nature had begun to take its effect in the genes. He had a theory about that—the genetic signals were all getting confused because of the poisons released into the natural environment. Animal intelligence had waned. Why not? If something attacked their physical health, it should influence their mental health as well. It worked that way with people. Why not animals, too?

He moved awkwardly deliberately so that the buck would see him and move off. Nevertheless, one of the men caught sight of the white tail. The man shouted and both of them charged through the bush. He stepped back behind a tree as they fired in the buck's direction. He waited until they went by, and then he leaned against the tree, bracing the gun. He took aim.

The first shot lifted off the top of the back of the head of the man on the left. His hunting cap actually flipped in the air. Chunks of his skull and fragments of his flesh and brain splattered on the trees in front of him. He lifted his arms as if he were attempting to fly. Then he stumbled and fell forward.

At first the man on the right didn't realize what had actually happened to his partner. He turned to chastise him for shooting from behind him. Moving with a slow motion gesture, he raised his rifle above his head. When he saw the blood pouring from his friend's shattered skull, his mouth opened and his eyes got wide. A movement directly in front of him drew his attention. He held his rifle out in front of himself as if to ward off a blow. Nevertheless, a bullet tore through his throat, dissecting an artery. Blood shot out like water from a punctured car radiator. The second bullet smacked him in the chest and drove him back on his bent legs. He died there in the awkward position, the blood still streaming down his neck, his eyes still wide open with the look of shock.

It took a while for the forest to grow still again. He stood there waiting as if he were afraid it might not happen. When he was satisfied that things had been restored to the way they were, he moved toward the dead men. For a few moments, he stood looking down at them. He put another bullet in each of their foreheads. It was a way of leaving more confusion, that's all. Then he rested his rifle against a tree. He undressed the one he had shot first and then he did the other, casting their clothes every which way.

Afterward, he moved in the direction of the fleeing buck. He followed in the deer's path long enough to satisfy himself that it hadn't been wounded. How many times had he come across one that had been? Most hunters today were terrible shots. They didn't use guns enough to be efficient, and the guns they had were too powerful for them to handle accurately. Many of them didn't handle guns but once a year. Some of them had no idea where to aim on a deer's body anyway. They simply pointed and shot. A wounded deer could go on for days, suffering terribly before it actually bled to death, the tale of its suffering frozen in its eyes.

He stood there for a few moments listening. Some clouds had moved in and made it even darker. There would be no help from the moon. He knew the direction home, but he couldn't move fast because he didn't want to scratch his face on a branch. That would be hard to explain.

When he was near the road, he stopped to be sure there was no one around. Then he ran out before anyone could come. He put his rifle away, standing there for a moment as if in silent prayer. His fingers were bent, both his hands looking more like hooves.

Then he drove off, soon forgetting why he had come and what he had done.

When he got home, he didn't know why he was dressed the way he was, but just as before, he didn't question the confusion. He put it aside like someone putting a puzzle into a drawer.

And then he went about the rest of his night being himself, being who he was, even though he hated it.

Three

DIANA BROOKS SAT BACK in her chair and clasped her hands behind her head. She closed her eyes and smiled. The editor in chief, Peter Benson, had approved her third straight major feature, pictures and all. With so much chatter about an editorial upheaval pending, and with Marion Heller, the publisher, quietly insisting that Peter give some of the women on the paper a chance to advance, Diana felt her career had reached a turning point. She would either stay with *The Middletown Post* or move on to a newspaper in New York City.

Actually, she hoped she would be promoted at the Middletown daily because the paper had grown considerably over the past few years. During the past year and a half, the daily had become a star in the Heller media chain. It was always Diana's intention to use it as a stepping stone to bigger and better things, but certainly those bigger and better things would loom even higher if she came out of an impressive editorial office. Actually, *The Middletown Post* had become the fifth largest upstate daily paper in New York. It was one thing to be a reporter for it, but quite another to be a feature editor.

At twenty-four, she couldn't complain that things had gone too slowly. Before she was twenty-three, she had graduated with a master's degree in journalism from Michigan State. In the beginning she intended to seek out a job out West. Like most young people in the area, she vowed in high school that she would "get the hell outta here" as soon as she could. She had grown up in a small community only ten miles north of Middletown, where her parents owned and operated a large furniture store.

But after graduation, openings didn't come her way as easily or as quickly as she had expected they would. Most of the opportunities she had found were in locations she had never considered and never wanted to consider. Because of her parents' heavy advertising in *The Middletown Post*, her father was friendly with Peter Benson. When her father called to tell her she could start with a job there and live at home to save money, she knew that this was her parents' way of keeping her a little longer. Being an only child, she could understand their motive, but she didn't trust her father's interest in her career. Her parents had always wanted her to settle down, get married and go into teaching.

"Journalism is such a gray area," he said. "You have no security."

"You didn't when you first started out in business, Dad," she reminded him.

"Yeah, but I was hoping things would be better for you than they were for me. That's the idea, you know, making things better for those who come after you."

"Whom do we know in journalism?" her mother added.

"That's not the point. I'm not looking for a safe little job that stuffs me away neatly in some part of the boondocks. It's the same old pattern women have been forced to follow since the Garden of Eden. I go to college. If I'm not engaged by the time I graduate, I go into teaching and try to meet a respectable guy. Then I get married."

"And what's so terrible about that plan?" her mother said.

"It's too dependent on my getting married. It sounds too much like an insurance policy. I want to be totally dependent on what I do, what my talents are."

"Look," her father finally said, "let her do what she wants to do."

Her mother nodded. They had obviously discussed it before. It was her father's way of saying, "She'll get tired, disillusioned, and defeated, and then she'll come home to do what we thought she would do from the beginning."

He had the look of a conspirator, someone who knew secret information as if he had a crystal ball in his office and he had seen her future.

Because of these suspicions, she was reluctant to take the position at *The Middletown Post*, but her adviser, Dr. Greer, told her it wasn't so bad an idea.

"People who start out in journalism really have to scrounge, Diana. Most of them begin at papers smaller than *The Middletown Post*. It's more than an adequate start. Make your mark there and be financially comfortable at the same time. When you feel you're ready to move on, it'll be easier than you think."

She considered. It had been easier than she expected for her to go off to college in another state. She was proud of the strength and independence she had already shown. There would be no quicksand at home, not for her.

Some of her college friends called her a "yo-yo." "You break away," they said, "but things pull you back."

She told this to her college advisor.

"Maybe they do," Dr. Greer said. He sat back and smiled after she told him. "However, things are changing. We used to be a country of nomads, but people are starting to see the value in roots and the emptiness in movement. We spend most of our lives trying to find ways to go home."

She liked that, although she didn't fully understand it at the time. Her roots were vague to her. When she began to work at the *Post*, she realized all the blanks she drew when she had to think about the area. She didn't know much about local government and very little about the intricacies of local industry and economics. She knew almost nothing about local history.

So she had to launch herself into a crash course in her own area. It had resulted in one of her successful features—a contrast between the area's economy and industry one hundred years ago and the economy and industry today. Some of the analogies were fascinating and the statistics intriguing. The paper had received good feedback from its readers.

Her quick success won her respect and admiration, but *The Middletown Post*, like any other fairly large news daily, had its infighting and politics. Before she had gotten the feature assignments, most of the big ones were done by Jeff Pearson, the present feature editor. He struck her as an insecure type, suspicious and jealous of everyone around him. There had been a shuffling in management only a year and a half ago and he had retained his position, but the word was that it was a hairline decision.

As far as Diana was concerned, Pearson had the physical appearance of a loser. A bachelor at forty-one, he was five feet eight inches tall and weighed close to two hundred ten pounds. The excess poundage distorted his facial features, giving him wide nostrils, large fishlike eyes, and thick lips. He was constantly panting and sweating, and there was nearly always a whiny tone in his voice.

Diana outclassed him from the start. She was always neat and immaculately dressed. Her hair was cut just to shoulder length. It was a rich, light brown, healthy and thick so it fell into place with a few short strokes of her brush. At five-nine, she still appeared to tower over the wide, plump Jeff Pearson. He hated to be caught standing next to her. He'd either sit and call her to him or approach her when she was seated.

Her strength and independence radiated through her eyes. She had the habit of looking directly at anyone she spoke to, rarely looking down or away. When she did an interview, the subject felt seized firmly in the grasp of her questions. Political figures, in particular, were made uncomfortable by this. On the other hand, Jeff Pearson tended to look down or at something when he spoke. He could rarely hold a gaze on Diana.

She carried her firm, well-proportioned body well, wearing outfits that emphasized her handsome long legs. Tony Manuchello, the sixty-one-year-old business manager, said she reminded him of Lauren Bacall. He was an old time movie fan with collector's posters of film noir, Bogart, and George Raft films. His compliment drove her to the American Movie Classics channel to catch Bacall. She started to imitate her hairdo, especially in *To Have and To Have Not*.

It really amused Tony, who couldn't stop sounding her horn, but in truth everyone at the paper envied her for her endless energy and exuberance. Her sense of organization and control made her stand out even more.

Other women and most of the men working in the editorial offices seemed continually overwhelmed by their labor. Their desks had disheveled appearances and they were in continuous frenzies about their work. A new assignment or an additional demand created near hysteria. Complaints, bitching, and groans were the currencies of conversational exchange.

They're not hungry enough, Diana thought. They lack the ambition. Her greatest fear was she would be unused, overlooked. She seized on whatever she could, seeing most everything as an opportunity.

Jeff Pearson knew this and he both envied and despised her for it.

It was not without some malicious intent then that he looked out his office window at the young female writer at her desk and thought, *Let her take this one and we'll see what a hotshot she'll be.* He nearly laughed aloud as he studied Benson's assignment. He stood up and went to his door.

"Diana, could you come in here a moment."

She contemplated him and then sat forwards, bringing her hands to her desk and instinctively grabbing up a notepad. Pearson sat down quickly as she entered.

"What's up?"

"I've got a new assignment for you, if you think you're up to it."

She caught the sound of a challenge in his voice, harking back to a childish dare, but she kept her look of indifference.

"What do you have?"

"Big story developing in Sullivan County today. Some gruesome hunting murder."

"More news desk, isn't it?"

"Facts are, but Benson and I have another angle," he said, obviously relishing the opportunity to include himself in an executive decision.

"And what would that be?"

"We want a series—an in-depth look at the

nature of big game hunting in the Catskills," he said, a wry smile forming. "Does violence breed violence? Do we have a budding Son of Sam out there, born during big game hunting season?

"We want to know about the type of people who trek through the forest all day to blow a deer out of the woods. Are people hunting because they're hungry for the meat or hungry for the kill? The bloodlust? Highlight a few hunters—some who do it yearly and some who just started, if you can. Get lots of authentic pictures. Get into the woods yourself. Get pictures of dead animals. The works. Don't worry about the expense budget either."

She stood there staring down at him for a moment, her indecision and confusion keeping her from an immediate response. Pearson began to feel that superiority he longed to feel. He curled his lips in at the corners.

"Of course, if you think this is too ugly for you to handle . . ."

"Ugly?"

"Well, I know women today are supposed to have the stomachs of men, but . . . ," he said widening his smile.

"Skip the sarcasm, Brad. I'll do it from the unisex point of view." She started out, paused and then turned slowly, nodding and smiling. "You know," she said, "this sounds like a damn interesting piece, especially in light of the debates about gun control today and the influence of the NRA. Charlton Heston hunting Bambi," she said writing the dramatic headline in the air between them. "Thanks for the opportunity to do something special."

The smile flew off his face as she walked out and he felt his throat closing. He already began regretting what he had done and she hadn't even typed her first word.

❧

Aaron stepped out on the porch after dinner. It was only six thirty, but the town was dark and deserted. There wasn't even a stray dog in the streets tonight. Every living thing had crawled into a warm space to sleep and wait for the reassurance that came with the morning sun. He watched the breeze bounce some light, discarded newspaper along the gutter. It looked like it was trying desperately to climb up and over the curb, but the breeze was relentless and it continued to bounce and fly until it was gone from sight, swallowed up by the darkness.

Suddenly, he saw Willie's patrol car turn slowly and start past his house and garage. He hurried down the steps to wave him over. Willie leaned across the front seat and rolled down his window.

"What's new?" Aaron asked quickly. "Something

happening? Usually don't see you around this time of the day."

"Just cruising. The murder's got everyone jittery. Tillie Trustman's sitting with a loaded shotgun in her lap. There's so much tension in the air, I feel like I'm walking through cobwebs."

"Yeah, I can see why. My mother reminded me that the last murder in this hamlet happened nearly fifty years ago. The famous Kaye Taylor murder of her husband."

"Cut him up and tried to cook him out of sight. My father used to tell me the story to scare the hell out of me if I misbehaved. I still dream about it," Willie said laughing.

Aaron just nodded as if he dreamed about it, too.

"You okay?" Willie asked. "I know that was quite a sight, the blood trickling over his face and down the sides of his chest."

"I try not to think about it."

"Me neither. I guess I'll get home and get some sleep. Who knows when I'll get another fuckin' chance?" Willie said and rolled up his window.

Aaron watched him drive off, his head turning slowly from side to side as if he truly expected to see something suspicious in these deserted hamlet's streets.

Even the police chief is spooked, Aaron thought, not that he especially considered him a brave man.

There was no doubt he was a tough man, a hard man, but demons had a way to slip under everyone's doors these days.

He continued to gaze down the street. Something deadly lingered here now. Murder put a stain on every shadow. You couldn't trust the darkness. It threw you back to childhood fears, he thought and continued to study the streets upon which he had played and lived all his life.

He had an instinctive feeling that the killer lived here, lived among them. He was local. He had to be. He couldn't just have stumbled on Al Jones. How would the killer know Al was going out a day before the season unless he had heard him say it? Or unless the killer was often out there. Maybe he was out there when he and Walker were hunting, too. Maybe that was who he had felt.

He looked up at the deer. It was time to take them down and get them butchered. No one made venison stew like his mother did. He wondered if it would taste as good this year or would all that has happened have an effect on even that?

He glanced down the empty main street again and then hurried inside just as Walker was going up the stairs.

"Where you heading tonight?" Aaron asked

"Old Mill." He smiled lustily. "Wanna come along? You might have a good time."

"Naw. Bunch of high school kids."

"You'd be surprised."

"I would."

Walker lost his smile. Aaron frustrated him. Why wasn't Aaron as hungry for fun and sex as he was? Why did he always make him feel immature just because he wanted to enjoy himself? Wasn't it true that all work and no play made Jack a dull boy?

"So what are ya gonna do, stay home and watch Archie Bunker reruns with the old lady again?" he asked, smirking and shaking his head in disapproval.

"Might."

"She doesn't need you by her side all the time, Aaron, not her, and she hates the idea that you think she does."

"I don't stay because I think she does. I'm tired of hanging around the bars with a bunch of losers all looking for the same piece of ass. Some of them are so bad off, they wouldn't know it if they fell over it."

"Beats staying home," Walker said. His voice lingered as if he wanted some reassurance.

Aaron was thoughtful.

"Maybe I'll go over to O'Heany's and play some pool with the stump jumpers."

"Waste of time. You'll never find a girl there. Lotta college girls around now. I heard the community college female population is at least two to one this year. Makes for a lotta hard-up coeds. And I can please them all," he said, pumping his arms out to the sides and doing a quick dance step.

Aaron thought his brother Walker was incorrigible ever since Barbara Rosen told him he reminded her of Richard Gere in *An Officer and a Gentleman*.

"Yeah, yeah. Just don't get loaded. Mom's a little on edge because of all this. Everyone is, Walker. Don't get into any arguments. There are people with hair triggers in every corner tonight."

"I'll be all right. Change your mind later, you'll find me on the dance floor at the Old Mill, broads all around me," Walker said and headed upstairs to put the finishing touches on his hair.

Aaron found his mother still cleaning in the kitchen. For a moment he watched her unseen. Cleanliness was such an important thing to her. She was always afraid someone would come in and find dust on the top of the refrigerator or a cobweb in the corner of a room. If anything wore out in this house, he thought, it was worn down by her constant scrubbing, not by age. He started to sit at the table.

She spoke without turning to him, which brought a smile to his face. How that woman could sense things, he thought.

"Don't hang around here Saturday night on my account, Aaron Kuhn," she said. Then she turned as he went for the chair.

"That ain't very hospitable, Marilyn Kuhn."

"Nevertheless, no one's gonna say I made a bachelor out of you," she said. She said it as if it had already been either implied or told to her, probably by the church committee women. "I can get along very well by myself evenings, thank you."

"Are you chasing me out to find some sort of woman?" Aaron teased.

"Not some sorta woman," she said turning quickly. "I never would think of suggesting anyone to you or your brother. That sort of thing never works out right in the end. I don't care about the way some of those old timers talk about how things were so much better when marriages were arranged."

"Wasn't your marriage arranged?"

"What? My marriage wasn't arranged. Maybe your father and I were nudged in the right direction, but as far as making up my own mind and . . ." She paused, catching herself in the middle of a familiar speech.

They stared at each other for a moment and then he laughed. She shook her head. "Just like your father, waitin' for me to bite and go on and on. Then you laugh at me. When am I gonna learn to ignore you two?"

The smile froze on his face. She realized what she had said and turned away quickly. Something in her would never permit her to bury her husband forever and ever.

"Never mind. You work hard all week, Aaron. You deserve whatever pleasure you can get," she said in a softer tone. "Go on and find whatever sort of woman you want."

"I'll wait until I find one like you," he said. She smiled but she didn't turn to let him see. "Oh all right. I guess I'll go over to O'Heany's for a while and see what's doin'."

"Is that the only place you know? Why don't you get dressed up and go to one of those hotel bars where they have singles weekends?"

He broke into a wide smile.

"What do you know about singles weekends, Ma?"

"What's this about singles weekends?" Walker came down the stairs quickly.

"I just said that your brother and you oughta get dressed up and go over to one of the hotels."

"Aaron? Get dressed up and go over to one of the hotels?" He held back a laugh. "I'll go if he goes. And besides, Ma, I am dressed up," Walker added turning around for her.

"Fancy jeans and a shirt opened to your navel is not my idea of dressed up."

Aaron laughed. Walker's smiled faded.

"Well things have changed since you were courting, Ma."

"Not for the better," she said. "I see the way young women dress today. Women had some self-respect back when I was younger and a decent man wouldn't want any other," she lectured. Aaron looked away, but kept his smile.

"Yeah, well, I'll see you all later."

"You take it easy," Marilyn Kuhn called out. "And don't get drunk!"

"I never do." The door slammed closed.

She stared out for a moment and then looked at Aaron.

"That boy worries me," she said more to herself than to him.

"He'll be all right, Ma."

"I pray," she said.

"You can't ride him. He's still young enough to do something just because you or I tell him not to."

"Well, why is that? Your father was raising a family at his age and being responsible."

"We can't be Dad," Aaron said. "No sense in your trying to get us to be."

She took a deep breath and then nodded.

"You're right, Aaron," she said softly.

He shook his head, regretting any words that gave her any pain. Then he rose. He had decided to go back up to change his clothes, shave, and comb his hair. Perhaps Walker was right, he thought. Maybe I have been using Mom as an excuse to avoid relationships with women.

It wasn't that he lacked confidence in himself. Women didn't run from him; he ran from them, but it wasn't because of shyness or a poor self-image. The Kuhns weren't good losers and he had once lost big when he committed his heart and soul to Tracy Cross, a high school sweetheart.

It's the hardest thing in the world to give yourself to someone, he thought. For many people it's become a near impossibility. Maybe I'm one of them and maybe there are more people like me than I first imagined. He gave that some serious consideration.

He had a theory couched in images and language from his own work: people had closed up like seized pistons in a car engine. The metals had merged, locked shut. In today's world it wasn't smart ever to reveal yourself. It was foolish to be honest. People used each other selfishly. It was no longer a process of one giving to another sincerely for mutual satisfaction. He was caught in a transition. He came from an old-fashioned house and his ties to it and its ways were strong. It was easier for Walker. Walker didn't remember his grandfathers as well, and he hadn't spent as much time with Dad. Walker was part of the newer world.

He laughed to himself. His thoughts made him

sound like a man of sixty or seventy years. But it was true—he was uncomfortable with most people his age. Also it was true that Tracy had been different. She seemed to want the same things and have the same values. He had trusted her and given her his most intimate self. Then he found out she had been seeing someone from Liberty Falls those night she claimed she was preparing for her community college classes. Her betrayal left him naked. He vowed never to be as vulnerable again. To compensate, he thought of her as someone who had died.

He turned to a quote he loved. His mother had read it to him from the old Bible in the courtin' room and he never forgot it.

"If you should die, I will hate all womankind."

For him she had died. And it was true: he had tried to bury all womankind. Deep in his heart, however, he knew it was something he shouldn't do and, when he was truly honest with himself, something he knew he really couldn't do.

Besides, it wasn't the time to think of things dying, not with all this going on. It was a time to throw sand in Death's face and go forward.

You give into the darkness and it will take over your dreams, he thought.

He liked that. It made him smile. It made him wonder if indeed he could tap into his family's well of ancient wisdom.

❦

O'Heany's was a rather big bar on a side street in the village of Monticello, a village much bigger than Centerville. Because it was the county seat, all the government buildings were located there. But it was mainly because of the trotter racetrack just outside the village that many of the new restaurants, motels, topless bars and nightclubs had sprouted up, building the population and the tempo of life in this once rather sedate Catskill Mountain town.

Actually, O'Heany's was really too far from the track to benefit from the track crowd. It was frequented instead by locals, mostly laborers and tradespeople. The menu consisted of a half dozen sandwiches, chicken, or shrimp in the basket, and steamed clams. In the center of the large room was a U-shaped bar with a television set high up enough and centrally located so that anyone sitting on any stool could see it. It was most always turned on, even when there was too much noise for anyone to hear anything. Off right of the bar was the pool table and to the left of that were a half dozen small tables surrounding a juke box. The kitchen was directly in the back.

The Irish family that had once owned O'Heany's had long since sold out. Now it was run by an Italian, Carmine Rosetti, and his brother Dick.

Dick's wife did most of the kitchen work. There was usually only one waitress on duty off season, but during the summer months and big game season, there were six, rotating the hours.

All the way back on the right side, the owners had placed a couch and a dartboard. There was a small table beside the couch. The speciality of the bar was a jug of beer. The regulars would play darts or pool to determine who would pay for the next jug. A large scorecard located just under the television set listed the names of high scorers.

O'Heany's was the closest thing to an old-fashioned pub. For the regulars who came there nightly, and especially on weekends, it took the place of a living room. Most of the men were single; some confirmed bachelors. A few came with their wives—hard-looking laboring women wearing men's jackets and pants. They sat at the bar and nibbled on peanuts and chips. If strangers came in on an exploratory visit, they usually remained for only one drink. It wasn't because the regulars were unfriendly either. There was just a special air of privacy to the place.

People who frequented O'Heany's were uncomplicated and unassuming types. They discussed their financial problems with an almost childish honesty; talked about family situations with one another as if they were all of the same family. They were suspicious of people who were subtle and closed-mouthed. Their first impression was that the person thought himself better, and if there was one characteristic they despised, it was social arrogance.

Rarely was there any violence. Arguments were settled by everyone who overheard any. Razzing and kidding would almost always be stopped short of any real anger or annoyance. If an occasional fight did break out, the parties usually made up shortly afterward. The small community that made up O'Heany's bar crowd wouldn't tolerate long term feuds. Such things made everyone uncomfortable, and O'Heany's was above all a place to be comfortable in a world that for so many reasons had become very uncomfortable.

Aaron liked it there because of all these things. He felt at ease; he felt he didn't have to be someone he wasn't. There was no one to impress. He could come dressed casually and be confident. For him, O'Heany's was safe. He didn't like Walker's hangouts because there were too many young, pretty, and sexy girls. They confused and unnerved him with their promiscuity, and it was too important to be macho and cool at Walker's places. All the hotel bars were too expensive, too sophisticated, and too plastic for him.

What's more, his father had brought him to O'Heany's. He had his first beer served over a bar to him here. This place was a personal landmark. He could vividly recall how his father would quickly become a center of interest. Men would gather around him as if he were the hub of a wheel.

Aaron hadn't anticipated how much Al Jones's brutal murder would change the atmosphere in O'Heany's and the nature of his relationship to the rest of the crowd. The moment he opened the door and stepped in and saw the faces turning to him, he realized it wasn't going to be one of his usually quiet evenings.

Just about every man who frequented O'Heany's was a hunter. Most of them were wearing their hunting jackets with their licenses pinned to the back. A few men still wore their bullet belts. The odors of steam clams, chicken, and shrimp mingled with the odors of the forest—mud and water, smoked wood and pine needles.

He paused for a second, almost deciding to turn around and go home. When he approached the bar, they made a place for him quickly. It was inevitable. He decided to get it over as quickly as he could. Everyone was eager to buy him a beer. Now that the story was out in the public view, he no longer had the burden of keeping it all secret. None of these people would have tolerated or appreciated his saying he was unable to talk about it because of legal restrictions anyway. He began to answer the questions and all other conversation ceased. Someone pulled the jukebox plug, and Dick Rosetti turned down the television volume. Aaron had no reason to hold back the gruesome details here. Just about everyone had known Al Jones and just about everyone could tolerate the description.

After Aaron finished and their curiosity had been satiated, he sat quietly. Side conversations started up again, theories argued. For a few moments afterward, all spoke in subdued, low tones. His story had spread a layer of gloom over the place. Most of the crowd moved away from him and he was left talking to a couple of old timers, each with his particular memory of a horrible hunting accident. He seemed to be attracting depressing tales, drawing them out of people.

Now he wondered if he might not have been better off going with Walker to his hangouts, places where people wouldn't know of or talk of the Al Jones's murder. He began to envy Walker for his night of escape.

Finally, he was able to get himself into a pool game. When the men around him continued to talk about the murder, he replied in monosyllabic words and grunts. It seemed hopeless. He couldn't even play pool well and decided he was better off if he left and made it an early evening. He was about to do so when Diana Brooks walked in.

The entrance of a strange woman her age unescorted would have attracted everyone's attention anyway, but there was a particular electricity generated in the air already because of the story of the murder. She merely highlighted the excitement. She had hoped to be unobtrusive. Her journalistic intention was to mingle quietly with these people and gather the kind of local color information she felt essential for the series. A phone call to the Sullivan County bureau chief had resulted in a list of a half dozen places favored by local hunters. She began with O'Heany's.

The small group of men clothed in red and black checkered flannel shirts and hunting jackets of bright orange and bright red parted to make way for her. Some of the faces collapsed into appreciative and lusty smiles; others remained stoically objective. She nodded and with tight lips, smiled back. Feigning a surge of gallantry, a young, wild dark brown-haired man of about twenty quickly slid off his bar stool. He whipped the handkerchief out of his back pocket and wiped down the imitation black leather. There were a few chuckles.

"What'cha doin', Timmy? You ain't cleaned nothing in years."

"Watch him, Miss," a tall, heavy man to her right said, "he's a lady killer."

"Yeah," someone from behind added, "they drop dead when they smell his breath."

There was a lot of laughter.

"Thanks for the advice," Diana said and took the stool. Then she turned to Timmy and said, "Thanks for the seat, 'lady killer.'"

There was a loud chorus of "whoa." She put her purse on the bar.

For her research among the locals, she had chosen to wear a ski jacket and tight black ski pants. There was a fluffy, white fur collar on the jacket and the color emphasized her rosy cheeks. All of the younger men began taunting each other and nodding in her direction. Throughout it all, Diana held her Mona Lisa smile and unzipped her jacket, aware that every one of her moves was under close scrutiny.

"Can I buy you a drink?" Timmy asked.

"If you let me pick your mind," she said.

"Huh?"

"He ain't got a mind," someone shouted. There was some laughter behind her, but most everyone's interest had been sharpened.

Aaron watched her entrance, just as the other men did, but when the stags gathered around her, he turned back to the pool table. He had always hated the idea of competing for a woman. For him it reduced the relationship to a game. Most women who liked that sort of thing were frivolous types anyway, he thought. Even if he succeeded in winning them to him, he wouldn't be satisfied.

Just for a moment though, when he looked up again, he felt sorry for this girl. Perhaps she had innocently wandered into this situation and didn't know how to gracefully extract herself from it. He looked over his next shot, but he kept half an ear on the dialogue at the bar.

"I'm looking for some information," she said. Carmine Rosetti stood before her. "Just a beer, please."

"Just a beer?" He looked at the men around her. They all laughed. She blushed.

First faux pas, she thought. This isn't going to be easy. She imagined Jeff Pearson's arrogant smile and dug in, however.

"Yes, just a beer," she repeated.

"Give her the best beer in the house," Timmy commanded.

There was more laughter and some applause. Everything said seemed to have the power of extracting some dramatic response. It was as if she had wandered into a recreation hall for lunatics.

"What kind of information are you after?" she heard someone ask.

The tall, heavy man behind her moved up to the bar, pushing others out of his way. He leaned toward her. She caught a stale, sickly sweet aroma coming from his clothing. When he smiled, the chewing tobacco in his mouth clung to his upper teeth. He looked as though he hadn't shaved for a week or more and there were small red hairs curling out from under his nostrils. Her stomach churned with revulsion, but she kept her smile.

"Hunting information."

"You wanna be a hunter?" Timmy said.

She didn't turn to him because the glass of beer was served and she welcomed the opportunity to look away from both of them.

"I don't want to be a hunter, no. I want to know something about hunting."

"Why?" the tall man asked. His shoulder nudged hers as he took over the stool beside her.

"I'm writing about it."

"Oh," Timmy said with some disappointment, but the tall man didn't seem to grasp her meaning. What did writing have to do with hunting?

"What do you mean?"

"I'm doing a story about hunting. I work for *The Middletown Post*," she said. Instinctively, she felt it was better to be straightforward with these people. He stared at her for a moment, blinking his bloodshot eyes.

"So that's it," Timmy said and then turned to the audience directly behind them. "She's a reporter," he announced as if announcing she was a spy.

"Not exactly a reporter," she said quickly. "I do features."

"Features? What's features?" he asked, grimacing. Everything he said was loud now and for the benefit of those behind them.

"Like essays. They're not news exactly. I mean, they're factual, but they're not totally objective."

"You better move away from her, Timmy. She's too smart for you. You didn't get outta high school," the tall, big man said.

"I did too. I broke out."

"Wait a minute," the tall man said, putting his hand on her forearms as she brought the beer glass to her lips. "You're not writing about Al Jones, are ya?"

"Well, in a way."

"Well, hell, lady," he said slapping the bar, "you walked right into the right place. See that fella over there playin' pool?"

She looked across the bar. Aaron deliberately turned his back and chalked his cue stick.

"Yes?"

"He's the one who found Al Jones in the woods all shot to hell."

"Really?"

"Hey, Aaron," the tall man called, "get your ass over here."

Aaron didn't turn around. Stan Collins, the tall, heavy man at the bar, was a boisterous, big-mouth type who made claims everyone knew were false.

Aaron remembered how much his father hated the type—loud people who talked a lot but did very little. They always claimed there was a time in the past when they had done something better than someone had done it in the present.

"It's better to ignore this type," his father told him. "If you don't, you'll end up poundin' him into the ground every time you see him."

"There's a pretty lady here who wants to talk to you about Al Jones. Come over here," Stan ordered as if he were the general of the O'Heany army.

"I'm busy," Aaron said without turning to him. "And I don't want to talk about it anymore."

"That ain't polite."

"It's all right," Diana said, but Collins had already committed himself to doing something for her. It had become a matter of his masculine pride.

"He'll talk," Stan said. "Just a minute."

"It's not really . . ."

Collins was up before she could stop him. He walked across the room, shoving people out of his way. Aaron didn't turn around, but when he lifted the pool stick to take a shot, Collins took hold of the back of it.

"Hey, don't you see that nice pussy over there just waitin' to be entertained."

Aaron pulled the stick from his grasp. They were nearly nose to nose.

"I said I was tired of talking about it."

Collins stared at him a moment and then he sneered and nodded.

"Feelin' like a big shot just 'cause you and your brother stumbled on a murdered dead man, huh?"

"Think what you like," Aaron said turning back to the pool table.

"Come on, Stan, leave him be," one of the men at the pool table said. Collins deliberately nudged the table and jolted Aaron's cue ball.

"Hey," another pool player said.

"Stubborn son of a bitch," Collins said. "Just like I heard your old man was."

Aaron could almost hear something click inside him. A gate was opened, a door jarred; everything rushed out—his father was dead and a man like this was alive, his mother's sad eyes, her lonely hours, his own bitter loneliness—all of it roared forth, raging, tearing. His body tightened, the muscles in his back tensing, the muscles in his neck turning to ropes of steel.

He spun around like a huge coil spring that had been released, and his fist shot out from waist level and caught Collins in his soft, protruding belly. The shirt and the flesh gave way like a sponge. The heavy man groaned and fell backward, clutching himself. His face turn bright red as he gasped for breath. He looked as though he would explode.

Instantly, every man around interceded. Four of them held Aaron's arms. A few placed themselves between the two men. They stood there with their arms out, holding away invisible forces. A couple of others helped Collins stand and held him from making any advances. For a few moments he had all he could do to catch his breath and recover from the blow.

"Fuckin' . . . son of a bitch . . . I'll tear the bastard . . ."

Aaron glared back at him. The weight of the men on his arms helped subdue the rage.

"It's all right," he finally said to rid himself of the human shackles. "I'm all right."

"Just take it easy, Collins," Carman said from behind the bar.

His brother came around and stood with his hands on his hips.

"Leave him be. Everyone told you to leave him be. If you can't stay away from him, get the hell out of here."

"Right," Dick said.

Collins relaxed and the men around him backed a few steps away. He raised his fist at Aaron.

"I'll get you, you bastard," he said, "when there aren't so many guys around to protect you."

Someone laughed up front, but when Collins turned to see who it was, the place grew deadly silent.

"He snuck one in on me," he whined, waving his hand toward Aaron.

"Come on, forget it. Come on," the men around him chanted.

"I'll buy you a beer," Timmy called. That seemed to satisfy him and he went back to the bar, mumbling curses and vows of revenge.

Aaron watched him carefully for a moment. He looked like he was still deciding on whether to fight him. Those around him stirred nervously. Someone put his cue stick back in his hand, but before he turned back to the pool table, he caught sight of Diana staring at him. Her face was flushed and excited. In the instant of that quick glance, he thought she was absolutely the prettiest thing he had ever seen, and he could do little to keep his heart from pounding.

Four

HE LOST ALL ENTHUSIASM FOR POOL. Collins was off to the other side, sitting at a table and complaining to a group of vaguely interested listeners. Aaron was disappointed in himself. What had come over him? He violated the advice his father had given him about people like Stan Collins, and in doing so, he had made himself the center of attention again. He didn't like it. The evening had gone sour for him. There was nothing to do but go home. He certainly couldn't give the game its proper concentration. Other men might stay, he thought, just to prove they weren't afraid and couldn't be intimidated. It took more courage to leave.

He put up his cue stick and reached for his jacket. None of the men around the table questioned him.

All pretended not to notice his preparations for departure. Carmine winked and lifted his hand as Aaron started out. He heard Stan Collins's loud laugh, but he didn't turn around. Out of the corner of his eye, he saw the girl at the bar staring at him, a great look of seriousness and concern on her face while Timmy Wylie talked at her.

As soon as he shut the door behind him, cutting off the music, the heat, and the noise, he felt a sense of relief and resurrection. He was alone again. There were no eyes on him. He was loose again and could move freely. He started down the sidewalk. His car was parked around the corner because all the spots on the side street had been taken when he arrived. He decided to drive around awhile, since going home so early might arouse his mother's concern. He even considered the possibility of looking for Walker, but when he was almost to the corner, he heard his name called. He turned around to see the girl walking quickly toward him.

The sight of her started his heart pounding. He never expected he would ever set eyes on her again and deep inside a part of him had already begun mourning over that conclusion.

"I'm sorry," she said coming up beside him. "It was all my fault back there."

"Your fault?"

"He wouldn't have bothered you if I hadn't come

in there inquiring. It was just bad luck all around for me to go in that place."

"You've got a right to go in there," Aaron said. "Not that I would put all that much value on it."

He kept his hands in his pockets and studied her. Small strands of hair had moved over her forehead. He liked the petite, delicate features in her face, but something in the shape of her mouth reminded him of Tracy. It brought his admiration to a fast halt.

"Were you really the hunter who found the murdered man?" she asked softly, handling him as if he was a soap bubble that might pop in her fingers.

"I wasn't hunting at the time. He was missing. His wife had called the police. I was just a part of a search party. I'm not any hero or anything."

"You don't hunt?" There was the sound of surprise and disappointment in her voice.

"Yeah, I hunt," he said, He looked away. "I had already gotten my deer."

"I see." She continued to stand there, staring at him. It piqued his curiosity.

"Just what is it you're after?"

"I'm a writer for *The Middletown Post*."

"I heard that," he said. "Exactly, what do they want you to do?"

She smiled, actually admiring his need to get right to the point.

"This murder in the woods has stimulated an interest in the hunting cult. At least for the editor and feature editor," she added with a small smirk.

"The hunting cult?"

"Well, the sport, the people who participate in it, the reasons why they do it—that kind of thing," she rushed out, sensing another faux pas.

Aaron nodded.

"Nothing like a brutal murder to stimulate the interest of a sensational news hound," he said.

She blanched, but she didn't turn away.

"I'm not concentrating on the murder," she said. "That's more news desk. I do a more in-depth study. Psychological factors, sociological."

"Good," he said. "O'Heany's is the place for an in-depth study. You'll especially find lots of psychological stuff to write about in there."

He started away. She watched him for a moment and then walked after him.

"I didn't pick this assignment," she said coming up beside him again. "The truth is I'm not happy about it. Hunting of any kind is brutal to me and I'm not anxious to go into places like that."

"So why do it?" he muttered as he continued to walk.

"Why do it? I was assigned it. If you want to be a professional, you take your job seriously and do what has to be done."

He stopped and turned around. The look of defiance and anger in her eyes intrigued him.

"Just following orders, eh?"

"Yes. Don't you do things you might not like, but do them because it's part of your work, whatever that is?" she countered.

He thought about Dr. Fern's wife's car and smiled.

"Yeah, I guess I do from time to time. Look," he said in a softer voice, "you didn't go to the wrong place. I'm not kidding. If that's what you're writing about, you'll learn a lot about hunters back there."

She glanced back at O'Heany's and shook her head.

"I don't think I'll learn the things I need for my articles," she said. "I'll spend most of my time keeping hands off my thighs."

He smiled and nodded.

"Can't argue with that," he said.

"Where are you going now?" she asked.

"Huh?"

"Are you heading somewhere special?" she asked, again with that timid, careful tone of voice.

"Why?" he demanded, not hiding his suspicion.

"Well you must know enough about hunting to be a professional if you've already gotten your deer. It is just the beginning of what they call the big game season, isn't it?" she asked and seemed to hold her breath. He could see she wasn't confident of that fact. She really didn't know much about hunting at all.

He shook his head.

"I'm not a professional. I'm just . . ."

"I don't want a professional," she followed quickly. She was determined not to lose him, it seemed. "Look, at least let me buy you a drink somewhere. I'd like to make up for what happened back there in Deliverance Inn."

"Deliverance Inn?" he thought aloud and then laughed "Oh. Yeah, I can see why you said that, although most of the guys in there are okay. They just look like they married their sisters."

She nodded. She would accept anything he said.

"I'm sure you're right. So, what about that drink?"

"We don't talk about the killing?"

"If you don't want to, no." He was silent. "I'm not going to hurt you," she said. She said it so seriously it made him laugh.

"Okay," he said, "but I'm not in the custom of letting women buy me drinks."

"Too bad. You won't be able to take advantage of women's liberation. My car's just down here," she said turning. He took her arm.

"And my car's just down this way," he said.

"I know, I know." She put her hands up. "You're not in the custom of having women drive you around. What are you, the last of the macho men?"

"The way it seems to me these days, I might be the first."

She laughed.

"Come on," he said, "before I change my mind."

"Something tells me you rarely do that," she countered and he smiled to himself as he opened the car door for her.

There was another place that was comfortable for Aaron, a very small bar only a mile out of Monticello. It catered mostly to the hotel workers at the Concord Hotel. He had done work for the owner once, a rather heavy but soft-spoken Hungarian named John Nussbaum. Although he had been in the area for more than twenty five years, he still maintained a strong European accent. Nussbaum's was never crowded. No real food was served. It was merely a bar. Aaron had been there recently when he had returned Nussbaum's car. Once he stopped there with Walker on a terribly hot summer day to get a cold beer. Walker hated the place and couldn't imagine why he liked it.

"There's a lot more local color at O'Heany's," Aaron said when he and Diana entered, "but this place has its charm."

There were only three small tables, so most of the clientele sat at the bar. One of the tables was free so they went right to it.

All of the hotel workers who sat at the bar were still in their uniforms. There were a number of busboys, dressed in white shirts and black pants. There were chambermaids and custodial personnel. There was no television set on here and the jukebox was dark, its plug out, the wire draped over it. The conversation was subdued; the people looked tired and bewildered.

"I didn't think the resort area was so busy now," Diana said.

"Conventions, hunters. It's a little quieter, but there are plenty of tourists and guests around. It gives the area a needed shot in the arm, especially these days."

"Aaron. Goot to see you." Nussbaum came out from around the bar, smiling and wiping his hands on a dishtowel that was tucked in his belt.

"John. This is Diana Brooks. She writes for *The Middletown Post* so don't give us any chipped glasses or anything."

"Would I do dat?" He smiled at Diana. "What'll it be?"

"Just two mugs of beer, John," Aaron replied and smiled at Diana. "That is your favorite drink, isn't it?" he asked, holding back a smile. "At least that was what I heard back at O'Heany's."

"I deserve that. Actually, I like beer."

"Two mugs," Nussbaum said turning to the bar.

There was no one else there, but it was as if he were giving orders to another bartender. Diana shook her head.

"One thing this area has plenty of—little bars and characters," she said.

"Yeah. So where are you from?"

"Pine Bush."

"No, I mean before you worked for the *Post*."

"Pine Bush," she repeated.

"Pine Bush? A local girl?" She nodded. "I don't get it. No one hunts down your way?"

"I suppose. To tell you the truth, I've never paid much attention to it. My parents own a furniture store and my father never hunted anything but customers. I knew hunting went on, but only vaguely knew. There's a great deal about my own area I've never paid much attention to," she confessed. "Like so many people my age, I grew up in my own little world."

"I'll bet."

"Why do you say it that way? With such agreement, I mean?" She asked, still looking more interested in his answers than he wanted her to be. It made him feel more like being in an oral examination or something than just with a pretty young woman, relaxing and having a beer.

"I dunno. You look like someone who has been sheltered and isolated most of her life."

"Sheltered? You sure you don't mean spoiled?"

"You're the writer. You chose the word. All right," he said feeling more generous now, "what is it you want to know about hunters?"

"For starters, how long have you been doing it and why do you do it?"

"Always have, long as I was able to. I suppose it's part of who we are. I come from generations of men who hunted, on both sides of my family. We just do it. I just do it. I don't analyze it."

"Are you saying it's in your nature, inherited?"

"No, not just mine. It's in everyone's in my family, but I do believe there's a little hunter in everyone. It is instinctive, part of the species."

She tilted her head and smiled.

"Deer hunting?"

"Not deer hunting, per se, but there was a time when people either hunted or starved to death."

"I guess I would have starved," she said quickly, shifting her eyes to avoid a look of condemnation.

"I doubt it. I don't think you've ever been hungry, really hungry, but if you were, you'd be surprised at what you'd chase for a meal. Besides," he said, "You're here hunting for a good story, aren't you?"

They stared at each other for a moment, neither breaking expression. Then the smile formed in his eyes and she laughed.

She turned her head to flip her hair back off her

face. That little gesture caught him by surprise, but it touched him. He thought it was something he would see forever. He would just pause wherever he was, in whatever he was doing and see her flip that hair. The feeling, the realization of the feeling, made him a little nervous, but he continued to stare at her. She was interesting. All the little things about her were interesting, not just the way she tossed her hair. He liked the way she raised the corner of her mouth when she wanted to listen intently. He liked the small dimple that flickered on and off in the base of her left cheek.

Nussbaum brought the beer.

"How's your mama?" he asked.

"She's fine, John. Thanks for asking."

"She's always so nice to me on the phone, never rushing me away."

"Yeah, she still believes in phone etiquette," Aaron said.

"Whatever it is, it's nice." Nussbaum looked at Diana and then glanced at Aaron and moved away quickly to leave them alone.

Diana had been thinking about what he had said. She looked up immediately and spoke as if nothing had interrupted them.

"Yes, I'm hunting up a story, but I don't kill anything in the process," she said, "And the point is we don't have to be hunters anymore. Your kind of hunting is a true blood sport. The hunt, the chase, the discovery, that's all one sort of thing; but pulling that trigger, killing something, that's another. Don't you think about it, think about the life you're taking?"

He ran his right forefinger along the rim of his mug. For a few moments she feared he wouldn't speak. In truth, her passionate reply surprised him, but it challenged him as well.

"I'm not a college graduate, so I'm not going to give you some deep explanation. As I said a while back just about everyone hunted because they needed the meat. It was an important source of food. I'm not going back as far as the cave man days, although I suppose it started with that and for some, it's still an important reason. Anyway, . . ." He stopped when he looked up from his beer. "Why are you smirking?"

"It's just that I refuse to believe people do it for that reason today."

"But many do. Really."

"With food stamps and welfare and . . ."

"Listen," he said, unable to prevent the anger from coming into his eyes, "there are a lot of people out there who eat their hearts out every day because they have to be on some form of welfare. They come from a stock of independent people. The hunt gives them a sense of dignity, even if it's just for a little while."

"But surely, the majority of hunters . . ."

"The majority of hunters? No. But what I was going to say . . . you'll think it's silly, I'm sure . . . was that hunting became part of our instinct. We're predators. The tendency, the urge, whatever you want to call it . . . it's there, under the skin. There are things in your blood that you cannot ignore. Maybe they are stronger for some than for others, but they are there in everyone nevertheless."

When he stopped talking, she simply stared at him for a few moments.

"What?" he asked.

This man was far more complicated than she had anticipated. She had underestimated him. She had considered the possibility of the hunting information as interesting from a novelty point of view, but never considered that she would find herself fascinated with the conversation. That was what was happening, and for some reason, it frightened her a little as well as pleased her. Was he right? Were there things within her, within everyone, that she would rather deny?

"You're a very deceptive fellow, Aaron Kuhn."

"Why? Because I don't talk like an idiot?" he asked sharply.

"And very defensive."

She leaned forward again. He saw the tiniest freckles at the peaks of her cheek bones and had the urge to run the tips of his fingers along the side of her face. He imagined the softness and the smoothness. She became aware of the intensity of his gaze and withdrew a few inches.

"Go on, what about those other hunters, the ones you haven't mentioned yet?"

"You mean sadists, guys out there to satisfy their need to inflict pain and death?"

She nodded slowly and sipped her beer, keeping her eyes on him.

"Of course, there are some of those, but there aren't many and they're not worth talking about. Maybe we're lucky they put it all in big game hunting," he added dryly. "I know there's some sort of ten-dollar word for that."

"Sublimation," she said.

"Yeah, right. I do read you know."

"Okay, okay. I'm sorry if I gave you any impression that I thought you were less intelligent than I am. You're probably more in many ways. And I'm not just saying that to placate you so you'll keep talking," she added quickly.

"Placate? I'm up to twenty dollars."

She laughed and sipped some beer.

"Do all men who hunt enjoy the kill?" she asked.

"Hell no." He laughed. "I've seen guys throw up immediately afterward."

"And you don't respect them when they do that, do you?"

He could see the sharpness in her eyes, that edge again. This was a woman of great passions, he thought.

"It's not that I don't respect them; I don't respect what's happened to them."

She raised her eyebrows.

"Oh, what's that? What's happened to them?"

"That they've been softened. It's the price we pay for progress. I don't know if I can say this so a writer with a college education can appreciate it," he added smiling, "even with twenty-dollar words, but hunting and things like it restore some of the lost strengths. Look at pets, for example. Don't feed your dog and he'll go out and scavenge, maybe turn back to the hunt, maybe not. It depends on how strong he is and how much he's been softened. Cats are more predatory. They're almost indifferent to being fed. If you forget, they'll go out and feed themselves. After a while they might not come back.

"Put a man from the eighteenth century out there and he'll survive. Put one from today out there, and he'll moan about the cold, the wet, the lack of salt and pepper."

She laughed.

"I don't know as I agree with all that, but you say it pretty well."

She leaned back and for a moment looked sad. Then she lifted her head and with a twinkle in her eye said, "Let's get back to your point. So by going out there in the woods and shooting a defenseless deer, you feel you've restored some strengths? You can beat your chest as you stand on Bambi and take a picture?"

He blanched and tightened the muscles in his back. There was too much sarcasm in her voice.

"It's not just shooting. There's more involved. And the deer isn't so defenseless," he added, raising his voice sharply. "Hunting, when it's done correctly, requires skill, instinct, a relationship with nature."

The smile sunk into her face and disappeared.

"How do you mean?"

"Nature gives the animal defenses. It's quiet; it's swift, and its hide is so much like the background I've seen men walk right past a deer that should have been in their sight, and not everyone who goes out there gets a deer. The truth is most of them don't and get tired and disgusted and cry about it over a beer before they go home with their tails between their legs."

The gradual rise in his volume drew attention. Some of the people at the bar turned completely around.

"Whoops," she said seeing the way they were all looking toward them. "Guess I finally touched a nerve."

"I thought reporters were supposed to be objective about their stories. You've made your mind up before you started. Why did they assign . . . ?"

"The story to a woman? Say it. Go on, get it over with. I could see it in your face the whole time."

"So? Don't tell me newspapers are like the army, train you for one thing and assign you for another."

"Hunting might be a masculine thing to you, but writing about it doesn't have to be. I can handle this. I assure you."

They both just stared at each other for a moment and drank their beer.

"I don't believe it's a masculine thing as such. I know a lot of women here who do it, too," he muttered.

"Look, I'm trying to be objective," she said, in a much softer tone of voice, "but just because I work for a newspaper, it doesn't mean I can drop off all my preconceived notions and my feelings. You try. That's the best anyone can expect."

"I'm not really qualified to tell you your business or tell the editor of your paper how to handle this. For all I know you may have the viewpoint they want or something. I don't know and I don't mean to suggest I do."

There was an apologetic tone in his voice too. She nodded, sat back, and contemplated him as if for the first time since they had met.

"What do you do for a living?"

"I have an auto body shop, a family business. We do all sorts of repairs, tires, welding. There's just me and my brother in the shop. My father died some time back. He had a bad reaction to an anesthetic when he went into the hospital for what was supposed to be a simple surgery, gall bladder. The doctor assured us it was nothing more serious than an appendectomy was these days. If it wasn't for the reaction, it probably would have been. My father was a very strong man. He was just fifty years old at the time."

"Oh, how terrible."

"Yeah." He looked down, fingering his glass. "It was a shocker. Happened just like that." He snapped his fingers. "One day he was one of the strongest men in town, and the next day, he was . . . I was seventeen and my brother was fourteen," he said looking up, "but we held on to the business."

She saw the pride in his face and for the first time, felt more than simple curiosity. The strength in his eyes excited her. Maybe there was something different about such a man.

"You became an instant head of the household, huh?"

"When I came back from his funeral, I went into the body shop and smashed every thing I could with a six-pound sledge—pounded a fender until it was practically flat against the floor. It was my way of crying, I suppose. My mother and brother didn't dare come in. They just . . ."

He stopped, conscious of the fact that he was telling her things he had never told anyone else. And here she was a complete stranger!

"Want another beer?" he asked to cover up his mental nudity.

"Do I have to let you pay for it?"

"You do."

"All right," she said. "I'll sacrifice my equality for the job."

He laughed and signaled to Nussbaum. The owner looked as though he had been anticipating the order.

"So what is this job, exactly? You say it's not to be about the actual murder story?"

"Not really. If I do the first segment well, it could be a series of in-depth articles on hunting and hunters. My editor, who strikes me as one of those men you thought would moan about no salt and pepper out there, wants to know if violence breeds violence. I suspect he's hoping I'll come to that conclusion."

"I don't think that's true at all. Most of the murders committed are acts of passion. There's no stalking of the victim the way a hunter goes after his prey. As I said, real hunting is an art. The kind of people you're talking about don't have the patience.

"And besides," he went on with more enthusiasm,

"there are other ways people exhibit the violence within them besides hunting. Vandalism, mugging, road rage. Heck, if that theory held any water, then every man who had been in war would be a candidate for murderer, more predisposed to it."

"So you don't think the killer of the hunter was a hunter then?"

"I don't know. I haven't given it all that much thought or that much deep thought, I should say."

"So do it now."

He thought for a moment. She waited as he sipped his new beer.

"All right. I'll tell you this. If he isn't a hunter, he's been around hunters and hunting," he said.

"What makes you so sure?"

"I got the feeling, just an instinctive thing, that he stalked him, the way a man stalks when he hunts. Al Jones was a hunter's hunter. He's been doing it for a lotta years. He would have realized he wasn't alone or in danger. It's more difficult for a man to hide in the woods, especially now, than it is for the deer, and Jones knew how to read the forest. His instincts would have sounded."

"You believe in the power of instincts," she said.

He smiled.

"What's funny now?"

"Another one of my ideas that I'm sure you'll find hard to believe."

"Try me."

"Well, whenever I am in the woods, when I go off alone or with my brother, and I'm in there a while, cut off from so-called civilization, I feel myself transform. It's as if I strip off the modern world and my ancestry emerges, my heritage. I feel . . . wild, as wild as the animals out there. It's as if I've been returned to an equal footing with creatures that rely on their instincts, their senses to survive. I not only feel like the hunter, but the hunted. What I mean is, I can see it all the way they see it."

He stopped talking. She didn't say anything, but she looked so serious.

"That's another thing I've never told anyone before," he added and downed the remainder of his beer. "It's not exactly the sort of talk I'd be doing with my friends in the shop. Most of them would laugh at me, I suppose."

"I think I understand and I don't think it's funny. I even . . ."

"Even believe it?"

"What if I said I do? What do you have to say to that?" she challenged.

He shrugged, smiling.

"If you can understand that, maybe you will be able to do a good job on this series."

"Thanks for the tentative vote of confidence. Will

you go back into the woods before the killer is discovered?"

"No, I'm satisfied. But my brother might. If I don't put up a big enough stink, that is."

"He didn't get his deer?"

"Yeah, he did, but the limit has been expanded this year to include a doe. Of course, you've got to get a doe permit too."

"A doe permit? There's so much I don't know about the rules and everything."

"Rules?"

"Well, what do you call it?"

"There are hunting laws. Rules makes it sound too much like a kid's game."

He paused and looked around. When he turned back, she was staring at him and for the first time, he felt he was being measured in a sexual way. It made him self-conscious.

"You driving back to Pine Bush tonight?"

"No, I'm staying in a motel in South Fallsburg for a few days. What I was planning to do was go out with some hunters."

"You're kidding?"

"There's no other way to do it, but get right into it. I've discovered that applies to everything I do lately. Maybe you know some reliable men I could hook up with. Just once. I can't pay them anything, but I won't be a bother."

He shook his head and smiled.

"I won't."

"Yeah," he said, "I do know some people over in Centerville who might agree to letting you tag along if you really want to do that. You probably have a hunting outfit too, I bet. Don't you?"

"You mean a special jacket and hat?" He nodded. "Is that really important?"

"It helps some dumb trigger-happy hunter from telling you're not a deer."

"Oh, that is important," she said. He laughed. "I wonder if I could rent them someplace."

"It's not exactly like renting a tuxedo or something." He thought a moment and nodded. "I have some things you might wear. Of course, you're going to look a little silly. They're not women's clothes. Might even cause a deer to die of laughter and then you'll be considered a hunter."

"Is that so? You did say there were women who hunt, didn't you?"

"Damn right there are, and some of them hunt better than a lotta men I know. People I'm thinking of sending you to see happen to include women in their hunting party."

"Really? That would be great. You tell me how to get to your place and I'll come down tomorrow, if that's all right."

"It's all right, but you've got to give me a day to

arrange it with these people. They leave pretty damn early in the morning and you won't make it tomorrow."

"How early?"

"Before sunup so they can get into the woods just at sunup. Early bird gets the worm sort of thing."

"Oh no." She grimaced. "Aren't there any late morning hunters?"

"Not any good ones and they won't be as authentic as these people. That's what you want, don't you, authenticity?"

She slumped back in her seat. He smiled widely.

"Well, I suppose you're right. I am looking for true local color," she said.

"Oh you'll get plenty of that," he said nodding with an impish grin.

It both annoyed and pleased her, reminding her of when she was much younger and she would enjoy the attention of young boys, even when they were taunting her. She could see the envy on some of her friends who never attracted a second look.

He finished his beer.

"Ready to go?"

"Yes, thank you," she said.

After they left Nussbaum's, he took her back to Monticello to pick up her car. When they made the turn onto Main Street, they were surprised to find a line of stalled traffic. Up ahead, police cars with their roof lights blinking, were parked on both sides of the highway. People were out of their cars and gathered around something.

"An accident?" she asked.

"I don't know. I guess we could get out and see. Doesn't look like this traffic's moving for a while."

They walked along the line of traffic until they reached the circle of people, a circle that was growing thicker every passing moment.

Aaron, holding Diana's hand now, inched his way through an opening.

Neither of them could believe what they saw. There, sprawled across the middle of the highway was a dead palomino stallion. The animal's head was all bloodied.

"Oh, my God," Diana said. "Did a car hit it?"

"Car hell," a man beside them said. "Don't you see that sign beside the horse? He wrote it in blood, the horse's blood."

"Sign?"

Aaron pushed his way further forward until they could read the sign. A half dozen local policemen and two state troopers stood beside it talking. The sign read, MY PRIZE HORSE. KILLED BY HUNTERS. It was signed, Sam Cohen.

"How horrible," Diana said. Who is Sam Cohen?"

"An egg farmer who lives about five miles or so

from here. Toward Forsterdale. Nice place, nice property. He has a couple of riding horses. Had a couple," he corrected.

"Why did he do this?"

"Anger."

"Anger?"

"Some bastards shot the horse."

"Oh, how terrible."

"Yeah. Look, there are the guys from your team," Aaron said pointing to a photographer and a reporter on the far end. "I'd say Sam's made his point, wouldn't you?"

"Why would they shoot a horse?"

"Frustrated because they didn't get a deer. Maybe they were drunk. Who knows?"

"Still think it's a manly sport?" she asked, her face tight with rage.

"The sport's manly, but not always the people who practice it. They'll probably arrest Cohen for this. Here comes a tow truck. What a sight this is going to be."

They stood by and watched the driver put a harness around the animal and then lift it from the pavement. It dangled awkwardly until they were able to get it securely onto the back of the truck to be carted off. Flashbulbs popped.

"Your front page photo," he muttered.

"It gives me the chills," she said embracing herself. She shook here shoulders. Even in the dim light, he could see her face had paled.

"You all right?" he asked.

"No," she said. "It is like being caught in a nightmare. That beautiful animal."

She looked like she was going to cry. Moved, he reached out and touched her shoulder. Without hesitation, she stepped into his arms and put her head against his shoulder.

"Just hold me for a minute," she said and he tightened his embrace. The scent of her hair was intoxicating. He didn't want to let her go. "Why are there so many miserable people in this world?"

He smiled when she lifted her head and looked into his eyes.

"Bad childhoods? Oppressive parents? Poverty? Social injustice. All of the things you studied in college and use in your writing, I'm sure."

"You just love kidding me, don't you?" she said, a little fire in her eyes, just the right touch to make her even more beautiful. It wasn't possible to resist. He kissed her, fast and hard at first, and then soft, lovingly and she welcomed it.

He felt his heart warm with expectations he had thought fantasies until then.

"I don't want to be alone," she whispered. It came from her lips as would a secret thought she let escape.

He said nothing. He nodded and took her hand and led her back to her car.

"Can you drive?"

"Yes," she said, but with disappointment.

"I'll follow you," he said and she smiled. He kissed her on the cheek and hurried back to his own vehicle.

He liked how when she pulled into the motel parking lot, she went directly to her room and just left the door opened for him, instead of standing there waiting for him to join her first. It was as if she wanted to be sure he was coming on his own steam. It brought a smile to his face. Doesn't she know that if I had an anvil tied to my ankle, I'd drag it all the way? he thought and got out of his car.

She was standing in front of the mirror by the dresser and looked at him through it. He closed the door behind him and she turned.

"I don't usually do this," she said.

He looked around as if he didn't understand.

"You mean, stay at a motel?"

"No." She widened her smile. "You know what I mean."

He nodded.

"You're not going to believe it," he said, "but neither do I."

That brought laughter to her lips. She took **off** her jacket and he moved toward her. She put her finger on his lips before he could bring them to hers. He widened his eyes.

"If anyone asks," she joked, "this is all part of my research."

"Mine too," he replied and they kissed.

His brother Walker carried contraceptives at all times. Aaron always felt it would make a woman feel she wasn't special, like he would do it with anyone. It was probably a stupid idea, but it was just who he was and how he thought.

"I don't have any . . ."

"I'm on the pill," she whispered to encourage him not to hold back. "Good girl precaution," she added.

"How do you know I don't have some sexually transmitted disease?"

"You've got to believe in someone sometimes," she said. "And besides, shut up. You talk too much. Twenty-dollar words and all."

He laughed and kissed her again.

After they were undressed and in bed, their lovemaking began so slowly, he felt like a young boy traveling sexual highways for the first time. She liked it though, liked the control he had of himself and therefore control of her. He kissed her neck and her shoulders in a way that suggested he had to taste each and every part of her and when he pressed his lips to her breasts and brought them gracefully over her nipples, she relaxed and then tightened her embrace, her body opening like a beautiful rose petal to take him in, to draw from him. In the dim light of the room, he saw her cheeks flush and her eyes take on a glow that excited him.

She continued to hold him tightly, as tightly as someone who thought she might drown or fall far if she didn't. He liked the way she made him feel even stronger, but his sex was so hungry, he was a bit embarrassed by his own passion. It brought tears to his eyes and he moaned louder than he wanted to moan. It made hm feel less manly, but apparently, not to her. She kept her fingers on his buttocks, pressing hard to keep him from even thinking about any sort of retreat. He fought hard to make sure he satisfied her, and when he came, he was disappointed in himself, even though it was clearly apparent she was not disappointed in him.

They held onto each other like two people not quite sure a storm had ended.

When it was over, they lay side by side just listening to each other catch his breath.

"I knew you would be a great lover," she said.

"Oh, how did you know that?"

"Instinct. Raw animal instinct," she replied and he laughed.

He rose to dress. She put her arms behind her head and watched him.

"Am I still part of the research?" he asked.

"Of course, and there is a lot more to do."

He laughed again.

"Tonight?"

"No, I'll get back to the story tomorrow. With your help, I hope."

"Okay. You know how to get to Centerville. Just follow Main Street up to the movie theater. We're right near by . . . Kuhn's Body Shop. Being it's the only one in town, you should have an easy time finding it. I'll be open by eight. Have some work to finish. That is, if you're still planning on going on a hunt after seeing all that tonight."

"Oh yes, yes," she said, but her expression changed as the memory of the dead horse returned. "It was like a scene from a Fellini movie back there tonight."

"Who?"

"A foreign film director. It's not important." She sat up and he could see by the expression on her face and the look in her eyes that she was back on story. "Listen, do you think that the man who killed that hunter . . ."

"Killed the horse too?"

"Yes."

"I don't think so."

"Just instinct talking or do you have some other reason for being so confident of that?"

"Right now, yes, mostly instinct, but that instinct

tells me there is something else going on with the murder. It's too . . . bizarre."

"Like the horse thing isn't?"

"It is, but there are different sort of bizarre events, I guess. You'll understand after a while maybe, but even for people like that, those who shot the horse, it's different, much harder to shoot your own kind."

She nodded and lowered herself to bed.

"Turn off the light as you leave, please," she said. "Not that I'll get much sleep."

He laughed, kissed her on the cheek, turned off the light, and made sure the door closed and locked.

As he drove home, he thought about the dead horse. Hanging in the air the way it was, the animal did look like part of a nightmare. For a moment though, he thought of the deer he and his brother had hung at the garage.

He reviewed the way Diana had challenged his love of hunting. Were his reasons as valid as he thought they were, or was he fantasizing about a world that no longer existed? In a way he welcomed Diana's questions, but in another way, he was afraid of them.

He pushed these thoughts aside and relived their lovemaking. He thought more about her face and the sound of her voice. The scent of her perfume lingered in his car. There was something warm in the air. He felt like a school boy again, dazzled by his first crush. He began to remember or rather to permit himself to remember how it had been with Tracy when they had begun. Was it as good? Was this something special? Was he wishing it was just so he could put his disappointment behind him? What isn't complicated in this life? he wondered.

When he pulled into Centerville, he was surprised to see a number of local men standing in front of Sam's Luncheonette so late. Looking down toward the municipal hall, he spotted a sheriff's department patrol car by the police station. He slowed down and parked in front of the group. Paul Carnesi came over to him.

"Something happen?"

"Billy Everett and Johnny Dumfort . . ."

"What about them?"

"They were hunting kind of late, with searchlights."

"Oh, jacklighting, huh? They arrested them?"

"Would have been good for them if they had. Moonlightin's bad enough, the danger and all. Scotty Burns heard some gunfire near his house. Enough of it to get him curious. He went out, his wife screaming after him for him to stay home, but he found Everett's car and assumed they were jacklighting. He fired off a round, shouted for them and then leaned on the car horn. Finally, he gave up, went home and called Willie. He didn't want to get them in trouble, but with what happened to Al Jones, he just thought he oughta call. Everyone's spooked."

"And?" Aaron asked, holding his breath.

"Willie and his deputy dog there, Bruce Sussman, checked it out. They tracked in about two hundred or so yards off of Everett's car and found them, flashlights at their side still on, which was why they found them so fast."

"Dead?"

Paul nodded.

"We were all playin' cards in the back of Sam's when Herb Heller's wife called him to tell him there was a call for an ambulance. Seems they were killed the same way, Aaron, naked, bullets in their foreheads . . ."

"What do you make of all this, Aaron?" Dan Longhair asked him. "Sid Klein here thinks it's some kind of mountain man who lives in the woods, maybe up around Neversink. There have been some of those anti-government people stacking out some space, just aching for a challenge."

"I don't know," he said. "This is one helluva night."

"Why?"

"Didn't you hear about Sam Cohen's horse in Monticello?"

"Monticello? What?"

"He dropped his prize palomino's carcass on Main Street. Killed by hunters."

"No shit. You're right. What a night."

"Yeah. Talk to you guys tomorrow."

"Right."

He pulled away quickly. He suddenly saw his home as a real sanctuary, and escape from the madness raging outside. The mad events of the night filled him with a quiet trembling. He sensed a horrible danger and thought only of protecting his mother and his brother. It was as though deer season had released the Angel of Death who now lurked somewhere in the shadows waiting and watching for its next victim. He welcomed the sight of the porch light. It made him feel good to see how his mother always remembered to keep it burning.

He had hoped she would be asleep when he entered, but she wasn't. At first he thought one of her friends had already called with the news and that was what kept her awake, but no one had called. She had fallen asleep watching television. When she awoke, she went to make herself some warm milk and honey and that was where he found her. She looked up expectantly when he walked into the room.

"What is it?" she asked after she had described her evening.

"More trouble."

"I can see that. Nothing with Walker?"

There wasn't any hysteria in her voice when she asked him that. There never was and that amazed him. She had such control, such stoicism. It was almost as if she always expected that trouble would come and she had prepared herself long ago to greet it.

"I'm sure his only problem is which girl to chase. No, there's been more killing."

He sat down and described the incident with Sam Cohen's horse and what he had discovered when he drove into Centerville. She didn't interrupt him.

When he was finished, she nodded slowly and said, "There's something very dark upon us, Aaron, something very dark and terrible."

She sighed so hard he thought she would crack her heart.

He got up and put his hands on his hips and stared down at her.

"You gonna sit down here all night or go to your bedroom and pretend to go to sleep?"

"Don't be such a smartass, Aaron Kuhn." She glared at him. Then she smiled and shook her head. "I'm going to go upstairs and pretend. You know how your brother gets when he finds me waiting up for him."

"Figured." He started away and then stopped. "Oh.

I met a girl tonight. She'll be over early tomorrow morning. Well," he thought remembering, "Maybe not now."

"What? What kind of a girl? Who is she? How did you meet her?"

He thought for a moment.

"She picked me up in a bar," he said and started away, smiling to himself.

"What? Aaron Kuhn. Damn," she said. "Why didn't I give birth to girls?"

Five

A SLEEK BLACK CADILLAC coasted into Center-ville. It emerged from the darkness like a thing born of the night. It seemed to move on a shelf of air as it glided over the highway. The two men silhouetted within were as still as corpses strapped to the seat. They had the air of fugitives. Their unobtrusive entrance into the village was unnecessary. The small group of men that had gathered at Sam's was gone. Even the stray dogs had left the streets to slumber in alleyways or in the warmth of abandoned buildings.

The now starless night added to the funereal atmosphere. Deserted storefronts and unlit build-ings presented a universal setting for nightmares. The lit up municipal building at the end of Main Street was an oasis of life in the land of the dead. The black Cadillac headed directly for it, slowing down to a halt when it reached the marked parking spaces. Its headlights went off, and for a moment it appeared as though it had brought itself there. Neither of the shadowy figures came out too quickly. It was as if they were deciding whether to turn into real people or not.

In the dull night, the click of the car door latches was quickly amplified through the street. The sounds disappeared within the crevices and alleyways. It was as though the darkness, starving for noise, greedily consumed anything that came its way.

District Attorney Steve Dickson stepped out of the passenger's side. His long, Lincolnesque body rose lethargically until he towered over the car roof. The driver, Tom Congemi, one of his assistants, got out more energetically. Dickson looked back over the small, darkened hamlet.

"What did you tell me?" Steve asked. "I won this precinct two to one?"

"More like three to one. You killed him in this township."

"Harvey Gold, our state party leader, probably thinks I took names off tombstones to get that vote outta here. But I'm not the first person elected by ghosts, eh?" Dickson asked. Tom laughed.

"A dog could go to sleep on Main Street and remain undisturbed for weeks."

"Who the hell would believe a place like this

would be giving us such a headache?" Dickson wondered aloud.

"Maybe we oughta just forget about it, pretend it doesn't exist. No one would know the difference."

"How I wish, but unfortunately, that is not to be the case, my friend."

Dickson turned toward the municipal hall and saw the Sheriff's Department car two spaces down from his. "Our illustrious sheriff got his ass down here fast enough."

"Election year coming up."

Both men started for the building. At five feet eight, Congemi looked like Jeff in the Mutt and Jeff cartoon when he stood beside Steve Dickson.

"If you were ever going to satirize a small-town police chief, you would choose Willie Brand. About five years ago, he arrested a couple of twelve-year-old kids who robbed a gum ball machine. Put them in handcuffs and made them feel they were going to the electric chair. The parents almost won a lawsuit," Dickson said.

"I've heard him called Gum Ball Brand, but never knew the reason," Congemi said.

"We have to get this thing out of his hands as fast as we can. He wasn't much help with the first death. Besides, I hear from the grapevine that he's into the sauce too much, not that I could blame him. If I had his life, I'd be comatose."

"Right."

"However," Dickson continued, contemplating the sleeping hamlet, "I'd say there's a headline or two to grab. Or maybe even three," he added, a cat-ate-the-mouse grin on his face.

Congemi laughed again and moved faster to keep up with Dickson, who moved in long, deliberate strides, his lanky legs appearing more like stilts. As he walked, he had to brush back the long strands of his ebony black hair that continually flopped over his forehead and into his vision.

Slowly, Dickson and Congemi entered the small lobby of the municipal hall almost like intruders trying not to be noticed. Stairs directly in front of the door led up to a meeting room and a small kitchen. The area was often used for volunteer ambulance dinners and volunteer firemen parties. Dickson recalled visiting it a few times during his campaigning. The government offices were off to the left in the lobby—village clerk, mayor, business office. Willie Brand's small police station was on the right. His deputy, Bruce Sussman, stepped out just as Steve Dickson and Tom Congemi entered the lobby.

"The chief inside?" Dickson asked.

"Yeah. I'm going back up to the scene to make a circuit and see if anyone's loitering. Willie's idea," he added as if to explain why he would do anything that stupid. Steve said nothing. He went right to the office.

Willie Brand looked up from his desk. His eyes were bloodshot, and his face was haggard and unshaven. His hair was wild from him running his fingers through it. There was more than mere fatigue written in his look. He appeared more like someone who had been hysterical for hours and had just calmed down.

Sheriff Roger Winn sat in the chair just to the right. He had his feet up on the desk when Steve and Tom entered. His hat drooped over his forehead and his unzipped jacket hung under his arms, the bottom of it nearly touching the floor. He was a short, muscular man with a slight paunch. Steve thought him more of a bureaucrat than a law enforcement officer, but he admired the way the sheriff remained in office. Twice Winn had run unopposed. He had a knack for being uncontroversial and well liked. Steve thought there was something to learn from him, despite the fact that the man never had much ambition. He had been sheriff nearly twenty-five years and had never sought another office.

"Looks like a bundle of activity here," Steve said turning to Congemi who smiled. The sheriff dropped his feet from the desk and Willie sat up.

"We were just waiting for you, Steve. We know

how much you like to be in charge," the sheriff said.

"Yeah, right. Okay, somebody bring us up to date."

Steve sat on the two seat wooden bench across from Willie's desk. The two-by-four office was sparse. An American flag had been pinned haphazardly over some plaques and awards. The inexpensive imitation wood paneling had begun to fade and there were scuff marks on the walls near the floor. The thin, dark-brown nylon rug was worn quite deeply in some areas, and burned in other places where cigarettes had been dropped and mashed into it. Willie's desk was cluttered with papers, ashtrays, a police scanner, and two-way base. There were cigar butts in the ashtrays and a small tree of used Styrofoam coffee cups stacked in the corner.

"Medical examiner finished about a half hour ago. The ambulance just took the bodies to the morgue," Willie said.

"Anybody know these two guys?"

"Yeah," Willie said. "One's Billy Everett, and the other's Johnny Dumfort. They've lived in Centerville all their lives, both about fifty-seven, fifty-eight. Johnny's a retired prison guard, and Billy still does various construction work when he isn't too drunk to hold a hammer."

"You mean *did* various construction work," Steve reminded him.

"Right." Willie shook his head. "I've got all their identification here."

He opened a plastic bag to display the two wallets, keys, and other odd items found in the hunters' pockets. When he raised it, Congemi stepped forward to take it and hand it to Steve who glanced at the contents.

"I guess this wasn't a robbery," Dickson said dryly.

"Guess not," Winn added with a cold smile. "We're not going to be that lucky."

Dickson grunted.

"What have you done so far?" Steve asked Willie. "Who've you questioned?"

"Questioned? It's a little late in the evening to go running around the village asking people questions. Everything but the New York Bar and Grill's closed up and the only ones in the grill are a few hotel handymen who don't know the time of day by now."

"He could have pulled over a few rabbits and squirrels, but you know how tight-lipped they can be," the sheriff said, widening his thick lips into a smile.

Steve felt a small headache beginning behind his right eye. It was a signal of his irritation and frustration. None of the old guard appreciated him.

"You two understand, I hope, that we have a rather big problem developing here. I mean, I don't want to upset anyone or stir up the natives, but by this time tomorrow, this community could be in something of a panic. In fact, the whole county could."

"I tried to make that point after Jones's killing," Willie said. "Remember?"

"We've done all the right things in relation to that, Willie. I brought in the BCI.

"On the other hand," he continued, his voice more testy,

"No one would suspect we had much concern if they saw this place at the moment."

"I don't think anyone else could have done anymore up to this point, Steve," Winn said quietly. "Not even some of your sharp, state investigators who haven't come up with anything from Al Jones's death yet."

"Yeah, well, this shoots to hell any theory that it was one hick taking revenge on another."

"If we didn't appreciate that before, I think we all understand that now," Winn said, the humor gone from his face and voice.

"He put a bullet in each of their foreheads as well?" Dickson asked and looked at the sheriff who just shook his head.

"Just like he did to Al," Willie said in almost a soft whisper.

"Professional hit man style after all," Steve said.

"Maybe it was a woman," the sheriff said. Everyone thought a moment.

"Can't eliminate anything at this point, I suppose," Congemi said nodding and looking at Dickson.

"All right. I'll be taking more direct charge of this thing," Dickson said. "Tom, here, will be my liaison officer."

"Liaison?"

"He'll be stationed right here in this office as of tomorrow morning," Steve said. For a moment everyone looked around. The absurdity of Willie's office was underlined.

"What are we going to use, a can opener to get in and out?" Sheriff Winn said and laughed quietly, his jowls shaking.

"We'll have to make do with what we have here as long as the crimes are confined to this hamlet."

"You mean, you really think this psychotic might start moving into other woods, other towns?" Winn asked, the idea just setting into his face like a rock in a bowl of sour cream. It lit up his eyes with new terror.

"Your guess is as good as mine about that, Sheriff. But as Tom just said, we can't eliminate any possibility, and that seems to me a very likely one if this thing continues. Depending on the killer's motives, of course, assuming he or she has any. Maybe we have some sort of a psychotic living in the woods. Who the hell knows? That's my point!"

"Shit," Winn said. Suddenly the immensity of the situation added weight to his girth. He looked like he was having trouble breathing. Steve looked at Tom Congemi who shook his head and smiled his disdain.

"That's why I want to centralize and control this investigation. For starters, nobody says anything to the press. I'll handle all of that. Just refer them to me when they start calling, Willie," Dickson said.

"No problem. I was never fond of newspaper people."

"What else do you have?"

"Well, we know the time of the murders. We'll have to wait for the ballistics reports of course, but I'd swear it was the same rifle. I know the kind of hole a 308 makes. Seen enough of them in deer," Willie said.

"Any suspects for this kind of thing?" Tom asked. Willie shrugged and looked at the sheriff.

"Any ideas at all, Willie? It is your hometown," Dickson asked with apparent impatience.

"To tell you the truth, I don't even know where to begin with something like this. Nobody's been going around town bad-mouthing hunters, if that's what you mean. There are people who don't like hunting, of course, but I can't think of anyone who'd do this. Not offhand."

"What makes you think it's someone local anyway?" Sheriff Winn asked.

"We're not saying it is," Steve responded. "You've got to start somewhere." Dickson thought a moment. "But the sheriff's got a point. It wouldn't be such a bad idea to get a handle on all the strangers in town. Check out all your motels, rooming houses."

"Do what I can," Willie said. "I'm not exactly overstaffed."

"What can you put on this, Roger?" Dickson asked the sheriff.

"I'll send a coupla patrol cars down tomorrow and one of my detectives. Keep the patrol cars here on shifts for a few days. But we're going to have a problem if this hospital thing isn't settled by Tuesday."

"What hospital thing?" Willie asked.

"Nonprofessionals are threatening a strike. They'll have a picket line set up by Wednesday morning and we'll have to station a car or two there around the clock," Winn said.

"I'll speak to Lieutenant Brokofski up at the State Police barracks in Ferndale to see what kind of assistance we can expect from them," Steve said. "Of course, I'll contact the BCI again and they'll have more investigators down here as well by late morning. It's important," Steve continued, leaning forward now and feeling a surge of energy and excitement building, "that we create the picture of a lot of police activity. The people have to feel we've got control of this. We don't, of course, and maybe won't have for a while, but it's the image we create that really counts."

"You oughta know about that," Sheriff Winn said, returning to his relaxed self.

"I don't think you do too badly for yourself, Sheriff," Steve Dickson countered.

The two politicians smiled at each other.

"In any case, Willie, we want you to know you're going to get a great deal of help on this. I've already sent for a criminal psychologist."

"Criminal psychologist?"

"To help us draw up a profile so we have a better handle on who we should be looking for out there. I thought with a similar M.O. so soon after the first, it was a good thing to do."

"Oh. Sure. Good idea," Willie said dryly. Anyone could see from his reaction and expression that forensic psychiatrists, criminal psychologists, fortune tellers, all of them were the same bullshit as far as he was concerned.

"Okay," Steve said. He slapped his knees hard to trigger his legs and stood up. "Let's get whatever sleep we can. It's going to be a long haul."

"I'll be back by seven a.m.," Congemi said.

"I won't be here until eight, eight-thirty," Willie said. "Never am here much earlier."

"That's a mistake," Steve snapped. "Chances are good they'll have a reporter down here waiting at your door."

"But I thought you said I shouldn't make any comments," Willie whined.

"Right, but you don't want his lead paragraph to say, 'The chief of police slept late while a psychotic murderer roamed the woods around the village.' You'll have people riding with their heads down on your roads and streets. Remember, image, image. We've got to make sure the people have confidence in us, in our actions."

Willie smirked and the sheriff smiled.

"See you later, boys," Steve said.

"Seven o'clock," Congemi repeated.

"Smartasses," Willie said as they walked out.

As soon as they closed the door behind them, Steve Dickson and Tom Congemi smiled at one another. They left the municipal hall quickly and moved silently to the car. At it, they paused and looked down Main Street.

"You know," Congemi said, "I got the feeling in there that this thing could turn out to be something really big for you, Steve. Know what I mean? You don't have much intelligence between the both of them. It's our show, all the way."

"Then we'd better do it right. I'll have a phone conversation with Harvey first thing in the morning and make sure he does all the right things politically."

"You're going to get some statewide headlines on this, maybe even national."

"No question about it, but something tells me, I would be better off if I got them for something else," Dickson said. The darkness and the eerie silence gave him a chill. "Let's get out of here. It's creepy."

The two of them slipped into the car quickly. In a moment the big Cadillac eased out of its spot, backed up, turned around, and headed out of Centerville, just as silently and as smoothly as it had entered.

The only thing it left in its wake was the darkness and the silence it had momentarily disturbed.

Aaron spun around in his garage the next morning when he heard the door being opened. He thought it would be Diana, but Gerald Spina, a high school senior, entered instead. Aaron liked the boy because he was a serious, hard-working person, polite, intelligent, and very athletic. He was captain of the wrestling team this year. Last year, he had won the 180-pound class at the statewide sectionals, so everyone assumed he would win a wrestling scholarship at one of the big universities.

Gerald lived with his mother in a small two-story

house on the outskirts of the village. The house had once been part of a tiny bungalow colony, consisting of four small units. The property had been in Anna Spina's family for years, but they had long since ceased to rent out the units. Bart Spina, Gerald's father, was never interested in running a resort property, small or otherwise. The grounds degenerated; the units fell into ruin beyond worthwhile repair. Now, with her husband gone, Anna Spina wouldn't even consider any sort of restoration. She had neither the money nor the inclination.

Gerald was an only child, and like Aaron, he had lost his father tragically. Bart Spina was killed in one of those freakish, yet all too familiar, household accidents. While repairing some shingling on his house roof, he lost his footing on the ladder when he was coming down, and he fell the full height. He broke his neck and died shortly afterward in the hospital. Since that time Anna Spina continued working as a secretary-clerk for an accountant, and Gerald took on every part-time job he could find. Lately, he was maintaining the grounds and doing odd jobs for Dr. Fern.

Aaron felt a natural sympathy for the boy. Although they didn't have that much to do with one another, whenever they did speak, Aaron sensed an affinity between them. Gerald was far from outgoing, but Aaron could see something in the way

Gerald looked at him and spoke to him. There was mutual admiration. It made Aaron proud to think that this highly successful go-getter saw something of value in him and enjoyed being around him and listening to him.

Sometimes, Gerald would linger a while and watch Aaron work. Usually Aaron couldn't tolerate the busybodies who would stand by and make casual comments. He felt they distracted him and endangered the quality of his work. But he didn't feel that when Gerald was there. He often thought that if they had kept the gas pumps and expanded the business, Gerald Spina would be the type of extra help he would hire. He was tempted to do it now, even though he couldn't justify the expense.

"Morning," Gerald said. Aaron nodded.

"She send you?" he asked nodding in the direction of the Fern house.

"Yeah. I was trimming the hedges and she stuck her head out of the bedroom window to tell me to come down here to get her car. I asked her if she called first, but she didn't give me an answer so I don't know if you wanted me here now or not," Gerald added.

"I've got to put this door trim back on and polish where I've painted. It's going to be a while yet."

"She ain't going to like that," Gerald predicted with uncharacteristic emphasis.

Aaron stopped working and turned to him again. Gerald stood there with his hands in his pockets. His shoulders seemed wider than Aaron realized. The boy had a naturally symmetrical physique, highlighted by an amazingly trim waist. Despite the cold morning, he wore a thin spring wrestling team jacket with his name embroidered on the front right. Although Gerald stood two inches shorter than Aaron did, he gave the appearance of being taller. He had perfect posture, an almost cocksure, confident way of holding his shoulders back and his chest out.

There was nothing characteristically arrogant in Gerald's face, though. He had deceptively soft eyes. Opponents, gazing into them when in combat on the mats, would relax their defenses, thinking Gerald was laid back and not very aggressive. But in an instant, those deep blue eyes would flash with an animal excitement and he would lunge like something born of the wild. When he was locked in a wrestler's hold or when he was in deep concentration, Gerald would tighten his mouth so firmly, the lips would whiten and practically disappear against each other.

Despite his hard, muscular body, he never completely lost his baby-soft cheeks. The roundness in his face was exaggerated by the short, military-like haircut he always wore. Everything about him was clean and correct. He looked like a graduate from a vigorous boot camp, a prime candidate for officer's training school.

Aaron once asked him if he had ever considered applying for admittance to West Point. Gerald shrugged and replied that he didn't think he was qualified. Somehow Aaron realized that the answer didn't stem from false modesty; it came from a coldly objective self-evaluation. Maybe he wasn't qualified to be an officer in the army, but if he wasn't, it wasn't because of his intelligence or his lack of grit. It was because of his temperament or personal ambition. He had been a successful boy scout, one of the few Eagle Scouts in the community.

"She's in a bad mood, is she?" Aaron asked. He wondered what it was like to work for the Ferns. The doctor was so oblivious to everything in his personal life, and Mrs. Fern was so unpredictable.

"I don't know. It's not that she's without any wheels. They got that Jaguar XK8 in the garage, you know."

"I remember when she ran it into a ditch. That's what I remember."

"Yeah, well, the doctor won't do anything with it since she dropped the transmission and you had to repair it. He acts like it's not even there."

"That's always the way it is with people who have too much," Aaron said with a nod.

"I know. If I didn't, I would have no trouble learning it over there," Gerald said without so much as suggesting the possibility of a smile.

Aaron shook his head and turned back to the car. Gerald came up behind him and watched for a while.

"You hear about Bill Everett and Johnny Dumfort?" Aaron asked without turning. Gerald was silent though, so he did turn. "Huh?"

"What about them?"

"Somebody shot them both in the head last night. They were in the woods, hunting."

"Oh, so that's what the ambulance was for. We heard it go by. Do they know who did it?"

"Whoever killed Al Jones, I'd say. Wouldn't you?"

"I don't know. I haven't heard any details about Jones's death either."

Aaron turned to look at him and smiled. Almost every other boy his age in this hamlet would want to know every grisly detail.

"Yeah, well, you'll hear more about it. I'm sure. That's all people are going to talk about." Aaron stepped back and ran a light over the door handle.

"What should I tell her? Time wise, that is?"

"Coupla hours. I want to touch this up here."

"Right."

"Tell her we'll bring it over when it's finished," Aaron added.

Gerald shrugged.

"Okay," he said raising his voice at the end to make it clear she wasn't going to be pleased.

Aaron worked on, almost forgetting Gerald was still there. When he turned, he found Gerald was staring at him.

"Saw your deer," he said. "One was an eight pointer, wasn't it?"

"Walker's. Mine was only six. Gave 'em to Meyer Bienstock to butcher up. Lotta meat between those two. Let me know if you and your mother want a few steaks or a roast. I know you used to eat it regularly."

"She and Dad did. I never got used to the wild flavor."

"Your father loved it, I know."

"He did. We haven't had it for a long time."

"Maybe you should go out and try your luck. After all this is over, I mean. I know how well you handle that rifle," Aaron said. Gerald shrugged off the compliment.

"Dad wanted me to learn, so I learned."

Aaron grunted.

"You learned well. I wouldn't recommend anyone go out there until they find out who's doing what though."

"I don't have the time for that anyway," Gerald said. Aaron thought he said it disdainfully.

"Well, everybody's got to take a break from what he's doing mainly with his time and energy. He'll get better at it if he does."

"Maybe," Gerald said shrugging. "I'll tell her what you said," Gerald said. Just as he turned, the door opened and Diana stepped in.

"Hi."

"Hi," Gerald said. The sudden appearance of a young woman startled him. He blushed for no reason and turned awkwardly to avoid brushing against her as she continued to come into the garage. Aaron dropped his tiny brush used for detail work and took up a rag to wipe his hands.

"Bye," Gerald said quickly and slipped through the door, taking care to close it gently. Diana laughed.

"Who's your bashful friend? He could give a girl a complex."

"Nice kid. Top wrestler. He made the all-state team last year. Stays away from girls," he added lowering his head and raising his eyes. "His coach told him they weaken the legs and he believed it."

"Really? How are your legs today?" she asked and Aaron felt his face redden and heat up. He realized it.

"So that's why I'm having a little more trouble kneeling down and straightening up," he quipped, and she laughed and then looked around the garage.

Diana's impression of most garages was that they

were disorganized, dirty, and greasy. Calendars with pictures of naked women were pinned on the walls and the floors were cluttered with cans of old oil, stray tools, parts, and tires. Whenever she had walked into one, she always kept her hands close to her body and moved as though she could get an electric shock by touching something.

But this garage was different. The tools were neatly organized on racks placed on Peg-Board on the wall to the left. Below it was a wide shelf on which were kept cans of paint, putty, and other materials, obviously arranged in some sensible order. The floor of the garage, although stained concrete, was cleanly swept. The garage was well lit by a series of long, low hanging fluorescent lamps.

When she had driven up to the garage, she hadn't realized how deep and wide it really was. Beyond the car on which Aaron was working, there was a truck and another area of tools. To the right of that was a big, old-fashioned potbelly stove. The pipe chimney ran straight up from it and disappeared into the ceiling. There were some chairs and stools near the stove and some wooden crates that were obviously turned over to serve as seats. The small area looked like a place set aside for an audience.

"Well," she said moving further into the garage, "I'm here. You looked surprised to see me, almost as much as that kid. I bet you didn't expect me, huh?"

"I wanted to see you again, but I guess you haven't heard the latest bad news," Aaron said.

He couldn't help studying her every time he looked at her; she had that effect on him. She was wearing the same ski jacket she wore last night, this time combining it with a pair of dark green slacks, which made her legs seem even longer. Her hair had been combed back neatly. It was held in place by dainty looking pearl-colored clips. Her strands hung straight over the collar of her jacket. He admired the fresh, healthy redness that had come into her cheeks. It brightened her face and made her green eyes even more dazzling.

He hadn't slept as well as he had last night, either. He was falling so hard and fast in love, he was afraid he'd break some bones. The funny thing was men were always thought of as slam-bam-thank-you ma'am characters. A one-night stand and then they were gone. His fear was she would do it to him.

"What happened now? Something more than what we saw?" she asked, holding her breath.

"Two more hunters were killed last night; each shot in the head for a final touch, the same as Al Jones," he told her. "Stripped naked, too. All hell's about to break loose around here."

He thought if she were shocked by the news, she

had a very cool way of containing it. Her eyes remained small and delicious. There was only that slight, nearly imperceptible movement in her cheek, flashing the dimple on and off.

"You mean, two more hunters were murdered?"

"I guess it's safe to make that conclusion. They couldn't accidentally shoot each in the back of the head and in the chest," he said, "and then strip and shoot each other in the forehead, so suicide's ruled out."

"This thing is developing into something very big, isn't it? National news," she muttered as if talking to herself. She looked more excited than terrified, which was what he had been anticipating.

Aaron shook his head and turned away.

"I guess you newspaper people are a different brand."

"Why? Oh, because of the way I view things first? Don't you see that this is going to make my series even more important?"

"More important? Two more men were murdered and you say, your series is going to be more important?"

"I mean interesting. To the readers," she added quickly. "There will be a greater demand for information."

"I see. Gruesome murders sell papers."

He went back to the car and started to tap the

trim gently to get it into place on the door. She stood up and walked to him.

"Well, if papers don't sell, there would be no reason to write stories for them and no one would be hired to work for them and people would be out of work and not able to buy cars to wreck so you could repair them," she rattled off with a smile.

"Right. I see. So the murders are good for the economy."

"What are you getting so uptight about?"

"I'm not uptight." He paused. "I thought you told me you weren't news desk. You were features."

"I still depend on reader interest. You're still going to help me, aren't you?"

"You mean, you're going to go into the woods even though it's obviously become more dangerous?" he asked, his voice full of disbelief.

"Will the hunters you mentioned still go?"

"The only thing that could stop them is an eclipse."

"Why an eclipse?"

"Because you're not permitted to hunt at night."

"But you just said those two hunters were killed at night. Come to think of it, how does anyone know they were hunting at night?"

"They went with flashlights. We call it jacklighting and that's not legal."

"There's so much I've got to learn and learn fast," she said.

He stared at her a moment. He wasn't sure if he admired her for her spunk or condemned her for her stupidity. He turned back to the Ferns' vehicle.

"You're just polishing this car?"

"No. Had to put a new door on it, repaint and finish. It was smashed in an accident."

"Looks beautiful." She drew closer to him to look at the car. He watched her run her fingers over the door. "I'd never know it."

"Thanks. Well," he said stumbling stupidly over some tools on the floor. She laughed.

"Might be more dangerous in here than in the woods," she quipped.

"Might."

His obvious nervousness caused by having her in the shop alone with him even after last night was amusing to her. There was something refreshing about his simple, yet honest reaction. She had been around supposedly sophisticated men too long. There was always a sense of competition, a sense of distrust. Things were usually not what they seemed; words had subtle meanings. Everything that was done had to be interpreted.

"I made that call for you. You can go along with them tomorrow."

"Don't they work? Tomorrow's Monday."

"These guys are unemployed most of the year. Besides, they think of this as work. They want to hunt during the weekdays because they know the woods are filled with weekenders from out of town."

"I see."

"And in some places in this county and the next, a day off to go hunting is treated like a national holiday. There are schools in the west end of the county that actually close so the older boys can join their fathers, and mothers."

"It's like another country," she said.

"That's America, full of different countries," he muttered.

As he turned back to the Ferns' car, she continued to look over the shop. She studied some of the machinery, felt the heat given off by an old wood stove, and tried to lift a small sledge hammer. The effort felt as if it would break her wrist bone.

He watched her move about. She certainly had nicely shaped legs, he thought. He admired the way her tight slacks clung to the curve of her thigh. He had to pinch himself every time he recalled making love to her. Was it a dream or did it really happen?

She turned and smiled at him, seeing how he was staring at her.

"I had a good time last night," she said. "Considering."

"Considering?"

"The horror of that dead horse."

"Oh, yes." He smiled. "To tell you the truth, it put some nightmares into me as well."

She drew closer.

"You can see I have to do this, don't you? If I back out, they won't give me any meaningful assignments. Thanks for helping me."

"I'm not completely sure you should thank me. I wouldn't go out now with all this killing going on." He paused. "You're set on it? Absolutely set on it?" She nodded. "All right. After I finish this door, I'll take you out to their place so you can meet them and make arrangements. I'll dig out some hunting gear for you. You got a good pair of boots, I hope."

"These aren't good?"

She wore a pair of fur-lined boots with zippers up the middle.

"You'll ruin 'em," he warned.

"The price of a good story," she said. He shook his head.

They both turned as the door opened and Walker stepped in. He stopped short when he saw her.

"Well, hello."

"My brother, Walker, " Aaron said. Diana nodded and smiled. "This is Diana Brooks. She's a deer hunter, " he added. Diana and he laughed.

Walker stood there with a dumb look of confusion on his face which only made Aaron laugh harder.

Denise Lester placed the cup of coffee down sharply on the kitchen table. Gary sat back quickly, thinking the liquid would spurt out at him and stain his uniform. Some of it did run over the edge and down the handle to the Formica top.

"Watch it, damn it!"

He looked up at her. She was glaring at him. Her small hands were clenched into fists and pressed tightly against her thighs.

"What the hell kind of a mood are you in anyway?" he demanded.

"You could have called," she said. The effort of her anger brought tears to her eyes. "You could have thought about us."

"I called you in the afternoon to tell you I wasn't coming home for supper, didn't I?"

"But you didn't say you wouldn't be home until after twelve," she protested.

Gary relaxed and sat forward to take the cup of coffee in both hands. She watched him sip it. He looked as though he were thinking up a good excuse. She folded her arms across her chest and bit her lower lip. They could hear the kids just waking up in the rooms upstairs.

"We all had to work late," he said and released a sigh of fatigue.

"Until that hour? I know hunters aren't around to hunt after dark. I know that much, Gary."

"Look," he said and slapped his hand on the table, "this is an emergency situation. There are piles of reports to make. If you don't like it, call Brian Donald and tell him to stop ordering me around."

"But so late?" Her voice began to weaken.

"Well what do you think I was doing? Huh? You think I was having fun? You think I have a woman on the side? Shit."

"You knew I'd be worried with the radio broadcasting that gruesome murder all day and you out there in the area where the hunter was killed. You knew it, Gary."

"All right, all right. I shoulda stopped someplace and called," he reluctantly granted. "I'm sorry."

"You always say you're sorry."

"What should I say, I'm not sorry?" His face took on that twisted smile, a smile she hated so much. It was almost sadistic. Sometimes he wore that smile when he punished the boys. Usually she had to rescue them. "All right, I'm not sorry. There, are you satisfied? Now let's eat."

"Fuck you, Gary, you know. Fuck you. I'm stuck up here all day and all night with the kids."

"So what am I supposed to do about that?" She didn't respond. "Damn it."

He pushed the coffee aside and turned away from

her. She went to the sink and began to sob softly.

It wasn't always like this, she thought. In the beginning he was kind and thoughtful; he treated her special, as though he were grateful for her love, as though he never thought anyone would love him. She knew what his family life had been, how there had been little love between him and his father and how his mother took his father's side against him most of the time. He used to spill it out to her, crying through his words. They'd be contented, lying together for hours in bed, talking about themselves, she holding his head against her breasts and running her fingers gently through his hair, and he calm, affectionate. Now, they hardly made love. And he was growing more and more intolerant of the boys. They had grown afraid of him. She was beginning to think that like a parent who had been a victim of child abuse, he was abusing his children, being the kind of father to them that his father had been to him. It was as though something evil ran in his blood. Dormant for a while, it had been awakened. Why? What had happened to change things? Was it something she had done? Her fault?

"You just don't . . . don't care about us," she said. "You act like you don't want us."

"Oh, shit. That's not true."

She turned on him again. Now she had something, she thought. She had him on the defensive.

"You never ask the boys to go anywhere with you. Before this thing happened, you could have taken them into the woods. Maybe you could have taken them hunting or something."

"What? You don't know what you're saying? Did you forget their ages?"

"They could learn things from you, things your father taught you about the woods."

"He didn't teach me anything. Let them join the Boy Scouts."

"Some father you're turning out to be."

"Well, I'm working most of the time, aren't I? It's not that I'm out there doing things for myself. Look," he said changing his tone of voice, "we'll do something next weekend, if I don't have to work. We'll go for a ride and stop somewhere nice for dinner."

"Will we?" she asked, hopeful but suspicious.

"Yeah, sure. All right, all right. I'm sorry. I shoulda called you. I had so much on my mind with Brian Donald pressuring everyone and . . ."

"Why is there so much pressure? What do they expect you to do?" He took a deep breath and shook his head. "What is it, Gary? Is there something you didn't tell me, something else?"

"Donald told me there was a strong possibility I'd be transferred," he blurted.

"Transferred?"

"Yeah."

"To where?"

"Farther upstate. There's been more cutbacks and guys with more seniority would have first choice. I might get the short end. I didn't want to tell you about it, because it might not happen yet," he added quickly.

"Oh," she said. She looked stunned. Then she looked around the kitchen. This house wasn't much, she thought, but she had grown so used to it. Despite her complaints, she felt secure here.

"I'll get your breakfast together," she said with a softer tone and went back to the counter.

To break the new heavy atmosphere, she turned on the radio. They caught the beginning of the local news and the headline brought them both to attention. "My God," she said, "two more men. What does this mean?"

"It means they'll have to bring more conservation officers into this area, not less."

She thought she saw that sarcastic smile on his face and was about to ask him if he could find some joy in such tragedy, but she turned to quiet the boys as they came screaming down the stairs and into the kitchen.

And the thought died like most thoughts in this house did lately.

Six

"HELL, YOU DON'T NEED those stump jumpers," Walker said after Aaron explained what Diana wanted. "I'll be glad to take you out and show you what hunting's all about. I've been planning on going for my doe anyhow."

Diana looked at Aaron for some guidance.

"You know Ma hopes we don't do that, Walker," he said softly. "We don't need it."

"We don't need it? Sure we need it. Got room in the freezer, don't we? We've got to do our bit for the conservation department too," he added turning to Diana

"Conservation department?" Diana looked from Walker to Aaron. "I don't get it."

"There's an overabundance of deer in this region," Walker said. "When they get to such numbers, the hunting limits are expanded. If we don't thin the herd, they'll starve to death. It's happened a few times."

"Oh right. If you don't go out and kill them, they'll die? I've heard that one already."

She started to laugh.

"It's more complicated than it sounds. Less die when the herd is thinned!" Walker protested.

"Relax, Walker," Aaron said sharply.

"Okay, whatever. What'dya say?" Walker asked, ignoring the banter between his brother and Diana. "This is your chance to go out with a real pro."

"I don't know. Aaron's already made other arrangements for me."

"With those backwoods stump jumpers? They can barely talk and walk at the same time. Forget it. You'll learn more with me."

Diana glanced again at Aaron.

"I don't want to be any source of conflict in the family. If your mother rather you didn't . . . it . . ."

"Hey, I'm a pretty big boy now," Walker said with some bravado and indignation.

"Sometimes you don't act it, " Aaron said quickly. "She wants to go out with a pack of hunters anyway. She's after local color for her article."

"Local color? Hell, I'm local, ain't I?"

"You're loco, not local."

"Very funny. Well," he said with some belligerence growing in his face, "if you want to pass up an expert for half-wit mountain people, it's your loss lady."

"Well, I . . ." She looked to Aaron again.

"Come on, " he said. "I'll show you the guns so you can seem to know what you're talking about and then I'll see about some gear. You can meet my mother too. She'll give you some insights about life in the sticks."

He wiped his hands and put the rag down. Then he pointed to the polishing cloth. "Still some touching up to be done," he said. Walker smirked.

"It's my day off."

"We told her we'd get the car back to her today," Aaron reminded him.

"So? What's she in such a rush about? She'll just drink herself into another accident."

"Okay," Aaron said. "I'll do it myself. Come on," he said to Diana.

"It's not that urgent," Diana said. "I can wait."

"Come on," he repeated, this time with authority. She followed him out of the shop. He stayed a foot ahead of her. "He's just showing off, that's all," Aaron muttered.

She walked quickly to catch up.

"I really don't want to be the cause of any trouble. Looks like that's all I do for you. Last night with that man and now with your brother."

"If trouble starts, it's been there waiting anyway," he said.

She took his arm as they stepped onto the porch. He turned around.

"Where'd you get all this wisdom?" she asked, the corner of her mouth up in a teasing smile.

He took a breath and calmed himself. There was no way he could look into her face and remain angry anyway, he thought.

"If it is wisdom, it just comes natural, I guess."

"That instinct thing again?"

"Something like that."

They both laughed as he opened the door.

The sound of a female voice brought Marilyn Kuhn to full attention in the courting room. She had just begun to do some dusting and as usual had a bandana tied around her hair.

"Ma," Aaron said, smiling at his mother's look of surprise, "this is Diana Brooks. She's a reporter for *The Middletown Post*."

"Reporter?"

"Hello, Mrs. Kuhn."

"Hello. Reporter?" She looked at Aaron and then at the dust cloth in her hand.

"Don't worry, Ma. She's not doing a story on this house and there will be no pictures."

"Well thank God for that."

"I'll bet there are quite a few stories that came out of this house," Diana said gazing around.

"She's doing a feature story on hunting," Aaron continued.

"Oh?"

"Yes. These terrible murders have brought some new attention to the . . . what do you call it?" she asked, turning to Aaron, "A sport?"

Aaron laughed.

"She's not exactly an objective writer," he muttered. Although he was talking to his mother, he kept his eyes on Diana.

"You doing the story on Aaron?" Marilyn Kuhn asked, her head tilted a bit with suspicion.

"I would if he was going hunting tomorrow, " she said, looking at him. Then she turned to Marilyn Kuhn. "But he's been kind enough to find me a hunting party to join."

"He has, has he? What's this all about, Aaron Kuhn?"

"Just what we told you, Ma. All right if I take Diana into the kitchen? I'm getting some hunting gear together for her."

"Well, it's not in the kitchen."

"Thought I'd treat her to some of your real coffee. Mine in the garage is a poor imitation."

"Just as long as you understand my house isn't usually this disorganized," she told Diana. "It's just that these two don't give me a moment's respite."

"He doesn't looks like the messy type when it comes to household things," Diana said gazing at Aaron, who turned a bright crimson.

"Oh, he doesn't?"

"Well, I saw how neatly organized his garage is."

"Yes. Just like most men, he takes care of what's important to him," Marilyn said nodding at Aaron. "Well, come on. I'll show you to the kitchen while he gets whatever he's getting."

"Thank you, " Diana said.

"Don't you go pumping her for all sorts of information," Aaron warned and went to the stairway.

"Is that an order?" She pointed a thumb at him. "Big shot. I'm the one who changed your diapers, Mr. Big Shot."

Aaron laughed and headed up the stairway. Marilyn watched him a moment and then turned toward the kitchen.

"So, you're a reporter doing a story on hunting? Tell me," she said, "where'd you meet Aaron?"

"Ma," Aaron called from the stairway.

"Oh, go on with you."

"I'll tell you everything, " Diana whispered. "Don't worry."

Marilyn Kuhn smiled. She liked this young woman and first impressions always proved the best.

❦

Steve Dickson touched fingers in cathedral fashion and rested the elbows of his arms on the shinny conference table as he leaned forward, his face in a grimace of deep concern.

Off to his right, Bob Foss, the county publicity chairman, and Lieutenant Brokofski of the local state police barracks spoke softly. It was as though they had met at a funeral parlor. Seated to the right of Dickson was a stocky five feet eleven inch man with hair that seemed to float in one solid wave from the front of his head to the back. The bushy dark brown eyebrows emphasized his prominent forehead and gave him a habitual look of deep intensity and concentration.

Sheriff Winn and Willie Brand were to his immediate right. Next to them was Dustin Collins of the BCI. There were all waiting for Bill Douglas, chairman of the County Board of Supervisors. Dickson's secretary had just told them Douglas was on the way into the office so they all looked at the door in anticipation when they heard the knob turning.

"Sorry I'm late, " Douglas said coming through the door. He was accompanied by Brian Donald of the Conservation department. "We were on the phone with Tom Matthews, head of ENCON. He's agreed to send down a dozen agents to help patrol the hunting if we request it. Willie," he said stopping by Brand's chair, "you've got some serious action in Centerville for a change, huh?"

"Unfortunately."

"Well, you've always been one of the best in the county. I'm sure you'll stay on top of things."

Willie blanched at the compliments. Out of the corner of his eye, he saw Dickson, Foss, Collins, and Brokofski smirk, with Brokofski's the most emphatic perhaps. Even the stranger looked disdainful. He could hear their thoughts in a chorus: Who'd believe Willie Brand could be on top of anything, much less something this serious? Only a career politician would say something so stupid.

Douglas took his seat at the head of the table. He was a short, stocky man with a long chin and heavy eyebrows. He had small, chubby hands and wore his jacket sleeves too long, ending right at his knuckles.

"More men will be some help," Brian Donald said seating himself beside Douglas, "but we do have thousands and thousands of acres to patrol so let's not anyone here have any false hopes about that alone putting a stop to all this."

"A good deal of the land is posted though, isn't it," Foss said sounding a note of optimism. He came to the table.

"Yes, but when many people are out there hunting, they don't stop to check for no hunting signs and I wouldn't count on some killer obeying them, would you?" Brian Donald tossed back at him. He had a very dry tone and a wry smile that twisted his lips so sharply, they looked made of rubber.

"Do we have an estimate as to how many hunters are out there?" Lieutenant Brokofski asked.

"Well, using our records of hunting licenses issued and considering what kinds of turnouts we've gotten so far. . . ." Sheriff Winn began.

"Along with what I reported from the resort people," Foss interjected.

"We expect close to a thousand men out there, scattered through the woods, over a period of forty-eight hours. Perhaps a few hundred more on the weekends," the sheriff said. "And don't forget," he added, "some of our public schools in the western end of the county actually take days off for hunting and are set to do so in two days."

"If they didn't take the days off, they'd have lousy attendance," Foss said. Every time he spoke, he sounded as if he was whining.

"I'm not complaining about it," Winn replied quickly as if he thought someone was taking notes and it would get out to his constituents.

The abject political fear in this room is thick enough to cut, Dickson thought, recognizing his own.

"Don't you think the heavy media coverage will discourage many?" Lieutenant Collins asked.

"Think? You're damn right it will. It already has," Foss said. "I've gotten a number of calls about cancellations from the motel people, rooming house people, and restaurant people. They're afraid of that publicity and they're afraid we'll have to come out with some sort of no hunting moratorium and destroy their season altogether."

"Can we do that?" Winn asked. "I mean solely on our own steam?"

"Oh, I don" t think we have to consider . . ."

"Gentleman," Steve interrupted. They all settled down and looked his way and at the gentleman beside him. "I asked you all to come here because I wanted you to meet and listen to Dr. Paul Wheeler. I thought it would be best if we could get some insight to what we might be facing and then come to some conclusions. Although Doctor Wheeler told me he doesn't like to be referred to this way, he's a national, if not worldwide expert in criminal psychology."

"I don't mind the national and worldwide, but expert suggests someone free from error," Wheeler said smiling. "And we are dealing with many intangibles here." He held his smile even though no one else relaxed a lip. "Just as long as we all understand that," he added.

"Nevertheless, he's here to draw up his mental picture of the killer for us based upon what information we have."

"Theories," Wheeler corrected. "Theories. We need more information to go beyond that description, I'm afraid, but I do have some early ideas which may or may not prove helpful to you, based upon what I already know, of course."

"I'd love to hear them. Before I retire," Winn muttered dryly.

Dr. Wheeler stood up, his rather large hazel brown eyes seizing onto the group before him, and cleared his throat. He liked to look directly at the people he spoke to because he felt it made them more attentive. Years of experience with college students taught him this, but this small audience would be attentive no matter what, he thought.

The right corner of his mouth lifted gently before each long sentence he spoke. Although he was shaven, there was a dark shadow around his chin and under his shortened sideburns. He looked down at some index cards and then cleared his throat. "Some people would say," he began, "that I'm a professional educated guesser. In a sense they're right, but I stress the word *educational.*"

He smiled again, but no one relaxed.

"Very well, " he continued, seeing there would be no light tone permitted, "Mr. Dickson asked me to direct myself to suggestions about where you should begin. Let me startle you immediately. I suggest you begin with yourselves."

He paused. The looks of confusion appeared in a chain reaction. It almost made him laugh.

"It has to do with my analysis of the situation. We can't ignore the fact that the every victim of this killer so far was in the process of violating one or more of the hunting laws at the time. Our first victim was hunting before the season actually started. The second and third were hunting at night. Fact one, then—our man could be obsessive about the law."

"I thought about that, but I also thought it might be just coincidence," Lieutenant Brokofski said.

"Yes, perhaps, but if it's not, it's a conscious, or perhaps subconscious, effort to deal with violators," Dr. Wheeler said with an air of confidence. "As you've just described, there are hundreds of men out there hunting in the woods, dozens in these woods alone, but the only men shot, hunted, whatever are the three who broke hunting laws. To me, this might suggest someone in law enforcement. Thus, I not so facetiously suggest, begin with yourselves."

"Why couldn't it just be some mad vigilante?" Sheriff Winn asked, "and not an actual law enforcement officer?"

"I suppose it could be. Maybe someone frustrated with the law enforcement agencies, taking things into his own hands to punish wrongdoers."

"He's not just punishing wrongdoers," Lieutenant Brokofski said. "He's executing them, stripping them down either before or afterward and then that shot in the head. It's like a military execution."

"Precisely," Wheeler said, his eyes brightening. "Execution follows conviction, which follows violation."

"But to strip them, make them run, hunt them so to speak . . ." Foss said looking from one to another.

"Maybe he's so crazy that he doesn't see them as people. He sees them as animals, deer, and no animals are dressed in the woods," Sheriff Winn muttered, half in jest.

"Interesting that you put it that way," Dr. Wheeler said quickly. "I've considered all that as well. To him, what is done to deer illegally might be a form of murder, and perhaps he sees these particular hunters as cruel beasts and wants to make that point."

"You really believe this guy goes through this thought process?" Bill Douglas asked.

"Serial killers, psychotics, have a certain method to their madness, yes. You have to recognize that and not underestimate them. Our killer follows a prescribed procedure, carefully. It helps him to feel justified, to feel he's doing something good for society. That's why I say it might not be simple coincidence that he hasn't harmed lawful hunters."

"We'll give out medals," Brian Donald said. Winn grunted.

"Are you suggesting that although this man is psychotic and lethal, he's still kept in check by some need for law and order?" Lieutenant Brokofski asked.

"Exactly. And that's why I'm leaning toward a law enforcement agent."

"Maybe we're simply dealing with a frustrated hunter who blames other hunters for his own failure," Sheriff Winn said, sounding like an amateur psychiatrist.

"Our man might not be a hunter at all," Bill Douglas suggested.

"Huh?" Winn said, turning to him. "What are you talking about, Bill?"

"I'm not the expert, or the educational guesser, but if he feels he's out there protecting the animals, he won't participate in killing any and therefore, he's not a hunter at all. We have to consider that as well."

"Then he would kill every hunter and not just violators, wouldn't he?" Dr. Wheeler said softly.

"I don't know. Maybe," Douglas said, reluctant to admit to any logic that defeated his theory.

"You're right. You're not the expert," Brian Donaldson said dryly.

"I'm just trying to add to the mix," Douglas cried.

"This is bullshit, Steve," Sheriff Winn muttered. "We're wasting time mentally playing with ourselves here. We have big decisions to make."

"Let's explore every possible concept," Steve said. "Doctor Wheeler comes highly recommended and there's no sense in investing in modern police technology and forensic psychology if we don't utilize it."

"What are you saying, I'm old fashioned or something? You want to blame something on my office?"

"No, just trying to get a handle here, Sheriff. No one is accusing anyone of anything," Dickson said.

"Let's not degenerate into infighting, gentlemen," Doctor Wheeler pleaded.

"He's right. If we start sniping at each other, this guy will continue sniping at people in the forest," Lt. Brokofski said.

Everyone was quiet a moment.

"So, we either have a lunatic out there protecting animals he sees as victims of crime or a law enforcement agent who's gone off the deep end?" Sheriff Winn asked. "Does that sum it up?"

"To a certain extent with what we know now, of course. It could change with every new piece of evidence and information," Dr. Wheeler replied.

"What if he just has a need to do this to people he knows?" Lieutenant Brokofski suggested.

"That is a third possibility and you might be right, about that," Wheeler replied turning to a map of the area, pinned on the wall to his immediate right. "It's true that up until now, he has been working, shall we say, within the Centerville area. There is a certain comfort zone at play. These could very well be his woods, in a sense, woods he knows as well as people know their own neighborhoods."

Everyone but Willie nodded. He looked unhappy with a conclusion that focused everything on his territory. Dickson saw it in his face and smiled to himself.

"Let's look at some other facts," Wheeler continued. "The man might know something about criminal investigations, ballistics, etc."

"Why do you say that?" Bill Douglas asked.

"Think of the caliber and make of the weapon he's using. Virtually every hunting weapon in this county would have to be checked out. It seems to make all hunters suspect."

"If the man is a hunter," Bill Douglas repeated.

"But even if he isn't, he might still have access to a common hunting rifle," Wheeler replied, "And had the smarts to utilize such a weapon."

"The gun used might be part of the family's possessions—a brother's, father's, father-in-law's," Sheriff Winn suggested.

"What scares me about all this is the possibility

that our man is otherwise a functioning person in society," Dickson said, "and not just some hermit in the woods or some crazed domestic terrorist."

"To the layman he could be that, yes," Wheeler replied. "We're dealing with a number of unknowns. His killing is compulsive, but calculated. He's psychotic, but only at a specific time and place and we see he's not stupid."

"He must be someone from outside of our area," Brian Donald concluded.

"Why do you say that?" Dr. Wheeler asked.

"Simple. If he lived here, what would set him off now?" Donald looked the others for support. "I mean, why didn't he commit these killings last hunting season or the season before that?"

"Well, I have two possible answers for your question. One is kind of frightening and it's this," Wheeler replied. "Perhaps he has."

"Huh?" Bill Douglas practically stood up. "What the hell's that supposed to mean?"

"Have you had any hunting accidents in the past that were not explained sufficiently? A man shot dead and everyone just assumed it was a hunting accident . . . maybe within this vicinity?" Dr. Wheeler pointed to the circle around the Centerville area.

"There was that Long Island man last year," Sheriff Winn said after a moment of silence. "The one not found until the week after season."

"Yeah," Brian Donald added. "No one had even inquired about him. Shot through the side of the neck, but he wasn't stripped naked and shot in the forehead."

"You remember that one, don't you, Willie?" Sheriff Winn asked.

"Sure," Willie said. "Billy Sills thought it was funny enough to put up a sign on his hardware store window: Deer . . . One, Man . . . Zero."

"More importantly, tell me this," Dr. Wheeler said softly, moving closer to the table. "Did this dead hunter commit any violations?"

"No. Not that we knew of," Brian Donald said.

"Maybe," the sheriff responded.

"What maybe? What?" Bill Douglas said defensively.

"How do we know he wasn't hunting during the week after the season? I think the coroner said he was dead for more than forty-eight hours. He could have been shot the day after deer season ended I think."

"That's possible," Lt. Brokofski said.

"I never thought of that," Brian Donald said, sitting back as if he had just been told he had terminal cancer. "We'd hafta check back on accidents over the past few years that might have involved someone bending or breaking laws."

"There's never been a year without some fatalities in the county," Sheriff Winn said nodding.

"You said there were two possible answers to Brian's question," Steve Dickson said. "What's the other?"

"Something could have served as a catalyst now. I couldn't say what that is without talking to the man," Dr. Wheeler replied.

"Anybody got his phone number?" Bill Douglas said. He laughed at his own joke.

"Is there anything different about this year's season as compared to the last few?" Doctor Wheeler asked.

"We have many more hunters up here," Brian said. "And there are doe permits issued."

"Doe permits?" Wheeler inquired.

"Because of the excess deer population," the sheriff added.

"I see. That is a change in the situation," Wheeler mused.

"But this isn't terribly unusual, this issuing of doe permits. We've done it many times before," the sheriff said.

"I think it is, if we work with our killer's train of thought. Doe hunting is otherwise illegal, is it not?" Wheeler proposed.

Brian Donald nodded.

"This year, because of this common rationalization for hunting, thinning out the herd, whatever, something usually illegal, is not," Wheeler shrugged.

"Just a guess, gentlemen, an educated guess," he added with a twinkle in his eye, "but our man's sub-conscious stream of anger might be stimulated by this view of the situation."

"In that case, he might stop murdering typical hunting violators and start murdering anyone with a doe permit as well, " Steve said.

"Perhaps even more so," Wheeler replied nod-ding.

"We can't stop it," Bob Foss muttered.

"Unless there is a moratorium in the vicinity," Bill Douglas said in a tired, dreary tone of voice.

"Putting a moratorium on hunting in the vicinity into effect might be a waste of time. He still might go off to other areas if Dr. Wheeler is right about the motivation," Lieutenant Brokofski said. There were nods of agreement.

"I think not, " Wheeler said with that mad scien-tist's twinkle in his eyes again, "but it's only a guess again."

"Why not?" Lieutenant Tooey asked quickly.

"For one, what I suggested, familiarity, and for another . . . territoriality."

"Huh?"

"He has a stake in this area. He protects it by pro-tecting its wildlife. He rages in madness here, not twenty miles from here, not in some other state. It's very characteristic of these kinds of serial murderers."

"Yeah, maybe," Sheriff Winn said, "but getting back to your theory that he's in law enforcement—this idea would eliminate that possibility, wouldn't it? Why would he kill men with doe permits? They're legal, aren't they? I mean, legal authorities have issued them."

"Not justifiable to him. His logic might go something like this—why don't we legalize mugging one year because people are carrying too much money now or walking the streets too much? Can what is illegal, with the added connotation of immoral, one year, suddenly become legal and moral with a Department of Conservation decree? For him, perhaps not."

The group was silent.

"All this," Dr. Wheeler concluded, "depends on your accepting my initial premise, and, I would like to remind you, as I said it's just an educated guess." He sat. "As I said, I'll refine my thoughts with every new piece of evidence, of course," he concluded.

Winn grunted.

"Any more questions?" Steve asked.

"Yeah," the sheriff said. "What do we do now—call in our own men for interrogation?"

"Willie," Douglas said. All the men looked at Brand. He had been so silent they had nearly forgotten he was there. "Three men have been killed in the Centerville area, possibly four if we count the guy killed last year. Do you have any suspects for some-thing like this? If you follow the doctor's theories, that is?"

Douglas turned to the others to explain.

"A man who's been a cop in a town as long and as effectively as Willie has knows his people. That's the benefit of the neighborhood policeman."

Everyone waited for Willie's response.

"Well, there are some men who I wouldn't trust for a moment, and of course, there are people who hate the big game season and hunting period, but I wouldn't mention any name in connection with this. Not without something concrete to go on."

"Very wise," Foss said. "You could ruin someone by pointing a finger and bring about some nasty lawsuits."

"I'm worrying about something else right now," Brian Donald said. "Panic in the woods . . . good men shooting one another. It's an ideal situation for paranoia."

"Is there no hope of catching him quickly?" Foss blurted, directing himself at Dr. Wheeler. The county publicity chairman's look of fear distorted his eyes and mouth.

"I can just give you a psychological overview. The police work is not my area of study. I'm sure you have detectives on this who have better ideas about it."

"Yeah, but there are literally no worthwhile clues at the moment that would single anyone out," Lieutenant Brokofski said. "There are no witnesses that we know of, not much in the way of forensics. We'll keep searching, of course."

"We're nowhere," Foss moaned, the realization of a total economic disaster on the horizon settling into him. "What the hell are you guys doing?"

"We're working hard," Steve Dickson said, glaring at Foss for a moment. "Around the clock, just as the sheriff is and the BCI are. We're all out there, but you heard why this isn't a typical criminal situation. We've got a mad sniper, an assassin loose on a battlefield. Imagine if a soldier was murdering his own men during an attack and all we knew was, the men were being shot by one of their own. Every soldier in the company would be suspect because every one would have the capability of committing the act. The killer hasn't left a calling card behind. He attacks, kills, and departs, disappearing into the woods almost without a trace. He's like a ghost, for crissakes."

"So you're saying the guy's too clever for us?" Foss said. "Is that what Bill and I are supposed to tell the county board of supervisors?"

"It's not a matter of his being clever," Lieutenant Brokofski said, coming to Steve's aid. "These murders are more difficult to solve for so many reasons including what's been pointed out here: his victims are away from population, are apparently unaware of what's about to happen, and unable to distinguish him from any other man out there."

"Or at least have reason to fear him if he's in anyway known to them or wearing any sort of law enforcement uniform," Wheeler interjected.

"We can only hope for the maniac to make a mistake," Lieutenant Brokofski said.

There was silence as each man contemplated his remark. Then Bill Douglas leaned back.

"Well," he said, his hands clasped, "from what the Lieutenant just suggested, the only hope we have of getting this creep is to keep things normal."

"But that makes every hunter out there human bait," Brian Donald said.

"Well, " Douglas said. "Let's see what beefed up patrols can do. We'll keep on top of it."

The district attorney smirked and shook his head. He turned to Willie Brand. Willie smiled slightly and nodded as if after all was said and done, there wasn't anyone in the room smarter than the small town cop after all.

"Anyone have anything else to say?" Steve asked. No one said a word. "Okay, then," he said standing. "Willie's office in Centerville remains our central location. Tom Congemi will run things for me from there. Please, gentlemen, keep any and all inquiries

from the media directed at either Bob Foss or
myself. We'll coordinate all that."

"You're welcome to it," Sheriff Winn said.

Dickson nodded.

"Thanks."

The meeting broke up. Each man got up slowly
and departed in silence. It was as though they had
each paid last respects to a corpse, some looking like
it had been their own.

❦

He wasn't home more than ten minutes before the
silence closed in on him. It always began this way.
Sounds, voices, music, anything drifted back, drifted
away until he was left in vacuum. At first he liked it
because it was soothing.

Then the distorted voices would start, voices
recorded and played on a speed too slow to me
understood. They came at him from every direction
until he covered his ears with his hands and closed
his eyes. For a while that would bring respite. He
took advantage of it to start for the old house, what
was left of it that is. He didn't see the broken window panes, the loose siding, the overgrown lawn
and rotted floor boards. He saw it the way it was.

He hurried around to the basement door and
found the rifle and the pistol. They emerged from

the shadows impatiently. He could almost hear the familiar complaints. They didn't die with him. They lingered in the shadows, in the corners, in the cavernous dark places in his mind.

"Where you been?"

"Why is it taking you so long?"

"What am I supposed to be doing, sitting on my hands here? Let's get this over with. You always took too long to do a chore."

He hurried back to his car and drove off, the voice still ringing in his ears, the complaints raining down so hard, he almost turned on his windshield wipers. It amazed him that he could see where to go anyway.

When he arrived, he stepped out and for a moment, only a moment, there was a lapse in purpose. Confusion almost sent him back, but the sound of a gunshot in the distance whipped his head around and he looked at the house.

Time for another, he vaguely thought. It didn't exactly come to him as a thought. It just came flowing in over a series of visuals, some old, some relatively new.

Then he walked forward, marching with determination. Sometimes, he looked behind and saw himself as a boy, trailing, his head down. He did this time.

"Catch up," he called. "By the time you get moving, it will all be over. I know that's what you'd like to see, too. You're soft, boy. You're more your mother than me and that's too bad for you, hear? Move it!"

The boy jumped and hurried. When he was close enough, he reached back and pulled his hair, hard. The boy knew enough to not cry out.

They marched on together.

"Just ahead of us," he said in a low voice. "You can get so you can smell it if you try hard enough. Walk softly. Remember the importance of surprise. Pay attention to the wind. You stink when it comes to being out here and baths don't make no difference. The soaps are perfumed. That doesn't disguise you.

"All right time to load. Go on, the way I showed you. Good. Now when I say, you flip off the safety, hear? You're taking this shot, boy. It's going to be all you."

He could hear the boy's fear. It was that palpable.

Damn, he thought.

Was I ever like that?

If I was, it will be over soon.

They marched on, he and his younger self, two shadows lifted from the past by a madness that frightened the very trees.

❧

Garth Allan came up from the basement carrying his rifle under his arm as if he were walking through the woods. His wife Lillian was just getting ready to go to work. She was secretary to the president of the farmer's cooperative, a job she had held for nearly twenty years. She and Garth were childless. Once, a little more than ten years ago, they fooled with the notion they might adopt, but when it came down to it, Garth didn't have the stomach for it. He didn't come out and say it, but the words lingered in the air between them. "I can't love any child that ain't of my own blood. He or she would always be a stranger to me."

With that sort of attitude on his part, Lillian let the idea slip through her fingers like just so much smoke and moved on to what she considered the next stage in their marriage: a quiet acceptance of each other's faults and weaknesses. It was as if the marriage had become a prison sentence, something to endure. They wore each other like old socks, mending the holes when they appeared, washing away the dirt and folding up at the end of their prospective work days. Words of affection, gestures and looks of passion drifted away with their youth. They had come to the point where they were merely used to each other and that put a cloud of depression over Lillian than hovered no matter how bright or how promising the day appeared to be.

She raised her eyebrows when Garth appeared.

"I thought you were going to wait. I thought you were mourning your friends," she said.

"Be damned if I let some psycho bulldoze me. This was the day I planned to go out. This is the day I go."

"But you were going to go with Billy and Johnny and seeing what happened to them . . ."

"More reason for me to go," he argued.

She turned away. When he was stubborn and stupid, she found it easier to pretend he wasn't there or he wasn't going to do what he was determined to do.

"I'm doing my shopping after work today," she said, "so dinner will be an hour later."

"Right," he said. He heard but he didn't hear. He was already wrapped up in his preparations.

This big game hunting has the power of a religious ritual, Lillian thought. There's very little they would put ahead of it or for which they would sacrifice it. It was as if it reinforced their manhood, confirmed their existence. It was as much a puzzle to her as most things men did in the name of masculinity. Cloistered by puritanical parents, Lillian never learned much about the opposite sex. Their hungers, lusts, and drives remained as much a mystery to her now as they were when she was an adolescent. Men were just . . . different and that difference was simply something else to be tolerated.

Life, Lillian had come to believe, was a matter of enduring, and death came when you simply no longer had the strength to be indifferent. Her lack of romance left her shallow and as light as a shadow. Any wind of change could blow her which way it wanted. She was just along for the ride.

"Are you going with anyone then?" she asked at the door. He turned from his gun.

"I'm only going on my own land," he said. "Saw a handsome buck down at the creek just last month. I'm sure he's still loitering about as if he owned the property."

"You'll show him," she said dryly.

He raised his eyebrows. Sarcasm was normally beyond her. He looked to see if she was going to laugh, but she just shook her head and walked out, closing the door softly behind her. He heard the car start and then heard her drive off.

His attention returned to his weapon and the memories of past hunts. All but one were joyful, satisfying. All but one was successful, and that one . . . was to be forgotten. He wouldn't even permit it to tinkle in his memory.

A little over a half hour later, he was strolling through his fields and entering the forest. He enjoyed the cool, clean aroma of the pine and the maple, especially when the maple syrup was running. This was prime land and he was proud he owned it. He cut over a small hill and down a well-worn path toward the creek, moving like someone who knew exactly the place he would find his prey.

At first, all he saw was a shadow that moved. It caught his eye and he turned to the right to look up the hill. The sun was just high enough to blind his sight. He put his hand over his eyes and stared. Someone was standing there. First, he was angered about being frightened and surprised, and then he was angered about someone else hunting on his posted property.

"Who's that?" he called.

When he lowered his hand, the man was gone. His heart began to race. He gazed around and then, instinctively, he moved to the side of the path and slowly, as quietly as he could, he started up the hill. When he reached the top, he found no one, but he saw the footprints in the mud. He could tell they were fresh of course.

"Bastard. WHOEVER THE HELL YOU ARE," he called, "THIS IS PRIVATE PROPERTY."

He waited, panned the area carefully and then relaxed. Whoever it was had been caught and probably fled, knowing he was on private land. Garth released his breath and started down the hill again. He walked quickly, but occasionally turned to check behind him. When he reached the creek, he paused. His buck wasn't there yet, but surely, he would be.

He found a comfortable place to wait, a rock behind a large blueberry bush. He lowered himself to the rock and stared quietly at the creek, listening to the sound of the water. At first, when he heard the man's voice, he thought it was something he had imagined. Then he heard it again.

"Hello, Garth."

He spun around to find himself staring down the barrel of a rifle. The barrel was jerked so it hit him right in the center of his forehead and the blow stunned him. He dropped his own gun and it was kicked away.

"What the fuck is this?" he demanded, wiping the blood from his temple.

"Your day to die," he was told.

"Why? Why are you doin' this? Why now? Did someone say somethin'?"

"Yes."

"Who? When?"

"Me. Every time I pulled the trigger," was the reply. "Take off your clothes."

Garth shook his head.

"You can do it yourself or I'll do it after. I'm giving you a chance, the same chance you give them."

"You're crazy. You're . . ."

"Come to think of it, I don't have the time to

hunt," Garth was told and then he felt the bullet split open his chest. He looked at the wound and his oncoming death like someone who thought he was immortal would look: full of surprise and anger and downright disgust.

Seven

"OKAY," Aaron said coming into the kitchen. "I got this hunter's jacket from a few years ago when I was a size smaller."

He held it up.

"A few? That's about ten years old, " his mother said. She turned to Diana. "The man won't throw anything out. The woman he marries better have a house with either a big attic or a big basement."

"And there's this hat," he added ignoring her. He held up a bright red cap with "Stoker's Oil" on the front.

"She'll be quite a sight in that," Marilyn said. "Is that the best you can offer?"

"It's not for fashion, Ma. It's for protection."

"Thank you," Diana said, taking the jacket and hat. She took off her ski parka and put it on the chair. Then she put the jacket on. The sleeves went five or six inches beyond the tips of her fingers. Marilyn Kuhn laughed.

"She's swimming in that thing."

"Maybe if I wear a few sweaters too," Diana thought aloud and looked up at Marilyn who just shook her head.

"I got a jacket for her," Walker said coming through the front door. "And it's not ten years old, either."

"This will be all right, " Diana said. She looked at Aaron for a moment. "He's right. I'm not wearing it to be fashionable."

"So you're determined to go out with Art Davis, huh?" Walker said. "Now how we gonna let a nice reporter do a dumb thing like that, Ma?"

"What do you mean, Walker?"

"Go out with a stump jumper like Art Davis."

"What do you have in mind, Walker?" Marilyn Kuhn raised her eyebrows and folded her arms across her chest.

"I offered to take her out myself, and show her what hunting's all about."

"You did, did you? I think you're all crazy. With that lunatic on the rampage in the woods? I'm sorry, Diana, but if you want the advice of a wise old lady, write about something else."

"I have my assignment, " Diana said gently.

"She's a stubborn one, Ma, " Aaron said. "When

she makes her mind up, she reminds me of you. But Walker and I aren't going back into the woods. We've got too much work in the shop," he said glaring at his brother.

"What's another day? We'll close tomorrow and . . ."

"Look. You know Steiner, Belski, Dan Gross, all made appointments to get snow tires put on tomorrow. Then we've got the Hinten's tractor to weld. And what about Tom Decker's snow blower? That's not even taking into account people who just drop in to have tires changed."

Walker just looked away. There was an embarrassing moment of silence.

Marilyn Kuhn sighed and shook her head.

"Let's have another cup of coffee," she said. Diana nodded and sat at the table again. "Walker?"

"Naw. I got things to do. Got to take advantage of every free moment I can get these days."

Aaron watched him walk back out. As long as he could remember, he was holding his brother in check. He recognized that Walker had a great deal less of a sense of responsibility. He barely graduated from high school because he never did homework or studied for tests. For a while he had tried to talk Walker into joining the army, figuring the experience might tighten him up. Walker almost did it, but pulled out at the last moment. There was no question in Aaron's mind that Walker would have easily become a drifter if it wasn't for the shop.

More often than not these day, he was tired of caring for him and driving him to do things. He was tempted to turn away and let him sink in his own degenerating procrastination. But then he'd think of his mother and the responsibility he owed her and his father. Only it was hard to continually be the good guy, the voice of sense, the control.

Devoid of worry and concern, his brother lived like some kind of free spirit taking life as it came, never spending much time planning or contriving for the future. He knew that most people simply called it a lack of ambition. While other men Walker's age had already settled down in a job or profession, married and begun to build a house, Walker continued to hang around with younger and younger guys. It was almost as if he believed time would stand still for him.

When he worked, he worked hard. He was master of the skills he needed to get by, but if Aaron ever tried to suggest that Walker take a new look at himself and consider his future, he was usually met with offhanded, silly remarks.

"I just wanna have a good time, " he'd say. "There's plenty of time to worry about those other things."

Occasionally, Walker would turn it on him like someone twisting a flashlight around.

"So why ain't you married and stuck with a mort-gage and insurance payments, big shot?"

"I just might do that soon," he threatened as if he was having a secret affair.

"Sure, sure. You're not even trying. Instead of going to the Playboy Club for a vacation, you go off with Ralph Lippen to fish in Canada."

Actually Aaron couldn't see much of a future in store for himself. At an early age, he had become sto-ical. The work insulated him. It was safe in the shop. There, he was in complete control. He was master. Men with five times his assets stood by stupidly, watching him remold the metals they had damaged. He could sense their softness and their fear and con-fusion of all things mechanical. They jabbered away nervously, talking of abstract things like politics or economics, while he dealt with realities.

When he was finished though, they wrote out checks with an ease he envied. They drove out in com-fort. If only there was a way to combine the two, he thought, to be real and yet comfortable and economi-cally safe. Why was it, he wondered, that softer men had taken control of the country's destiny? There was nothing independent and hard about their spirits. They were shrewd, arrogant, and schooled in deceit, but there was nothing of the pioneer in them. Or at least most of them. These thoughts made him cyni-cal when he longed to be optimistic and houseful.

"No, I never went hunting," Marilyn Kuhn was saying when Aaron came out of his reverie. "These women who Aaron's talking about aren't my breed. But I don't want to influence your story."

"That's all right," Diana said. Aaron smiled at her enthusiasm. She wanted his mother to talk. "I don't think of it in terms of equalizing the sexes."

Marilyn put her hand up.

"I know you modern girls are putting everything in those terms these days. Maybe we were wrong, and maybe . . . maybe we were even abused some . . . although I'll never say maliciously or deliberately, but I saw the world divided into things masculine and things feminine. It gave it some balance. Children always knew where things would be found."

She paused and smiled down at her cup. Diana didn't move a muscle for fear Marilyn would become self-conscious and stop.

"My husband was never above helping me in the kitchen if I was sick and there were many times when I went out to chop some kindling for the wood stove. Even changed a tire on a car for him once in the middle of a snow storm."

"You never told me that story, Ma," Aaron said.

"Of course not. Don't want you asking me to help out in the shop too," she said.

Diana laughed.

"What I mean to say, Diana, is we respected each

other. We never felt this competition men and women seemed wrapped up in today."

"I understand."

"Maybe you do and maybe you don't. I'd never go hunting deer. I've shot a gun. Killed a rat once out in the shed in back. But I'd never go out on the hunt. I'll prepare the kill though. Without hesitation. Food's food when it comes down to it. Not to use it would be the bigger sin, it seems to me."

"I'm getting the best material right here," Diana said, turning to Aaron.

He looked at his mother and then looked down.

"Then be smart," Marilyn Kuhn said, "and stay outta those woods until they catch the maniac."

"If I did that, I'd be a mighty poor example of your modern woman," Diana said. "And just like you had to do what you had to do, I have to live up to my responsibilities."

Marilyn Kuhn smiled and then nodded at her son. He caught the pleased look in her eyes and felt a warmth in his heart. His mother didn't approve of many young women these days.

But along with this pleasure and happiness came a new sense of fear and anxiety. Why was he helping to put her in danger's way and how could he talk her out of it now?

Walker worked his frustration out on the car, finishing the polish job. It was difficult for him to verbalize his feelings, even to himself. Vaguely he understood that he was jealous of the apparent interest this pretty girl had taken in Aaron. Aaron was never a lady's man. It was the one major thing he felt he had over Aaron. Whenever girls were around him, he was usually awkward, shy, and unimpressive. He'd back away from them.

Walker knew that Aaron had been hurt by a girl once, but he felt there were deeper reasons for his brother's failure with women. Usually it was like struggling with a stubborn tire rim when he tried to get him to go out on a double date. He would find every excuse imaginable not to, and if he couldn't think of one, he would just say, "I'm not interested." That would be it. No amount of persuasion would make a difference. It got so he never bothered anymore.

Where had he picked up this girl and why did she find him so interesting? She was fine, he thought. He could show her a time. Why was Aaron palming her off on Art Davis? He knew more about hunting than that backwoods redneck. Certainly it wasn't because he was afraid of going in the woods now. It's just like Aaron, he thought, letting something like her slip out of his hands. Girl stupid. That was his problem. He just didn't understand them. He had spent too much of his life in this dumb shop, working, working, working. When he wasn't doing that, he was sitting around with Mom or talking to the jerks about fishing.

He threw the polishing cloth down and stood up. It was done. Looked better than before it was smashed, he thought. He went to the window and looked at the house. Got to find out more about her. Maybe I can get in on this yet. Aaron won't follow up on it most likely. I can get away for a while tomorrow. He's trying to make it sound busy just so I won't go out for the doe. Screw it. I work hard enough as it is. Lots of guys are taking off from their work to hunt. Why should we be any different? People around here expect it, he concluded.

He saw them come out of the house. She carried his hunting jacket and a hat, and they were both laughing. Damn good looking piece of ass, he thought and opened the door.

"Hey, where are you going?"

"Like I said before, up to Art's."

"The Fern car's all done," he said approaching. He stared at her. She kept this innocent smile on her face, but he knew what she was thinking. He knew this type really well, he thought.

"I'd better get that car over there," Aaron said.

"Sure. Want me to take her up to Art's?"

Walker smiled, but Diana looked away. Coy and tricky. Just the way I like them, he thought.

"Naw. I've got to talk to him about this," Aaron said, obviously embarrassed by Walker's interest. "I feel kind of responsible."

Aaron gazed at Diana and saw she liked his reasoning.

"Besides," Diana said, "there's no real rush. I'm not going out until tomorrow."

"Just trying to be helpful and friendly."

"Okay," Aaron said turning back to Diana. "I'm going to break one of those rules you've come to love. You follow me in your car so I can make this delivery to Mrs. Fern, and I'll let you drive up to Art Davis' place after."

"Oh my," she said with her eyes blinking quickly. She took his arm to pretend she was a weak, hanging vine type. "Do you think us poor fragile types could do all that?"

Aaron turned blood red.

"Very funny. All right, get into your car and wait until I pull out of the shop."

He left her standing with Walker, who wore a look of total confusion. They were both silent for a moment.

"My brother's a character. A little behind the times, I'm afraid."

"Yes," she said. "Isn't it refreshing?"

"Huh?"

"I mean, with all these pushy types around, guys

who just pump up their chests like balloons trying to impress you when all they have is a lot of hot air. I bet you run into types like that all the time in those singles watering holes."

"Yeah, yeah, sure." He looked after Aaron and scratched his head. "Where the hell did you two meet?"

"O'Heany's."

"O'Heany's? But that's a . . . you mean, you went to O'Heany's?"

"Swinging place. You oughta try it some time," she said and walked to her car as the shop door opened.

Walker stood there, staring after her.

Could it be? Was there a female type he didn't understand?

❧

Maria peered out the doorway and then opened it wider. Although the Ferns paid her well and the work was not difficult, she had always considered the job dangerous. Their home was the most likely target for any thief. She was suspicious about every ring of the buzzer. The area had changed since she was a little girl. House break-ins were unheard of then, and drug problems were virtually nonexistent. But just the other day, she read about a doctor who

was robbed and beaten for his drug supplies. It happened only forty miles away. Who could know what loomed outside, and with Mrs. Fern the way she was a good deal of the time ... it was all just too much of a responsibility. Her face revealed the fear as she looked at Aaron.

He smiled and looked back once at Diana, as if to be sure she was still there, waiting.

"Yes?"

"You can tell Mrs. Fern her car's ready. I'll leave it in the driveway."

"Is that Aaron, Maria?" He heard her call from the hallway.

"It's him," Maria said sullenly.

"Well, let him in."

Maria stepped back. Aaron moved forward, but stayed just inside the doorway. Rose Fern was dressed in a house coat. Her hair was loose and unbrushed, and she was barefoot. She had the look of someone who had just gotten out of bed, only she carried a drink in her right hand.

So early, Aaron thought. This must be the sign of a real alcoholic. He wondered why the doctor didn't do something about her.

"We fail to see what's closest to us, " his mother always said. He nodded slightly, hearing her say it in his memory.

"Your car's all done."

"Oh good. Gerald told me it would be. Let me see it," she said coming forward.

"It's cold out there, Mrs. Fern," Maria said. The maid gave Aaron an angry glance. It was as if she blamed him for causing a disturbance by bringing the finished car. He stepped away so Rose Fern could look out.

"Oh, the mess is on the other side, isn't it?"

"Not any more," Aaron said. He felt stupid stating something so obvious. He was playing a part in the insanity.

Rose Fern saw Diana.

"Who's that?"

"She's giving me a ride, Mrs. Fern."

Rose gave him a skeptical, sly smile that made him uncomfortable.

"If you have any problems, call the shop," he said turning to go.

"Well, where's the bill?"

She stepped toward him and smiled flirtatiously, standing much too closely. He wondered if Diana could see it.

"Oh, I'll give it to the doctor later. No rush."

"The doctor?" She laughed and turned to her maid standing to the side in the hallway. "Tell him how the doctor's spending Sunday, Maria. Tell him," she commanded.

He looked at the housekeeper, but she just turned and walked away.

"The doctor decided he would go on playing hunter until he caught a deer," she said and laughed again, waving her arm so emphatically the contents of her glass spilled out. She didn't seem to notice.

"Still hunting?"

"I told you it was your two deer that did it. That's all he talked about for two days. Even brought Dr. Friedman down here to gape at them. He's just not as good at it as he used to be. Of course, he blames it on everyone and everything else. Everyone is cheating or doing something wrong, but him and so he's a failure. How much does it cost to buy one already shot, because that's what he'll probably end up doing."

"Didn't he hear about all the trouble? I mean . . ."

"He's oblivious to anything that contradicts what he wants. He always has been. That even includes me sometimes," she said. She finished the contents of the glass. He stepped out of the doorway, edging away like someone who was trying to effect an escape.

"Yeah, well no problem. I'll give him the bill when I see him."

"If you're going into the woods, you'll see him before I will," she said and laughed. "Give him the bill in the woods," she added as she closed the door.

He paused to take a deep breath. While he walked to Diana's car, he caught sight of Gerald Spina watching him from the corner of the property where he was digging up a dead maple tree. He waved, and Gerald waved back.

"That's the boy who was in your garage this morning?" Diana asked and nodded toward Gerald, who stood watching them.

"Yes. He does some handyman work here."

"Ambitious for a teenager these days," she said.

"He's the type who would rather work than waste time mingling with friends."

She smiled at him.

"I bet you were like that when you were his age, huh?"

"Yes. And no," he added as they backed out of the driveway.

"No?"

"Gerald's . . . different."

"How so?"

"There's something driving him, something . . . painful," he said surprised at his sudden ability to verbalize a thought he had always had.

She looked back at Gerald thoughtfully and nodded.

"This town is full of interesting characters," she said.

"No different from any other small town, except . . ."

"Except? Aaron?" she pursued when he didn't respond. "Except what?"

"Except it just might be that someone who lives in it has gone dead mad."

It sent a shudder through her and she turned to look back at Gerald Spina who was still standing and staring after them.

❦

The two men sat on a large boulder situated just at the rim of the clearing. They rested their rifles against the rock and passed the pint of whiskey back and forth. The partly cloudy sky had rapidly become a dreary grey unbroken ceiling, shutting out the sun. Weather forecasts had predicted a snow a little heavier than the powdering they had already gotten in the county, but the two hunters were not depressed about it. Snow made for easier deer tracking.

The whiskey warmed their stomachs and helped swell their waning optimism. They had trekked through the woods for over an hour, and aside from a jackrabbit, they hadn't seen a thing. Like so many out-of-towners, they entered the Catskill forests with misconceptions. They had been told the deer population was so heavy that there were practically herds of them everywhere. It wasn't even a matter of getting a deer; it was a matter of how big you wanted it to be.

"Probably a bunch of guys in here before us," the taller of the two said. His partner nodded, although he didn't really understand the significance of the statement. His friend continued as if he was really some sort of an expert on hunting. "Drove the deer deeper into the woods."

"Oh. Yeah, yeah."

"We'll go off to the right. It looks thicker there. If I was a deer, I'd go for thicker woods."

The area he pointed to was overgrown with white birch. The trees grew in clumps, many branching off the same trunk. Weaker ones had already been starved out in the competition for nourishment. Some decayed and cracked, while others were covered with wild mushroom growths that looked like tumors. Because of its rot, this section of the forest suggested death. It was a ghetto for poorer trees of the wilderness. It was depressing and gloomy.

"Let's get at it," the shorter man said, revving up his enthusiasm.

They put the bottle away and took up their rifles. As they crossed the field, something stirred on their immediate right. They stopped to listen. The taller man's eyes got wider as he smiled and walked on with exaggerated care, practically tiptoeing. They entered the woods and waited. It stirred again, a little further to their left this time.

The shorter man crouched, and although the taller one wasn't sure why, he did the same thing. It seemed like something he had seen in a movie anyway. They moved against the brush, finding it impossible to be silent as they did so. The stirring got louder. There was a rustling of leaves, a swish of branches. Was the forest toying with them? It was as though the over-growth had become animated simply to tease them. It brought a flush of excitement to both of them. Nothing but a deer could make that much noise, they concluded. Deer or bear. What if it were a bear? They were both suddenly charged with excitement, their eyes wide. They were about to get their first big kill.

Suddenly the stirring got even louder and the movement in the bushes became faster. The tall man spun to his right and his partner lifted his rifle impulsively. Both of them fired at once, the sound of their rifles merging into one terrific blast.

"Did you see it?" the tall man asked.

"Yeah," his friend said, but not convincingly.

"I think I saw it too. I saw it!"

"We might have gotten it then, huh?"

"Maybe," the tall man said, but he didn't move forward. "Wait and listen," he added.

They were silent. The forest had grown still around them again. Ruptured white birch peered down at them. The tall man felt as if the forest had closed in. It was as though they had been drawn into a trap. The neutral woods had become an antagonist.

"All right," the tall man said, eyeing the surroundings carefully, "Let's see."

They started through the brush. Almost immediately after the first branch cracked, a rifle shot echoed back at them. The bullet split branches to their left and they both dove forward.

"Hey. HEY. WHAT THE . . . WHAT THE HELL'S GOIN' ON?" the tall man shouted.

"FUCK YOU," a voice called back. "YOU MANIAC MURDERIN' BASTARD."

Another shot tore up the tops of the bushes above them.

"It must be him, " the tall man said. His friend's eyes reflected the wild fear running through him.

"Fucking shit," he said and began firing into the woods.

The tall man took the same action, although neither of them saw anything. They emptied their rifles in a maddening and hysterical barrage of bullets. Shots were fired back. They reloaded and began answering them.

"Careful," the tall man said as his friend moved to the right. "This ain't no dumb deer. We gotta try to flank him. He's got us pinned down here."

"Son of a bitch," the tall man said and pressed his body closer to the earth.

"Jesus," his partner moaned. "Jesus, Mary, and Joseph. He's going to kill us."

"Keep your head down," he told his partner.

But the dank odor of rotten bark and decaying

leaves created waves of nausea. The sudden cessation of firing was even more frightening. Panic rushed through his veins. He swallowed hard and let out a small moan of despair. In minutes, he could be dead. This wasn't why he had come up here. It wasn't supposed to be him who was hung to dry.

"Christ!" he screamed. "Get the fuck away from us, you bastard!"

He closed his eyes, found a pool of courage to dip into, jumped to his feet and fired blindly. Then he dropped to the ground again.

Whoever it was he was firing at, continued to fire back with just as much blind anger. A shower of branches came down around them.

"That's seems like more than one rifle, don't it?" he partner asked.

"Maybe he has an automatic. We're probably sitting ducks here."

"Jesus."

They clutched the earth. His partner realized he had pissed in his pants. The strong odor of urine came up into both their nostrils, but neither of them complained.

When you pissed in your pants, you were still alive at least, they both thought.

The dead don't piss.

The dead just rot.

Eight

THE DAVISES LIVED in a small wooden frame house on a secondary highway between Sandburg and Centerville. A 1965 Ford was jacked up on cement blocks to the immediate right of the house. A late model dark-blue pickup truck was parked in the driveway. The house itself was depressingly dilapidated. It looked tired and sick. Diana couldn't be positive, but to her it seemed as though the house actually leaned forward and to the right. Perhaps a strong wind could blow it down. The shingles were painted a dull grey and the chipped black shutters were loose at every window.

"This is what you call poor white," Aaron said. "On and off welfare. When he works, it's construction labor, but there isn't all that much building going on around here these days. These are people who really do hunt to eat."

Diana nodded. It still amazed her how somehow she had grown up in the vicinity of all this and yet been blind to it. There were more invisible people in her area than she had imagined, or maybe it was just that she had refused to see.

Snow had begun to fall lightly when they had left Centerville, but it was obviously growing heavier with every passing minute. She had the windshield wipers going and the monotonous rhythm seemed the proper background for such a dismal setting.

"How old a man is he?"

"Late forties," Aaron said. "Although he looks a lot older. They have two very young kids though, and a few older ones. Babies just seemed to rain down on these kind of people."

"Seem?"

"They break out in children, sorta like other people break out in the measles," he said.

"Measles? Never quite heard it put that way," she said. She laughed and pulled into the driveway.

"I'm just chock full of local color."

"Don't worry, I'm taking notes. So how many people live in that house?"

"Six or seven. Can't remember exactly. His mother lives with them, too."

The house door opened and a very heavy man wearing only a tee shirt and jeans stepped out. His thin hair blew wildly about his forehead and temples. When he smiled, Diana could see that he was missing many teeth. He waved and walked forward. As he drew closer, she noted that he limped. The puffiness in his face was emphasized by the tiny eyebrows and small mouth. His eyes were lost in swollen cheeks. He spit something out and put his hands on the car door.

"Howdy, Kuhn. This here the reporter woman, huh?"

"Yep. Diana Brooks, meet Art Davis."

"Hello. Aren't you cold in just an undershirt?" she asked.

"Undershirt?" He laughed, but when he did, he didn't make sounds. His body simply bounced and he closed and opened his eyes.

"So," he said, "you wanna be a real hunter, huh?"

"I'd like to go along and observe. I promise I won't be in your way," she said.

Davis simply stared at her. The sight of such a woman at his house intrigued him. It was as if he was talking to a movie star, and for a moment, the wonder of her beauty and youth took his breath away and left him dumbfounded. Aaron could almost read his thoughts on his forehead: she wants to be with me?

"Maggie around?" Aaron asked leaning over. "Thought they could chat for a few minutes."

"Yeah, yeah. I"ll call her out. She don"t want nobody in the house canna it's a mess. I told her it's always a mess so what the hell's the difference?"

He laughed at his own remark. Aaron just smiled and shook his head.

"What time you planning on going tomorrow?"

"We'll go out by six-thirty. Don't start getting light now till nearly seven and I don't need no Smokey the Bear or anyone on my tail. He's been snoopin' around here quite a bit lately. Surprised to see him this far out of his way."

"Oh? Well, you know how seriously Gary takes his job."

"Who asked him to?" Art snapped back. "He should be hauntin' them city slickers, not good folk like us just tryin' to put meat on the table."

Aaron nodded in agreement. He harbored the idea that for people like the Davises, hunting season should be an all-year round thing. They didn't kill extravagantly, and no one appreciated a good kill as much. But he was afraid to utter such a thought, especially in the shop where it would start a debate that would go on for weeks.

"Where you plan on going this time?" he asked Art Davis.

"Figure we'll try around Krasek's lake there. Saw three buck this fall."

"Good spot."

Art turned back to Diana and smiled as he pulled his chest up.

"So we's goin' to be in the papers, huh?"

"Yes, you will," Diana promised.

"Gonna tell us when so we can buy one?"

"Better than that. I'll get you a few copies," Diana said.

He stared at her a moment and chewed on his inner lip as if he was still considering whether or not to permit her to go along with them.

"We wouldn't like it if you wrote that we did somethin' wrong," he muttered.

"I promise to have you approve of any copy beforehand," she said.

"Copy?"

"What she writes, Art. That's reporter talk," Aaron said.

"Oh. Yeah, sure. Yeah, well, I'll get Maggie out."

He started back to the house and then turned.

"Don't build her up too much," he warned. "She's got a swelled-up head about it already, figurin' her picture's gonna be in the paper."

"I understand," Diana said. She turned and looked at Aaron. He smiled and shrugged.

"You wanted real local color. I got you real local color."

"Now that I've met him, I'm terrified of what his wife's going to be like."

"She's a nice person—quiet and simple. Don't expect a lot of discussion, or big answers to questions."

"Like I'm getting from you, you mean?"

"Exactly," he said smiling. It took all his self-control to keep himself from leaning over and kissing her. She moved her lips as if she anticipated he would, but before he could think about it again, the door opened and Maggie Davis stepped out, dressed in a man's hunting coat and jeans.

She was nearly as big as her husband, only her face did not appear as swollen. Her hair was cut short and had the look of a homemade job. Her light brown eyebrows were untrimmed, but she wore lipstick. She had small facial features and Diana thought when she was very young, she must have been pretty. Her smile was weak and uncertain. She looked quickly from her husband to the car and then back at her husband as if she was looking to get permission to take another step forward.

"This is the little lady," Art said.

"Hi, Maggie. I'm Diana Brooks." She extended her hand.

Maggie stared at it for a moment before taking it firmly and shaking.

"Please to meet you," Maggie said.

"I appreciate you people permitting me to go along with you. I'll try not to get in your way tomorrow."

Maggie just smiled.

"You'll see she's a pretty damn good shot with a 308," Art said.

"Oh, I am not," Maggie said. She smiled shyly immediately after she spoke.

"Did you ever shoot a deer?" Diana asked.

"Four out of the last six years," Art said quickly with pride.

"I was lucky," Maggie said. "You ever shoot a rifle?"

"Never even held one," Diana said.

"It ain't hard once you get use to it," Maggie said.

"You want her to meet you people right here?" Aaron asked.

"Unless she can find her way to Krasek's Lake herself," Art Davis said with a wry smile.

"I'm not even sure I can find my way back here," Diana said. She smiled at Maggie, but the big woman wasn't sure she was joking.

"Can't do a lotta talkin' in the woods," Art admonished with as serious an expression as he could make.

"I understand."

"She's really there just to observe," Aaron said.

"Right. I'll save my questions for before or after the hunting expedition."

"Hunting expedition?"

"I mean . . ."

"Ain't you afraid of this here mystery killer?" Art teased with a wide smile.

"Well," Diana said with a reporter's keen quickness. "Aren't you? You're hunting deer and apparently he's killed deer hunters only."

"I'll tell you this," Davis said, his lips tightening and his eyes growing beady and cold. "If he shoots at me, he better get me on the first damn shot."

"Who-all's in your party tomorrow, Art?" Aaron asked.

"My brother and Peter Braddock. Pete's pretty upset about Johnny Domfort."

"Yeah. But he's going out anyway?" Aaron commented, almost under his breath.

"You know Pete. He even went deer hunting the day after his mother died. Now how's that for determination?" he asked Diana.

"The others won't mind my being there?" she replied.

"Naw. You ain't carryin' a gun. Just you come though. Don't want to have no more fresh fish tracking near us that's all."

"Fresh fish?" She looked at Aaron.

"He means first time hunters. Okay," Aaron said. "If she's not here by six thirty, go on without her."

"Would anyway. Picture or no picture in the paper," Art said sternly.

"I'll be here," Diana said with a firmness Art Davis appreciated. She started the car again.

"I'd have you in the house," Maggie said. "But it's a mess with the children and all."

"That's all right. I've got to get back to the shop," Aaron explained.

"See you tomorrow," Diana said. Art Davis grunted. Maggie continued to smile and nod. They both stood there watching as Diana backed out of the driveway.

She saw the woman wave slightly as they pulled away.

"Still wanna go through with this?" Aaron asked her.

"Just how good are they?"

"Oh, they're good. They always get their game. It's just that they're raw about it."

"Raw? What do you mean, raw?"

"It's not easy to explain. You have to be there with them. You'll see what it is tomorrow. If you really go," he added. He looked out the side window.

"Oh, I'll go," she said with a firmness that drew back his attention. "I'm the type who makes her mind up and follows through, come hell or high water."

He smiled at her.

"Look who's using old-fashioned expressions now."

"Must be contagious." She paused and looked at him. "Do you really have to go right back to the shop?"

"Not right back, why?"

"How about showing me some hunter's haunts. Some place where I can buy you lunch."

"Buy me lunch?"

"How's a working girl supposed to work up an expense account?"

He shook his head.

"What's wrong with that?"

"The place I'm thinking of taking you to is filled with guys who wouldn't understand. Make a right turn at the intersection and pull over."

"What for?"

"It's easier if I drive rather than give you directions every five minutes."

She looked at him suspiciously.

"Sure it's not because you don't want to be seen driven around by a woman?"

He laughed, but when she didn't, he stopped.

"Don't start that stuff about my insecure masculine image," he warned.

"Oh, you know about that sort of thing," she said pulling over. "I wouldn't have thought so after last night."

He blanched again.

"I know about it, but don't pay it any attention," he said opening the door.

"You would if you worked in my office," she quipped.

He leaned back and smiled.

"That's why I don't work in your office," he said. "In fact, that's why I don't work in an office period."

"I have to admit," she said sliding over, "that I like the working atmosphere more in the field myself."

"So this is the field?"

"Sorta," she teased moving closer to him. They held each other's gaze for a moment and then he kissed her and she moaned and let herself slip farther into his arms.

"More research?" he whispered.

"It never stops," she said and they kissed again.

"Ever neck in a car in the woods?"

"Now that you mention it, no," she said. "But I'm up here to do things for the first time."

He smiled and started the engine. Then he drove off the road and deeper into the woods. He turned off the engine and started to kiss her again.

"Is it safe?" she asked with some concern in her eyes.

He started to nod, but reached over to lock the car doors instead.

"It is now," he said.

She leaned back and he kissed her on the neck. She sat up and took off her coat and then he did the same.

"It's better in the rear," she said.

"I thought you never did this before," he quickly commented.

"Just being logical," she replied.

"Sure," he said nodding and smiling. She crawled over the front seat and he followed.

It was like being a teenager again, the struggle to get comfortable, the excitement of peeling off their clothing in broad daylight and then the way their passion took over to make them cling to each other, twist and turn and fill their lips with each other's lips until they coupled and made love with an intensity that brought surprise to both their faces, surprise and pleasure and great wonder. The more she enjoyed him, the more he wanted to please her. He wanted to lose himself forever in her. His intensity increased until she kissed his forehead and held his head in his hands and whispered, "It's all right. Easy."

Her words brought him back to reality and he regained control. He took a deep breath and was about to say something to her, when he saw her eyes widen with fear. Instinctively, he pulled himself back.

"What?" he cried.

"Something, someone . . . I'm not sure . . . there was a shadow."

He started to dress as he looked out the windows. He could see no one, but the moment was lost. Fear was what was palpable now. She was dressing quickly.

"Are you sure you saw something?"

"No, not positive. I thought I did," she said.

He opened the car door and stood outside, studying the forest. It was deadly quiet.

Damn, he thought. He didn't want to frighten her any more than she was, but he did feel something. He could see no one, but he knew in his heart that they weren't alone.

"Is there anyone there?" she asked.

"Not that I can see," he said. He continued to study the woods.

"I'm sorry," she told him.

"Forget it. It's all right," he said getting back into the car and starting the engine.

He was in deep thought.

"What is it, Aaron?"

"Nothing," he said forcing a smile. She held her intense look. "Just that until this is over, we'll all be seeing something in the shadows."

She nodded, glanced at the woods and then cuddle up to him as he backed them out and back onto the road. It wasn't until they were miles along that she felt she could let out her breath.

❦

Steve Dickson's buzzer jerked him out of deep thought. He was daydreaming a scenario of events that led him to a senatorial seat. People were hungry for strong, vigorous law enforcement. The district attorney's office was a perfect place to work good publicity and build popularity with the electorate. It was all a matter of timing. He could start with Congress because this congressional district was a tailor-made one for a strong running Democrat, even though the county had a significant Republican registration. When a Democrat won the county, he usually won the congressional district.

Steve believed he was destined for great things; he felt it. Everyone around him felt it. All he had to do now was come out a winner with this hunting maniac situation. It had already given him much wider exposure than he had anticipated so early in office. He had drawn another phone call from Harvey Gold, the state party chairman, who had suggested liaisons with the governor.

"Do everything on a big scale," Harvey Gold had advised him. "It gives people the impression you're a real mover. You're in contact with the governor; you're in contact with the BCI. You're in contact with the army, for Crissakes. Whatever. Be in contact with the President, if you can. Every statement's a headline and every headline drives you deeper and deeper into their minds."

"I appreciate the advice," Steve told him. "It's a tough situation here. We're . . ."

"I know it's tough, but just be careful. Don't make promises you can't keep. I watched your campaign. It was beautiful, but you can fuck your whole career with one blunder in a situation like this one. Don't shoot from the hip. Talk, talk, talk, but make few actual commitments. If possible, get some other official to stick his neck out with the controversial actions. Take your pick of the best fruit. Understand?"

"Yes, I do."

"Good. We've got you pegged for big time stuff, Steve. You impressed a helluva lot of people in high places. Call me any time if you need any advice."

"I will."

"Get that liaison going with the governor's office."

"Right away," he said. He did make the call and got the governor's personal secretary.

"The governor's been briefed," he told Steve, "but we'd appreciate details as you get them."

"I'll put my man on it right now. His name is Tom Congemi and I'll make sure he stays in close touch."

"Any other killing?"

"No."

"Call us immediately if it gets much worse."

Steve promised he would, but afterward he wondered if calling for all this extra help didn't make it look as though he and the people in his command were incapable of handling the situation. Early expe-

riences in the political arena had made him some-
what paranoid and distrustful of everyone's motives.
Maybe the governor hoped to get some mileage out
of it. Maybe Harvey Gold was part of that? He and
the governor could have worked it out together.
Gold was very close to him. It just could be they were
planning behind his back, planning to take over and
take advantage.

When it came to politics, paranoia was a good
thing, a very good thing to have.

The buzz of the intercom cut his thoughts
abruptly.

"Yes?"

"Sheriff Winn on three."

"Thank you. What's happening, Roger?"

"First gunfight. Up behind Woodbourne Flats."

"Shit. How bad?"

"One man hit in the leg before it was stopped.
Both sides claim the other fired first. I had a feeling
this sorta thing was inevitable."

"Did you call Bill Douglas?"

"Not yet. Thought I'd tell you first. You wanna
call or should I?"

"You call. He'll only want to know the details.
Where are they?"

"The wounded man's up at Harris Hospital
emergency room. I got his partner and the other guy
here. There are a couple of news hounds outside my

door already, and I think there's a television remote pulling up as I speak."

"Hold them off. I'll call Congemi and we'll be right over," Dickson said.

"Right."

After he hung up, he sat back and tried to sort out his options. Images of cheering crowds continually interrupted his thoughts. It was tantalizing. Instinctively, he sensed that this situation could go either way. It had the potential of destroying him as well as launching him faster into a waiting political future. It would do no good to think about it. He realized that immediately. Like a man on a tightrope, he'd only grow nervous realizing the possibilities. The best thing to do was move forward, determined and never, never look down.

He stood up so quickly he surprised himself. Then he laughed at the burlesque picture he presented.

Thank goodness I'm alone whenever I'm like this, he thought, otherwise, no one would invest a moment in my future.

He hurried on to make a deal with destiny, confident he could do well in this negotiation. After all, no one else involved with this situation in the county was as well equipped to benefit from it than he was.

❦

Willie Brand stood on the end of the small hill and looked down at the forensic team that had rushed to the site. Everyone seemed oblivious to the nasty turn in the weather. A light, cold rain had replaced the flurries.

He turned when he heard the sheriff's four by four bouncing over the ruts. Winn's deputy drove it as far in as he could, and the sheriff got out. The sports vehicle's door sounded like a gunshot when he slammed it behind him. Below the hill, the BCI forensic men looked up and then back at Garth Allan's body sprawled naked on the ground. From this angle, every time the forensic men moved to the right or left, Willie could see Allan's eyes, wide open, frozen in a death stare at the sky. Half of the top of his head was blown away.

"Why can't people kill people in nice weather?" Winn quipped. He whipped a cigar out of his top pocket and began to peal away the cellophane.

"Lieutenant Brokofski's on it," Willie said. "Bruce called him as soon as the call came into my office. "I told him to call you immediately."

"Sorry it took me so long to get here. I was dealing with that situation in Woodbourne Flats. You hear about it?"

Willie shook his head and Winn described the gunfight.

"It's all going to shit," Willie said.

"That's why I told Dickson. I haven't told him about this yet. He was wrapped in reporters so I left the office and got your patrolman's call. Fill me in."

"Those two over there," Willie said, nodding toward two men in hunting outfits speaking to a BCI detective, "found him. This is private property, posted, but they didn't pay attention or notice the signs," he added with anger. He looked like he wanted to arrest them for it.

"I don't think Allan's in a position to lodge a complaint, do you, Willie? Besides, it probably would have been hours and hours, if not a whole other day before we found him out here if they hadn't," Winn suggested.

Willie grunted.

"I guess this shoots to hell the expert's theories," Winn continued.

Willie turned slowly, his eyebrows hoisted.

"How so?"

"Well, Garth Allan's hunting on his own land, daylight . . . what's the violation?"

Willie gazed back at the corpse being examined.

"No license," he muttered.

"How's that?"

"Never bothered to get himself a hunting license. You don't own the wildlife, even if it wanders onto your property. There's still laws and regulations about it."

"No license? Shit." Winn shook his head, his eyes widening. You think that guy's right, then?"

Off in the distance, they could hear a siren. Both men turned.

"That'll be Buzzy bringing Garth' wife home."

"Maybe she'll know something. Maybe he went out hunting with someone," Winn said nodding at the body below them.

"No," Willie said. "She was already asked. He went out alone."

The sheriff nodded, impressed.

"Shit's going to hit the fan around here now. Big time," he muttered.

"It already has."

The two law enforcement officers were silent as one of the forensic men came walking up the hill toward them.

"Considering the temperature, I'd say less than six hours ago," he remarked.

"Did you find the bullet?" the sheriff asked.

"Yes sir. Just dug it out. It was a nine millimeter."

"Pistol?"

"Looks that way, Sheriff. A change in the M.O."

"What'dya know? Anything else?"

"We isolated some footprints in the muddy areas and already determined they're not Allan's. We'll have the size and maybe the boot style. Lieutenant Brokofski tracked them back," he added nodding toward the state police detective returning to the scene of the murder.

"Anything?" Winn called to him.

"He started near the house," he said approaching. "Looks to me like he was waiting for him to emerge, expecting him."

"That's interesting too."

"Yes sir, it is," Lieutenant Brokofski said. "We might conclude now that he's choosing his targets carefully. Willie tell you the victim had no hunting license."

The sheriff nodded, took his hat off and ran his fingers through his thinning hair.

"Not the first time Garth's done that," Willie said. "And I'm sorry to say, he's not the only one around here."

"Whoever the killer is, he's got a way of knowing who violates the hunting laws," Lieutenant Brokofski said.

"That narrows it some," Winn said. "I guess that expert guesser or whatever he is has something. The killer would have to have some in with law enforcement."

Willie grunted.

The rain grew harder and colder. He pulled up his jacket collar.

"If there's ever a right sort of day for death like this, it's today," Winn said.

Nine

AARON PULLED INTO THE JOE CREEK DINER parking lot. It was located off a major highway, but far enough out of the way so that it only serviced travelers and hunters. They could see the red hats and jackets through the diner windows. Unshaven men seated in the booths peered out at them. For a moment it looked as though they were all of one face.

The snow here at a higher elevation had changed to a fine, powdery crystals and the grey overcast lightened toward the horizon. On the wet, silky highway behind them, cars rode by, their drivers impervious to the precipitation. The tires spun in a continuous wet kiss. When Diana opened the door and stepped out, the combination of breeze and droplets put a soft spray over her face.

"Warming up," Aaron said coming around the car. "Probably turn into rain and melt the little snow that's fallen."

They hurried into the diner, laughing at their eagerness to get out of the weather. Everyone turned to look at them as they unbuttoned their coats and searched for an empty booth. A short, dark-haired waitress to their left smiled and beckoned.

"Hi Toby," Aaron said directing Diana toward the empty seats.

"How's Walker?" she said immediately. He saw she waited for a real answer.

"Same as always."

"Too bad," she said smirking. He smiled at Diana and reached for the menus.

"What's the special?"

"Bean soup, creamed turkey."

"Sounds good. How about it?" he asked. Diana studied the menu.

"Just a turkey burger, I think. Well done. And coffee, please."

He looked about for familiar faces and found none nearby. When he turned back, she had a small notebook out on the table and was scribbling rapidly. He smiled and sat back.

"You don't mind, do you?" she said without looking up. "I don't want to forget some things, and first impressions are always valuable."

"Why should I mind? That's your job."

She gazed around.

"Do you know anyone?"

"Nope. These are mostly outsiders, up for the hunting season. You can see why the local economy benefits."

She nodded and continued to gaze around. He smiled to himself at the way her soft eyes narrowed with her thoughts.

"Tell me," she said after a few moments. "Do you think it's possible that he's in here?"

"He?"

"The mad killer of hunters. I mean, maybe he's one of them. It's logical that would be, don't you think?" she added quickly.

"Oh, that because hunters are killers again," he said nodding, a slight smile on his face.

"Exactly."

"I really don't think it's that easy to make the transition from animals to people," he said.

"Why not?"

"It's different when you kill your own kind. Most animals don't unless it's over territoriality."

"I realize that, but don't you get to a point when killing comes easier . . . sorta something you get use to? The first deer and the twentieth are not the same, are they?"

"It's still a deer and not a man. Look, I told you

before—men are by nature hunters, predators, but that doesn't mean they're cold-blooded killers. I find a distinction between hunting and murdering."

"I'm giving you that," she said, encouraged by his response, "but I still think it would be easier for someone who has hunted all his life to kill a man, than for someone who hasn't hunted at all? Do you really think I'm totally wrong about that?"

"Yes," he said quickly. Then he paused. "Well, yes and no."

She stared at him, waiting for an explanation. He looked around to be sure that no one was eavesdropping on their conversation.

"Hunters are accustomed to weapons. It's easier for someone who has had experience using a gun to use it in a murder. That's all I would give you. Most murderers are not hunters first. You can do a minimum of research and learn that most murders are murders of passion, done in a moment of anger. Even premeditated ones are motivated by the simplest of things like greed, jealousy, that sort of stuff."

"How do you know all this?"

"I read some mystery novels," he confessed with a smile. "I'm not all metal and muscle."

"I see. Okay, that all makes sense, but . . ."

"And another thing," he said, leaning forward and lowering his voice as if he was embarrassed by the discussion, "they're by nature two different things entirely. Hunting in the pure sense is a life process. It's actually a means of coexistence with nature. If it's done intelligently, it can help nature."

"Cull out the herds so they don't starve. I heard your brother," She said. "I know, I know." she said with a note of skepticism.

"Well, it's true." His face blanched a little as he stressed the words. "I know these groups of bleeding hearts, like Friends of Animals or something, ridicule it, but it's true. Civilization has disrupted the balances that once existed in nature. I think nature's fighting for its very survival, especially with all this land and home development that doesn't take the natural balance of things into consideration."

"People who murder sometimes think they're doing it for their survival," she pointed out. "Don't they?"

"Murder's still different."

"I'm not convinced. How else is it different?" she pursued.

He thought a moment.

"Murder is a form of communication."

"A what?" She started to smile.

"Communication."

He sat back as the waitress placed his bowl of soup before him and Diana's turkey burger and coffee in front of her. As soon as she left, he leaned forward.

"Murderers are trying to say something to society and to their victims. It's an unreasonable form of communication, but a form nevertheless."

She stared at him a moment, studying his eyes.

"You know," she said, "sometimes I get the feeling you're toying with me."

"Not at all. I really believe that. All of it." She bit into her burger.

"Okay. So what's our maniac killer trying to say?"

"I don't know. The most obvious thing is he's against hunting, I suppose."

"Maybe he's just a serial killer who just came into the area," she offered.

"Maybe."

"You don't believe that?"

"I really get the feeling that he's someone local. He seems to know the area. It's just a feeling so don't quote me in any article," he added quickly and went to his soup. They ate quietly for a while. Occasionally, she scribbled another note in her pad.

"Do you think these guys would mind if I snapped a few pictures before we left?"

He shrugged.

"Of course, I'll ask them first."

"Do that." He leaned toward her to whisper. "Only, if the killer's sitting in here, he might get nervous. You could be risking your life," he teased.

"Very funny," she said but then gazed around

again and wondered if what he said couldn't be so.

When she looked back, she caught him staring at her. He looked down quickly.

"Maybe you're right. I think I'll err on the side of caution and wait for pictures until tomorrow."

"Wise decision," he said. They ate quietly for a few moments and then he sat back.

"Before we left the house, my mother asked me to ask you to dinner. I told her you probably would be working on your article, but . . ."

"No," she said. "I'd love to come to dinner at your house. Like I told you, your mother's a gold mine for a feature writer."

He nodded. He wished she had come up with another reason first, but he didn't mind being second fiddle to his mother. She seemed to read his mind.

"Of course, I want to see you."

"Oh?"

"Check out that masculine image again in a different setting, maybe."

He had to look down, even though he smiled.

"Afterward . . . I mean, after dinner, if you'd like . . . we could take a ride up to the Neversink Dam. The view of the sky and the countryside is beautiful this time of year, especially if it clears up. It's no big deal but it's something to see and I just thought . . ."

"That sounds terrific," she said. "If you think it's safe," she added, reminding him of what they had just experienced.

"It'll be safe," he assured her, "but if you think you'll be too nervous."

"No, it's all right. I was probably just spooked back there. I'm sure it was nothing. Right? Right?" she asked again when he didn't respond.

"Sure."

"You don't believe that," she challenged. "You and your instinct."

He shrugged.

Before either of them could say anything else, however, they both turned to watch two state police cars come into the parking lot and from the way the officers were walking toward the diner, Aaron knew they weren't stopping just to have some lunch.

"Uh oh," he muttered and she turned to them quickly.

"If we could just have everyone's attention for a moment," one of the state policemen said. All talking stopped in the diner. The countermen stopped clanking dishes and silverware and waited. Aaron turned around.

"We're making a check of weapons, hunting pistols in particular. And we want to see your licenses. Please remain in the diner until we have spoken to all of you. Thank you," he said.

As soon as he and his partner approached the first booth, the talking resumed, but at a much louder and noisier level.

"Is this routine?" Diana asked.

"Hell no."

"Then maybe the killer really is in here," she said, looking back at the men at the counter. Did anyone seem more nervous? "What do you think?"

He just shook his head and wore an expression of deep thought. Diana looked back at the rest of the diner again and watched the state police going from table to table. They stopped at one and asked the hunter to show them his pistol. After they looked it over, they handed it back to him.

"This might be something more," she said. She opened her pocketbook and took out some change.

"What are you doing?"

"I'll be right back," she said. "I want to call the news desk."

"Always the reporter."

"Of course," she said, getting up.

He watched her go to the phone booth.

His attention was broken when the state policemen arrived at his table.

"Are you carrying any weapons here or in your car?"

"No. Where did the new one happen?" he asked quickly. They both looked at him for a moment.

"Just checking hunting weapons," the one on the left said. Aaron smiled and nodded. After they left, Diana came back to the table. She saw that they had already covered their booth.

"Did they say anything about it?"

"Closed-mouthed. What did you find out?"

"News desk doesn't have anything yet on any new killing but there was some sort of shooting incident in Woodbourne. Spooked hunters shot at each other."

"I thought that might happen," he said, "but this looks like something else."

"What? It's another killing, isn't it?"

"I really think you oughta stay out of the woods tomorrow, Diana."

"Are you kidding? This thing's grown so big my feature's gonna win the Pulitzer."

"If you live to write it."

"He hasn't shot a woman yet."

"That we know of and really, Diana, I don't think he's going to care if it's a woman or a man he shoots."

"Doe permit," she muttered.

"What?"

"This is the season when female deer are permitted to be shot, right? "Maybe he thinks of us as doe," she mused.

He lost his smile. She didn't seem to notice. She

was too involved in her own thoughts now. "Diana, this is way past being amusing or an interesting game or . . ."

"I think I'd better get back to the bureau office and start my piece," she said, not listening.

He waved toward Toby and indicated the check.

"Come on," she said. "Don't look so worried. I'll let you pay the bill."

He shook his head, but he didn't have good feelings. There was static everywhere.

Something even more terrible was yet to happen. He was sure of it.

Steve Dickson and his three assistants sat silently waiting for the phone to ring. Fifteen minutes earlier, he had put his call in to Harvey Gold. They had been successful in keeping the news of the latest killing out of the media for the time being, but Steve knew the delay wouldn't last much longer. The pressure was on; a major decision had to be made. For the first time since this thing started, Dickson felt a sense of impending personal disaster. Perhaps he shouldn't have been so out front on this after all. Pessimism worked its way out of the darkness of his mind. It was raging free and clear and it would have its say. He was about to be blown right off the map.

This killer continue to kill again so quickly. There wasn't even time to come up for air.

The buzzer sounded. He didn't say a word. He simply lifted the receiver.

"Mr. Gold on three, sir."

"Okay. Hello."

"Steve, I got this much," Gold said without pause for a greeting. "He'll give you an hour then he's taking the initiative."

"An hour?"

"You know hunters are a strong voting group. We're talking about conservatives, members of the NRA, lobbyists against strict gun control, the whole gambit. They have to feel protected."

"What would he do if he was in my shoes?"

"A moratorium on hunting in your county until you guys get it safe again."

"But that puts all the pressure on us. On me," he added.

"You've got one out, as I see it," Gold said in a hoarse whisper.

"What's that?"

"Get Bill Douglas to ask for it."

"I suggested that to him already. He didn't buy it."

"Suggest it again. If he does it, then the resort industry will direct its frustration against him and not you. In the end it's always the guy up front who gets hurt."

"Isn't the governor worried about that?"

"Are you kidding? Big Daddy had to take action because you guys are all incapable. Believe me. He's going to state it right. They're drawing up the language now and there's nobody in his inner circle worried about your ass. There are a number of people out there just waiting to jump out and say, "See, we told you he was too young and too inexperienced."

Steve couldn't contain his moan.

"You've got an hour. Be a politician and work Douglas into it. Let me know how you make out."

"Yeah. Thanks," he said and hung up. His assistants waited. "We've got to get Bill Douglas to declare a moratorium on hunting in this county."

"Fat chance," Tom Congemi said. Steve's political advisors, Ken McKinny and Jeff Kaplan, grunted.

"Maybe we can overwhelm him into it. Let's get over to his office."

"You're dead if Bob Foss is there," McKinny said. "The hotel, restaurant and motel people's strings are attached directly to his mouth."

"Maybe he's not there," Dickson said, but when they got to Douglas's office, Bob Foss was already seated on the small couch to the left of the desk. They both looked as though they knew exactly what was coming.

"I'll lay it right out for you quickly," Steve said

going right to the seat in front of the desk. His assistants stood back, looking as glum and as serious as possible. They served as a chorus. "They have been three occasions already where men have fired on one another out of fear they were being attacked by the killer. Two men were wounded. Fortunately, no one yet has been killed that way. An hour ago, we received word from Centerville. There's been another murder."

"Another murder! Why the fuck didn't you call me right away?" Douglas demanded.

"I've been working to keep it out of the press as long as possible. Words leaked already. It's a matter of minutes before it hits the air waves. I've refused a number of interviews."

"Big deal, so have I. What do I have to do, hang out in your fucking office to find out what's happening?"

"I came over here personally, for Christ sakes," Steve whined. "Give me credit for that, at least."

"You didn't do it to pass the time of day. What do you want from us?" Bob Foss said. His mouth went up in the corner and his left eye narrowed.

"Spill it out," Douglas told him.

"You as county leader," he said, ignoring the publicity man, "ought to take the initiative and call a halt to hunting in the county."

To Dickson's surprise, Foss didn't explode. He looked thoughtful for a moment.

"Did you get any decent leads out of this last killing?" he asked.

"We've got a little from forensics . . . foot size, boot style . . ."

"That's it?"

"One other thing. He's changed his weapon. He killed this man with a pistol, a nine millimeter. No rifle first this time. It was all done close, a real confrontation."

"A pistol?"

The two politicians looked at each other.

"More sophisticated than just a wild lunatic in the woods," Steve suggested. "The killer lay in waiting for this specific victim. That's what they're telling me now."

"Great. What's your criminal psychologist got to say about it?"

"I'm meeting with him after this and the law enforcement team will be there."

Everyone was silent a moment. Then Foss sat forward.

"Do you realize if we halt hunting and you never catch this guy, we'd damage the economy of this area for years to come?"

"He's right," Douglas said. "People might get it in their heads that skiers are in danger next and then what?"

"That's stupid. We've got to end hunting and give

us the time to investigate without the threat of death," Steve said.

"What would you investigate?" Douglas said. "So far you have nothing very concrete to work with except a possible shoe size and some abracadabra from a profiler."

"Your only hope," Foss said, "is the maniac making an error and he'll only do that if he goes back into the woods. You end hunting and he'll disappear in the woodwork. Then what?"

"But we're letting men risk their lives just so we can get a lead," Steve protested.

"Some of our local people plan all year for this event," Douglas said. "And I don't mean just hunters. I'm talking about all the retailers who benefit." He spoke softly, almost as if he were thinking aloud.

Rationalization, like the common cold, suddenly became infectious.

"You'd be surprised at how many people need the meat," Foss said.

"People are going to go out anyway. We don't have the manpower to enforce such a ban," Douglas added. "Even with the added conservation officers."

Steve felt the hot potato being passed around the room.

"None of that justifies such a risk of human life," he insisted.

"Is that your public recommendation?" Foss said. Dickson stared at him.

"Sure."

"Then go on the air and call for it yourself and we'll support you."

"That's bullshit," Steve said, his face reddening.

"I'm sorry, Steve," Douglas said. "But the mayor of New York doesn't tell his citizens to keep off the streets when citizens are mugged. He tells his police force to get on the ball and work harder."

"Work harder, Steve," Foss said with a small smile.

"When this is over," Steve said standing up and glaring at Foss, "someone's gonna look stupid. And I'm telling you now. It's not going to be me."

He turned and marched out of the office, his assistants following in dead silence.

❧

Just before Aaron pulled Diana's car to a stop in front of the shop, they heard the news bulletin come over the radio.

"*The governor has called for a moratorium on hunting in the woods of Sullivan County. He announced his decision in Albany only moments ago.*"

The governor then spoke.

"*I have been in touch with the Department of*

Conservation. Additional wardens are being sent into Sullivan county to help patrol the moratorium. The failure of local and state authorities to make any significant advancements in the investigation of what is being popularly termed the Maniac Hunter Murders requires us to take this action. Of course, if the situation should improve, or a significant arrest made, we would consider ending the moratorium."

Reporters' voices were heard shouting in the background. One got his attention.

"Governor, what if this maniac goes into another upstate area and kills hunters?"

"We'll face that situation if and when it occurs. I don't want to get into too many questions at this time. We're just beginning to formulate policies and actions and it is important for communications between my office and the local law enforcement offices to solidify."

"Do you think the local authorities have botched this up?" a reporter asked, but the governor didn't respond.

The announcer came on.

"District attorney Steve Dickson couldn't be reached for comment. However, Bill Douglas, chairman of the county board of supervisors, said the moratorium was regrettable. He said the economy of the area has suffered enough with the decline of the resort industry and this situation does not help it. However, he offered to do anything he could to cooper-

ate with the governor. Repeating once again—a moratorium on hunting has been declared in Sullivan County. All of this has resulted from reports of a fourth slaying in the woods. WSUL has also learned that a number of gun fights erupted yesterday and early today between hunters and groups of hunters that thought they were under an attack by the killer.

"*Reports from Los Angeles . . .*"

Aaron shut the radio off and sat back.

"So much for all that business in the diner," Diana said.

"This pistol thing bugged me from the start," Aaron thought aloud. "It's got to mean something."

"What?"

"I don't know. Pistols are used after a firing squad shoots the victim. Someone puts a bullet in his head. That's what he has been doing."

"Oh, how gross." She grimaced and then moaned. "It's so scary. Maybe this is too much for me to stomach," she admitted.

"You oughta be grateful to the governor. He might have saved your life."

"I still have to do some sort of story," Diana said.

"We'll give you plenty of information about the art and business of hunting. I'll pick you up at six," he said as they drove up to the shop. "I'll feel safer about you're not driving alone tonight."

"Okay. No false bravery on my part."

"Well, there's a confession," he said. "Hey, come on, cheer up. You're still in the middle of a big story."

"I know," she said, smiling again. Her expression changed when she saw the look that was now on his face. "What is it, Aaron?"

"My mother's on the porch. She must have been waiting for us in the front window. Something's up."

He got out of the car and Diana quickly followed.

"I just heard about the new killing," she said when he and Diana stepped up to the porch. "It was Garth Allan."

"Garth Allan?" Aaron shook his head. "Jesus."

"Another local man," Marilyn told Diana.

"Oh."

"That's not the worst of it for us," Marilyn added.

"What do you mean, Ma?"

"He went out," Marilyn Kuhn said.

"Went where?"

"Who went?" Diana asked.

"Walker. He went out for the doe. About an hour ago. I couldn't stop him. It was before the news came on about the moratorium. He said he was tired of just hanging around."

"That idiot."

"Do you have any idea where he might have gone?" Diana asked.

"He promised he'd try to find someone to go along with him. That was as much of a compromise as I could get," Marilyn said.

Aaron turned around and started away.

"You're not going to go look for him," Marilyn Kuhn said, more hysteria in her voice than command. "I don't need two of you out there with all this going on."

"She's right, Aaron."

"I should have never gone for those doe permits. Let him talk me into it. Damn."

"You didn't know what was going to happen at the time," Diana said.

"My father never hunted doe, no matter what was permitted," he said, but it was more like a voiced thought than a statement in response. He snapped out of his reverie quickly. "Go on back inside Ma. It's cold and nasty."

"Promise me you won't go looking for him, Aaron. Promise," she pleaded.

"I'm not going anywhere. Go inside before you get sick."

She hesitated a moment and then went in.

"I'm sorry your mother's so upset. I guess I shouldn't come tonight."

"No. It'll be better if she works on the dinner. Keep her from worrying so much."

"Well, call me as soon as Walker returns, will you.

I'll be at the local, Sullivan County news office until
five and then at the motel."

"Right."

"Thanks for showing me around," she said stepping closer and touching his arm. He looked at her
for a moment, and for a moment, he forgot about
Walker. "I'm looking forward to going up to the
dam too," she said, brought her lips close to his ear,
and added, "to continue what was so unnecessarily
interrupted."

She kissed him, but it was far from a goodbye
kiss. It was slow and soft and revved up his memories of what they had started in the woods to the
extent that his body warmed all over.

"See you later," she said softly holding his hand
until she had to let go. Then she turned and walked
back to her car.

He stood there, watching her. She waved after she
got in and then she backed out and drove off.

Before he turned to go into the house, Dr. Fern
turned into the garage.

"You did a great job on the car, Aaron," he said
getting out.

"Thanks. How you do?"

"Didn't see anything. Not even a rabbit. Then
when we got out of the woods and heard the news, I
was glad. Got my bill?"

"Just inside," Aaron said and the doctor followed

him into the garage. He was tall, lean man with a dark complexion. He looked younger than his fifty-eight years.

Aaron handed him the bill and he dipped into his pocket to pay it in cash.

"Any leads yet?" he asked as Aaron took the money.

"I haven't heard anything."

"Where's Walker?" he asked.

"He went out before the moratorium was declared."

"Going for doe?"

"Yeah," Aaron replied not showing his disapproval.

"I'm sure they'll flush him out quickly. Although," the doctor said with a twinkle in his eyes, "you guys probably know places no one else knows."

"Not really," Aaron said.

"Where do you think he went?"

"Probably west of the Dennison's Ford," Aaron said.

The doctor stared at him a moment and then smiled.

"Yeah, I thought of that area, but chose somewhere else. Oh well, it's too late now, I suppose."

Aaron nodded and the doctor went out. When Aaron emerged, he saw him drive off, only not toward his office and home. Despite what he had told Diana about the nature of a real hunter, all that business about being outdoors, using your instincts, culling out the herds, etc., there was something incongruous about the town doctor being a hunter, even though he had grown up in the area and had hunted with his own father.

It was just another one of those inexplicable things bothering him these few days.

He gazed up at the sky. The clouds looked bruised, angry. Walker should be home soon.

He hoped.

Ten

"I CAN'T JUST HANG AROUND HERE LIKE THIS," Aaron said after another hour had passed and Walker had still not returned. He had gone upstairs, taken a hot shower, shaved and dressed in nicer clothing, anticipating Diana's return and a good dinner. When he came down, he was both surprised and annoyed that his brother was still not back.

Despite her stoic expression, his mother did not hide her anxiety. He could see it in the way she held her shoulders up, tightening her neck, moving her hands sharply, almost angrily, and occasionally releasing a sigh as if she was releasing hot air.

His mother turned from the sink counter and looked at him, her eyes narrowing.

"What good would it do for you to go treapsin' through the woods? In a few more hours, it'll be dark and he'll hafta come out anyway," she said. It wasn't hard to see that was her prayer.

"Maybe he never went out. We could be worrying over nothing, Ma. He's like that sometimes—blowing off about doing something and then ending up at one of his hangouts or riding around with one of his idiot buddies."

She thought he might be right. He saw it gave her a sense of relief.

"How would we know for sure?"

"I'll go down to Sam's and see if he was there. Maybe somebody knows something."

She gave him those scrutinizing eyes.

"Aaron Kuhn . . ."

"I'm not going into the woods," he emphasized. "It won't hurt to see what's what. He could be sitting around jawin' off with busybodies."

"Okay," she relented. "Oh," she said as he turned to go down the hallway. "I almost forgot. Mrs. Fern called while you were upstairs sprucing yourself up for dinner."

"Mrs. Fern? What did she want?"

"She wanted to know if you had seen her husband?"

"Seen him? Sure. He came to pay for the car. He said he was going home."

"Did he?"

"I don't know. He didn't head that way, but I thought he would be there soon."

"Well, she sound the way she usually does. Her voice shaking. She probably was hitting the bottle and doesn't even know he's home."

"Yeah, maybe," he said and shrugged. "I'm sure it's probably something stupid like that. I'll call her back later," he said and left.

There was quite a crowd at Sam's Luncheonette. All the locals who had heard the news about the moratorium gathered here to discuss it. The four small booths were filled, as well as the three tables. All the counter stools were taken. Sam and his wife, Gladys, were scurrying about like workers in a fast food restaurant. They had no one to wait on tables during the fall and winter months, so consequently, they both doubled as counter workers and short order cooks as well as serve the customers at the booths and tables.

Aaron was greeted by the warm, moist air and the loud chatter as he opened the door and entered. Some faces turned his way and there were a few waves and hellos. He searched the crowd quickly, hoping to see Walker seated amongst the men, but he wasn't there. Sam's wife smiled at him as she broiled hamburgers.

"You're a lucky son of a bitch," Murray Burns said. He was seated at the corner of the counter, his large, soft rear end and heavy legs practically swallowing up the small cushioned stool. There were some grunts of agreement. "Gettin' yours before this trouble started."

"You couldn't get one if they extended the season two months," one of the men at a nearby table said. There was some laughter.

"He who hesitates is lost," Aaron said smiling. He walked over to the counter.

"Buy ya a coffee," Burns offered.

"Naw. I'm looking for Walker."

"Walker? He was here some time ago."

"Was he?"

"Lookin' for someone to go huntin' doe with him. I woulda gone, but I had been out all day. To tell ya the truth," Burns said whispering, "I'd be damn happy to just get my buck and run, much less get a buck and go back for a doe."

"Anybody go with him?"

"I don't know. Hey Sam. Sam!"

"Hold your bippy," Sam screamed back at him. "No one else will."

It brought more laughter.

"Another hamburger?" Gladys asked. She wore a smile of incredulity.

"No. Aaron's lookin' for Walker. Anybody seen Walker Kuhn since he was in here?"

"Saw him drive outta town," a voice called. Aaron looked at Eddie Morris.

"Which way?"

"Toward Greenfield Park."

"Anybody go with him?"

"Nobody in his car when I saw him."

"He still out there?" Burns asked.

"I don't know. Maybe," Aaron said. Everybody nearby grew silent.

"To tell you the truth," Burns said, "I didn't think he was really going to go after he couldn't find anyone to go with him. I asked him where you were and he said somethin' about chasing some broad all over."

"He's always been a stubborn bastard," Aaron said.

Just at that moment the place grew quiet as Gary Lester entered. He stood at the doorway, contemplating the group as if he was trying to decide if anyone would take him seriously. For the hunters there was great expectation in those moment of silence. Then someone shouted from the back.

"IF IT AIN'T SMOKEY THE BEAR."

Great laughter followed. Gary smirked and shook his head.

"Smartass," he shouted back. Then he lifted his hand up in stop traffic fashion. It immediately grew silent again. Gladys and Sam froze in position behind the counter. This time when Gary glared at the group he seemed to swell in his uniform.

"I'm just here to be sure everyone understands

the meaning of this moratorium. Let there be no doubt about it," he continued with a firm, strong voice. "This situation is out of control. Forget about the deer."

"That go for family-owned land as well?" someone asked.

"It does if you think about Garth Allen," Gary said. There was a heavier silence. "You might own the land, but you don't own the wildlife."

"How long's this gonna last?"

"Nobody can say," Gary said. "Now does anyone know of anybody still in the forest?"

"Yeah," Burns said. He pointed to Aaron. "His brother might be."

"That true, Aaron?"

"I don't know for sure. Been trying to find out. He told my mother he was going in after a doe."

"What do you mean, you don't know for sure?" Gary asked, as if Aaron was deliberately being vague.

"He came here looking for a partner, but from what I can gather, no one joined him. Eddie Morris said he saw him drive toward Greenfield Park though."

"You call home?"

"Just came from there."

Gary looked at his watch and then at Aaron.

"Well," he said, "I'll go up to Greenfield Park and look around. See if I can find his car."

"I'll go with you," Aaron said.

"We don't want to encourage any civilians from going into the woods until this is over," Gary retorted.

"Aaron Kuhn ain't no civilian," someone shouted. There was a chorus of "Yeas."

"He knows more about these woods than you do, Gary, and it's his brother we're worryin' about here," Eddie Morris point out sharply.

"Why wouldn't you want him along?" someone shouted.

Gary looked at Aaron.

"All right," he said. "Let's move. You gotta go home for anything?"

"No," Aaron said thinking about the promise he had made to his mother. "I got a pair of boots in the car trunk. That's all I need."

"Good," Gary Lester said.

Not more than a moment after they left and the door closed, the place came back to life. It was as though the world had been momentarily put in freeze frame and then released to play out its remaining scenes.

❧

"Afternoon, Denise," Brian Donald said when Denise Lester opened the front door. Her eyes were wide and glassy, almost the eyes of a doe.

"Mr. Donald!" she exclaimed and brought her hands to the base of her throat as a terrible thought snapped like lightning through her brain.

"This is Lieutenant Brokofski of the BCI, Denise," Brian Donald continued, holding his smile. "He's down here as part of our countywide investigation of these terrible hunting incidents," he added.

She looked from him to Brokofski and then back to him, shaking her head as if to throw off the thoughts.

"Somethin's happened to Gary, hasn't it? That's why he hasn't called me," she said quickly. Her hand flew up to her mouth like a small bird, to perch on her stick thin lips.

"No, no," Brian Donald said. "It's nothing like that."

"Then why are you here?"

Although Brian Donald was Gary's immediate supervisor, he had never set foot in their home and they had never set foot in his. Except for an annual picnic the department had, in fact, she never saw Brian Donald.

"The investigators are doing a routine check of the private weapons owned by all state employees," Brian Donald said in as matter-of-fact a voice as he could muster.

"Weapons?"

There was a loud crash behind her.

She turned and screamed.

"I TOLD YOU NOT TO PLAY WITH THOSE CANS IN THE HOUSE!" She looked out at Brian Donald and Lieutenant Brokofski. "The boys," she explained as if identifying their gender was explanation enough.

Brian nodded, smiling.

"When they get home from school, they're like released prisoners. They go wild."

"Know what you mean," Lieutenant Brokofski said smiling, too. His handsome face and soft blue eyes relaxed her shoulders. "Got three like that at home myself and my wife's climbing the walls these days, too."

She nodded and then blinked her eyes as Brian Donald's words echoed in her mind.

"You said weapons?" she asked.

"Firearms," Brian Donald said. "I believe Gary owns a 308. I know he has a nine-millimeter pistol, right?"

She shook her head.

"I don't know very much about the guns. I hate the sight of them, in fact. He keeps them all locked in the spare bedroom upstairs. The room's a mess," she added as if they were already in it.

"Uh huh. Do you know if he took any of the rifle, or the pistol with him to work?" Lieutenant Brokofski asked.

"No, I don't know, she replied. She studied their faces a little closer. "Has Gary done something wrong?"

"No, no," Brian Donald said quickly.

"I don't understand all this. Then why are you here?"

"I told you, Denise. This is just routine," Brian Donald said. "I've got to visit the homes of five of my other officers today, in fact."

"Oh."

"Red tape, you know," he said and closed his eyes gently.

Even though she didn't know, she nodded and relaxed.

"So, do you think we could have a look at that spare bedroom?" Brian asked, his smile returning.

"I suppose so," she said. She started to turn to make room for them to enter and stopped. "I shouldn't without him here. Gary isn't goin' to like this."

"Don't you trouble your little head about it, Denise. I'll explain it to him. He'll understand. I'd tell him about it now, only he's out in the field," Brian Donald assured her.

She thought a moment.

"Can't you raise him on the radio?"

"Oh, we can, but I'm not bothering an officer in the field with all that's going on unless it's important and as I said, this is just a routine thing."

She hesitated and then nodded.

"I gotta dig up the key to the gun cabinet. He hides it somewhere in our bedroom. Come on in and have a seat in the living room," she said, "only please excuse the mess the boys made."

They entered the house and immediately, the two Lester boys came out and stared at them. The older of the two was lean and muscular. The younger looked like a miniature version of Gary.

"Hi boys, Brian said. "Raisin' a little hell for your mother again?" Both of them shook their heads quickly. "Well you'd better behave. This here's a man from the Bureau of Criminal Investigation."

"He is?" the older one said. They had no idea what it meant, but their faces reflected that it sounded very serious to them and very important. They looked at Brokofski with almost as much fear in their eyes as they had when their father went into a rage over something they had done.

"So let's behave and listen to whatever your mother tells you, understand?" Brian asked them.

They both nodded dumbly. Denise laughed nervously.

"Right through here, she said and led them into the livingroom. The boys stayed behind, but watched through the doorway.

"As I said, please excuse the mess. I haven't gotten to this room yet."

The toys were scattered about. The two men took note of the disarray. It looked as though the room had gotten so far ahead of her it didn't matter when she had time for it. There were toys everywhere—on chairs, the couch, under the small table. The boys' coats and hats had been thrown over the easy chair, and papers were scattered over the floor.

"I don't even try to straighten up until they go to sleep, " Denise said. "I'll see if I can find the key," she said.

"Thanks, Denise, " Brian said. "Oh." He looked up at the buck's head mounted on the right wall. "Was this one of Gary's trophies?"

"No. It was his father's."

"It's a beaut. Now that I think about it," he said glancing at Brokofski and then back to her, "I don't think I remember Gary talking much about his own hunting."

"He never did," she said. "He hasn't hunted for years and years now," she said. "He hates hunting and what he says it's become," she added and went upstairs.

It was a good ten minutes before she returned.

"Sorry, she said, "but he does a real job on hiding this. He moved it from where he had it before, but I found it."

She held the key up like a prize she had just won.

"He wants to be sure the boys don't get to it."

"Understandable," Brian said. "We just wanna take a quick look, touch all bases."

"What makes such a thing necessary?" she asked, still holding the key close to her. Brian glanced at Brokofski. "Oh, as I said, a routine thing."

"We get orders from the top," Brokofski added. "Sometimes they put us through the wringer. Someone gets an idea and the whole investigative department's gotta jump. And half the time they don't tell us why."

"Just like the department of conservation," Brian said. "No different."

He looked at Denise to see how she accepted their explanations.

It was clear she wasn't satisfied, but she felt uncomfortable interrogating the two officers.

"It's upstairs, first door on the right," she said and walked out.

They followed her up and silently waited as she opened the door. She looked around the room quickly, as they stepped in beside her. All of them looked up at the empty gun rack.

"Was there a rifle in the there, Denise?" Brian Donald asked her.

She nodded.

"Yes, I saw it a few days ago, in fact. Gary lets me dust around the guns."

"Maybe it's in the closet," Brokofski said. He went

to it without waiting for permission, but there were no rifles there.

"Would he keep these guns anywhere else in the house?" Brian asked. Denise shrugged again.

"I can't imagine where else," she said.

The two men looked at each other.

"Think. Do you remember him taking them with him when he left this morning?"

"This morning?" She turned to him. For a moment she looked to be in a total daze. "I don't know. I didn't see."

"What about his pistols?" Lieutenant Brokofski asked her, a little more authoritatively.

"In here," she said opening the cabinet.

The two men moved quickly to examine the contents. Brian Donald shook his head.

"No nine millimeter," he remarked. He turned to Denise. "You don't know what that pistol looks like?"

"I don't know one from the other, sorry."

The two men stared at each other a moment. She picked up the vibrations.

"He's in some sort of trouble, isn't he?" she asked quietly. "This isn't any routine visit. What is it?"

She looked from one to the other, waiting.

"We told you, Denise," Brian Donald began.

"Don't you know where he is? What is it?" she followed, her voice more shrill.

"Take it easy, Denise. I know where he is. I'll be seeing him soon. It's all right. It's routine. Just like we told you," Brian Donald insisted.

She shook her head.

"I want him to call me. As soon as you see him, you tell him to call."

"Absolutely," Brian assured her.

She followed them down the stairs, her arms folded under her small bosom.

"Thank you, Ma'am," Lieutenant Brokofski said tipping his hat.

She watched them go to their car.

"You tell him to call me!" she cried after them, her voice full of desperation.

They left her, fingering the collar of her blouse and staring after them.

❧

Diana had come to the end of her first installment and had just pulled the last page out of the typewriter when Martin Kahn came out of his office. He was a tall, thin, nervous man who had a reputation for tenacity. It was chiefly through his effort and energy that *The Middletown Post* was able to expose the county purchasing scandal five years ago. As a reward, he was pushed up to Sullivan County Bureau Chief. Unlike the other bureau chiefs, he spent a good part of his time outside the office, keeping in contact with sources, finding the story possibilities first hand, and then assigning them.

"Where's Roy?" he shouted to no one in particular. Everyone turned, but only a very young-looking man dressed in a sweater jacket and pants replied.

"Went to the race track."

"Oh yeah," Kahn said. "Okay, Steine, come in here."

The young man knocked some papers off his desk in his enthusiasm. This was Steine's first year in the office and his excitement often attracted laughter and snide remarks from the other bureau employees.

"I got a call from Maggie," Kahn said. He held Steine's arm as though the man would rush off before getting his assignment. "She didn't know much. But something's definitely brewing in Centerville. Check it out, sniff around. Call me the moment you get something."

"Right." He turned quickly.

"Wait a minute, Steine."

The young man turned, his face falling into disappointment. The chief had change mind.

"Who's the chief of police there?"

"Brand. Willie Brand," Steine replied quickly.

Kahn smiled.

"Good boy. Okay . . . remember. As soon as you learn something substantial, call."

Kahn stood there watching as Steine got his coat and rushed out of the building. Then he shook his head and smiled.

"Mr. Kahn?" Diana called.

He turned to her.

"You've got a credible source at the Sullivan County District Attorney's office?"

"Well," he said walking over. "I know this girl who mans the information desk at the county building. It's probably nothing, but ..."

"What?"

"She overheard one of the D.A.'s assistants say he was going out there because there's been another. If another means what I think it means ..."

Diana thought about Walker Kuhn.

"You think it's another killing?"

"What else?" He was about to say something else when the phone rang in his office. She watched him walk off and then she brought her article over to the dispatcher.

"Mark it for the feature editor," she said. "I don't want it mistakenly sent to the Sunday Magazine editor."

"Heard that happened to your last story," the dispatcher said nodding. "These things happen."

"Please, not again to me. I've got enough problems down there," she emphasized.

"Well," Martin Kahn said coming out of his office

quickly, "looks like I didn't take this seriously enough. It's too much for young Steine to handle."

"What do you mean?" Diana asked. Her heart began to beat faster. Kahn went for his coat.

"All the sheriff's units have been directed to Centerville. Somethin's coming together." He started for the door.

"Wait for me," she said. "I want to go with you."

She scooped up the notepad on her desk as she went for her coat. Her own action took her by surprises and for a moment, she hesitated and looked at the pad in her hand.

Newspaper work was surely in my blood, she thought with a vague sense of sadness she couldn't explain.

Eleven

"WELL," Gary Lester said as he slowed down and turned onto the shale layered side road, "looks like they were right." He smiled, but Aaron continued to look ahead.

Walker's car was parked on the side of the road. It was an area for hunting that they had discovered together years ago. He wondered why his brother had been so determined to go hunting now. Whom was he trying to impress? He could only vaguely recall Walker's comments. Diana had taken his full attention, and he couldn't remember the last things he had said to Walker or Walker had said to him. Maybe his brother had indicated then that he was going to hunt doe no matter what. He couldn't be sure, but if he had been paying attention, he might have stopped it before it had started.

"We just lucked out," Aaron finally said. "There were other possible areas for him to go hunting in around here. I wouldn't have put this area at the top of the list."

"I've never been very lucky at finding anyone," Gary Lester replied, steering the conservation department vehicle off the road and pulling up behind Walker's car.

Aaron looked at him. What an odd thing to say, he thought. Gary and he hadn't carried on much conversation on the way up to the woods because he was too deep in thought. For a while he had actually forgotten he was riding with Gary Lester. Now he contemplated him more seriously.

"How often have you gone looking for someone?" he asked.

Lester shrugged.

"Enough," he said.

Aaron had never particularly cared for the man. He was more like someone to tolerate than to like. Sometimes he felt sorry for Gary Lester because of the way the other guys viewed him. It was true that he took himself a lot more seriously than others took him, but maybe . . . maybe that wasn't such a bad thing, Aaron charitably thought. Too few people are serious enough about their work. Other men resented Gary Lester because he was uncompromising.

"He'd charge his own brother with a violation if he had a brother," Ralph Lippen once said. Everyone in the shop agreed and chanted, "Smokey the Bear!"

Just like before at Sam's there was always a lot of laughter when that was said. The man was a law enforcement office, but he achieved little respect. Was he oblivious to the low image he held in the community or did she simply not give a damn? Whatever the answer, it didn't raise any respect in Aaron.

"Let's blast away and see if that, gets him," Gary Lester said and pressed down on the car horn. He did four long blasts and then they waited, staring at the woods.

"He probably went in over there," Aaron said pointing to a separation in the bushes.

"You have hunted here before, huh?"

"Sure. We usually make a full circle, peaking near the old railroad track bed, but like I said, it wouldn't have been my first choice." He looked at his watch. "He should be on his way back. He knows when the sun's going down."

"Think he heard the horn?"

"Maybe. Even though those trees are bare, you'd be surprised at how sound can be sucked up in those woods," Aaron said and then thought, why am I telling him all this? He's been involved with the forest more than I have.

They sat silently a while longer, waiting and then Gary Lester's eyes grew smaller.

"What's that up ahead? Looks like another car just peekin' around the bend, doesn't it?"

Aaron leaned forward.

"Yeah."

"What the hell . . ."

Gary Lester started the engine and edged up the road. He paused when the car came into view.

"Look familiar to you?"

Aaron was speechless for a moment and then nodded.

"It should. I just worked on it."

"Huh?"

"It's Dr. Fern's wife's car."

"Wife? I don't get it."

"Me neither."

"Well, whoever is in there . . . there's not that much daylight left," Gary Lester warned. There was little emotion in his voice. He wasn't thinking about Walker's welfare as much as he was about the hunting law. Aaron smirked.

"Let's back up to where your brother walked in," Gary Lester said. "Maybe he's comin' out already."

"Walker's stubborn and determined. If he hasn't been successful, he'll go the full limit." Aaron said, nodding to himself. "Always been like that. More like my father in that way."

After they parked again, Gary Lester opened his door.

"Well, let's go in a ways, call out and see if we can raise him. He could be stashin' himself somewhere and waitin' for one to trot by."

"Doesn't feel right to me," Aaron said, hesitating after he opened his door and looked about. The forest was too silent. Nothing moved. It was as if it was holding its breath. He found himself doing the same thing.

"You have any other ideas? Like you said, daylight is dwindling."

"All right," Aaron said. He stepped out of the car. Gary got out slowly and then went to the trunk. He opened it and took out a 308.

"What's that for?"

"Just in case," he said. "Being prepared is my middle name. Besides, we might want to let one go to rouse him."

Aaron nodded slowly and looked around. There were no signs of anyone else, yet all the talk, all the excitement and the publicity put something in the air. He could feel it. The world that he had often turned to in order to escape madness had now gone mad itself. Everything looked dangerous. A wide tree could be hiding someone. A branch cracking, leaves crunching, brush moving and touching, all of it could indicate there was someone out there watching them, following them.

He felt a chill and closed his jacket tighter. Gary Lester came up beside him and studied the forest.

"Damned if I'd want to hunt with something like this goin' on," Gary Lester said. "Either takes a lot of self-confidence or just a lot of stupidity."

Aaron didn't reply. He started for the path, thinking suddenly about the promise he had made his mother. He should have called her before he left, he thought, just so she'd know he wasn't going after Walker alone. Maybe they'd find him soon and it would all be over. Maybe.

Gary Lester followed close behind. The wind had come up and he could hear it whipping around tree tops. The clouds were moving so fast it looked as though they were being pulled across the sky by invisible strings. When they were a little more than a thousand yards in, they both began shouting. They stopped and listened, but there was no response and there wasn't the sound of anyone moving toward them.

"Think he's takin' another route back?" Gary Lester asked.

"I don't know," Aaron said, surprised himself at the tone of defeat in his answer. "Who the hell knows? Never thought he'd do this," he said, but he lowered his voice so it was more like a voiced thought.

"That so?" Gary Lester said. He said it so strangely

that Aaron stopped and looked back at him. He was gazing off to the right.

"What's up?"

"I thought I heard somethin' off there. Did you hear a car after we had gone into the woods a ways?"

"Sure, but I just thought it was someone traveling the road. What of it?"

"I don't know," Gary Lester said, but he looked worried about it. He panned the forest for a few more moments and then shook his head and walked on. "What's the doctor's wife's car doin' here?"

"Well, I know he's been hunting," Aaron said.

"Doc Fern?"

"Always did as long as I've known him. I knew his father, too and he was a hunter. Hunted with my father."

"Didn't he know about the moratorium? Doctor or no doctor, he's violating it if he's in here. Did he know about it?"

"I don't know, Gary."

Aaron didn't want to get anyone in trouble.

"Big game hunting season," Gary Lester mumbled. "All the great white hunters treating guns like toys. They think they're in a carnival shooting at metal ducks. It's all become another game. Nothing is like it was. Except maybe for you," he added with some distinct bitterness in his voice.

"That's not true," Aaron said. "I wish it was."

"You hear someone?" Lester said sharply and pointed his rifle to the right.

"WALKER?" Aaron shouted.

They listened. The forest was dead silent again. Aaron's heart starting to pound with that instinctive sense of danger. His eyes were everywhere, searching ever heavily overgrown area of bushes, every fallen tree.

They continued to call and listen, moving further and further into the forest. Aaron's concern for Walker intensified. He was barely holding back a sense of panic. His brother should have returned to this point, he thought. By now he should be at least this far. Once, when they stopped to listen, he thought he did hear someone moving through the forest. They both screamed loudly, but when they were finished, there was no response and no sound of movement.

It had already grown a few shades darker. The forest took on a gloomier appearance. Skeletonlike trees became distorted figures against the bleak, grey sky. The absence of any real forest life lent a tone of desolation to the wooded scene. Aaron felt different signals coming at him. There wasn't the sense of calm and balance here now. Rather there was something high pitched and shrill in the air.

What was more disconcerting was he felt no kinship to the man who accompanied him. Now, deep in the forest, he felt alone. Gary Lester had suddenly become eerily silent as if the loss of light closed in on his ability to voice anything but an occasional grunt. There was none of the typical idle chatter going between them that hunters had, sometimes to cover their own innate sense of fear. There were no words to link them together, no common bond in Nature that he usually felt with a companion.

As a result Aaron's mind was left free to think, to imagine horrid thoughts. Before long he began to envision Walker's body, sprawled out and butchered just the way Al Jones had been. The possibility of such a scene terrorized him. Once, he stopped and jumped back when he mistook a broken hanging branch in the distance for a man's dangling body. Even more vivid recollections of Al Jones returned, rushing over his mind, tormenting him with the threat.

"I don't know." Gary Lester finally said. "We might better think of starting back. It's getting too dark and too late, and maybe he's gone out another way and we're just wasting time and energy. What'dya think?"

"Maybe." Actually, that was just what Aaron was hoping for now. "If we go to that ridge there and shout a bit, it should carry pretty far."

"Um. I'll let go a round with this too," Gary Lester said tapping the rifle.

Aaron walked faster. He placed all his optimism on this final attempt to raise his brother. Surely from this position, they could be heard. Walker had to respond. He just had to. Gary Lester didn't keep up with the increased pace, so Aaron reached the ridge about thirty seconds before him. He shouted and listened. Then he turned to look back.

Gary Lester had raised his rifle. For a moment, Aaron thought he was pointing it at him. He remembered thinking that the man was carelessly slow about it. He was going to say something to him and took one step forward before the shot rang out. It sounded like a clap made by two giant metal hands. Everything was so quiet around him just before it, creating a striking contrast and amplifying the gun's rapport.

He felt his body snap so hard to attention, he thought he might have cracked his spine. All of his reflexes jumped. A hot streak passed across the nape of his neck. The very life inside him shuddered.

He saw the left side of Gary Lester's neck explode in a pulpy mass of flesh. The blood shot out and created an instant spray of red droplets. Gary's head fell to the left, tipping over like a jolted bowling pin. He shrugged as would a man who had just experienced a terrible chill, and then his body folded to the earth in the manner of a puppet whose strings had just been cut.

Aaron reached forward dumbly, as if the gesture could pump life back into Gary Lester's body. His hand folded instinctively into a fist and then he went into a crouch. The gunshot had reverberated throughout the forest, but to him it seemed to go mostly directly behind, traveling in waves, rolling over the forest floor, winding around trees until it died out in the depth of the woods.

A number of thoughts went through his mind— get Gary Lester's rifle, dive over the ridge, hit the earth quickly, run. All the options lined themselves up in computer speed. However, choice was taken away from him by the advent of a second shot. The bullet tore up the soggy ground in front of him, spitting earth and small rocks up at him and around him.

He turned and somersaulted down the ridge, tucking his head in with a gymnast's expertise, and rolled over and over until he landed on his back, his arms out to his sides. Then he rolled onto his stomach, looked back once, and jolted forward into the forest, running with all his might, slapping down branches and bushes in his way. After what seemed to be minutes, but what was really no more than twenty to thirty seconds, he slowed down and got control of himself.

Visually, he replayed the events that had just occurred, while he listened hard for sounds of his pursuer and caught his breath. Branches cracked in his wake. Someone was coming and coming quicky.

Aaron dropped to all fours. His only chance might be to jump the man. He held his breath. He could see a figure silhouetted in the trees. He seemed to run right into one, spin and then start again. As he drew closer, Aaron hugged the earth, but kept his eyes up and then, the man burst out and Aaron's heart felt like it had just done a total flip.

There, standing only ten yards away was Dr. Fern. Totally naked.

❦

Aaron rose cautiously. The doctor was just turning in a mad circle. His face, his chest and his legs were all badly scratched from the branches and bushes he surely had run through, probably without even feeling the pain. He looked in too deep a shock to feel anything.

"Doc," Aaron called.

Doctor Fern brought his hands to his face to prevent himself from seeing something horrible.

"Doc, it's me, Aaron Kuhn," Aaron called as he walked toward him. "What the hell is happening?"

Slowly, Doctor Fern lowered his hands. He contemplated Aaron.

"Doc." Aaron shook him.

His eyes cleared, but then another bullet ripped through the trees and sizzled by the both of them.

Doc Fern didn't wait. He charged ahead again. Aaron followed, pausing and crouching at the top of the next crest. Doc Fern tripped and toppled down the other side.

Whoever it was who was shooting at them, he wasn't coming with frantic pursuit. He was coming through the woods with the slow, deliberateness of one who knew he had control, one who knew he would get his game. It was this sense of calm pursuit that Aaron knew well. It came with the confidence and the knowledge that he had the game where he wanted it and he was getting it to do what he wanted it to do. All that remained was to follow the path and close in. The harder work had been done. This was the finishing.

For many hunters, the kill always seemed too quick. One pulled the trigger and instantly ended the chase. There was no long, drawn out struggle. The strategy had been worked out well and the job had been done. Sometimes it reminded him of when he built up an event in his mind—planned it out, waited for it and waited for it. When it finally came and went, there was always a sense of letdown. So it was with the finishing. At times he had almost wished the deer could get up again and go off so that the hunt could go on.

He had once discussed this in the shop with a few of the guys who hunted, and someone suggested they all use anesthetic bullets. Then someone else said they were all nuts. He felt relieved when he finally got the deer. Eventually, everyone but him were swayed to that point of view. Funny thinking about that now, he thought. He chastised himself for being too calm, too philosophical precisely at the wrong moment.

He turned and hurried down the hill to help Doc Fern back to his feet.

"Who's after us?" he asked.

Doc Fern looked at him, his eyes widening. He shook his head. And then as if Doc Fern believed Aaron was holding him to set him up for an execution, he ripped out of Aaron's grip and charged on.

"Damn. Not that way at least," he cried, ran up beside him and cuffed the doctor's right wrist, tugging him forcefully toward a bank of pine trees. The much older man followed, but he was nearly at the end of his energy tank. He stumbled and fell forward, gasping for breath before his eyes went back in his head and he dropped to the earth.

Aaron still held his wrist, but the older man's arm was totally limp.

Another bullet ripped through the trees around them.

Aaron pulled the naked man up and threw him

over his shoulder in a fireman's carry and continued on. For a while he didn't seem slowed much by the man's weight. He was driven now by his own raging panic and that had given him a surge of energy and strength he didn't know he had.

As he ran deeper into the forest, he wondered about Walker. A sense of confirmed doom came offer him. The killer was out here now; he was most likely out here before. He slowed down, and then the foreboding turned into a rage. Whoever it was who had been hunting the doctor and who had killed Gary Lester might have already killed his brother. He wanted to confront this evil. He wanted to turn and face this evil force, not flee from it and leave it out here to do more damage, issue more death.

Something deep within him stirred. He had sensed it was there, but he had never felt it as strongly as he did now. Whenever he lost his temper badly, it came out slightly. It bad nudged him that night in O'Heany's when he struck Collins. It was something primeval; something held back, coated with generations and generations of civilized ways. It had been quieted and contained, but never completely destroyed. He had always sensed it was there, but not until now did he welcome it so much.

With the doctor on his back he certainly couldn't outrun the killer. The man would come straight on, gaining more and more until he had him in range. He couldn't help but think of the man as the hunter and himself as the game. As long as that relationship existed, he was at a disadvantage.

This man was clever. When he stopped, the man stopped, listened and moved forward carefully, moving with a precision that reminded Aaron of himself. It was eerie—as if he was actually hunting himself down. He couldn't afford to stand still and think about it. He had to do something to change the relationship.

He carried no weapons. He hadn't even worn a hunting knife. For a few moments, he chastised himself for that and then he realized he hadn't gone downtown with the intention of ending up in the woods. What was he doing here like this? He tried to reason out events in order to understand what had happened so quickly. It frightened him because it made him feel as though fate or destiny had worked this out.

A branch cracked close enough for him to panic. He plodded on, trying to think as he moved. It was clear that both he and Gary Lester had walked right into another pursuit and vicious murder. They must have interrupted his chasing Doctor Fern. How did the doc come to be here? How did the killer know he was? Was he something supernatural? It seemed as though he just appeared. Did he cruise looking for parked vehicles and then enter the forest?

As he spun around trees and cut through the brush, he thought about the buck he had killed. He had tracked it well and come upon it so stealthily that it didn't sense his presence until moments before he fired. He brought it down with one clean shot. He did not look back now as he ran, but he couldn't help imagining the same for himself—a shot would ring out and he would fall, pierced fatally by the bullet. The thought terrorized him.

He was slowing down. His legs were beginning to sing with pain. The doc was too heavy a burden after all. How did I get into this place? he wondered. There was really no comparison between himself and a deer. The deer had no foresight, no imagination. It had no idea about the impending doom. It could fear, but it couldn't envision. It couldn't see itself killed in this manner. He could and he suffered for not using that intuition to its fullest. Was his death now inevitable?

He stopped and listened. The branches cracked under foot. He lowered the doc and studied the forest. Why couldn't he see him? The noises stopped, too. Was he looking right at him, waiting for Aaron to make a move one way or another? Still toying with him?

Aaron heard Doc Fern groan and looked down at

him. If he left him behind, he was sure to leave him to be killed, but if he tried to carry him any farther, he would surely ensure his own death as well. He's watching, waiting to see what I will decide, he thought. That has to be it.

He suddenly realized that the very clothing meant to protect him under normal circumstances now helped mark him for death. His bright red and black checkered coat made him feel like a dog with a can tied to its tail. No matter how hard it ran, it couldn't shake it off. Here he was trying to seek sanctuary in the depth of the forest, heading for deeper woods, and all the while he forgot he was wearing a loud announcement of his very presence. How stupid.

He peeled it off quickly and threw it to his right, treating it like a bomb about to explode. It got hung up on a bush.

Sorry, Doc, he thought. There's no chance for the two of us, but if I can get out, I can get so help maybe. Perhaps, if the doc was still . . .

Aaron fell to his knees and scooped up as many fallen leaves and other forest debris as he could, spreading it over the physician's body. Maybe the killer would be confident of getting the doc and concentrate on him, anyway. If he had to bother with him, he might lose me, Aaron thought. That's a hope.

"It's all I can do for you, Doc," he muttered.

The older man moaned and turned slightly, his eyes still closed.

Aaron started away, determined to run his heart out, but suddenly he stopped and looked at his hanging jacket. It clung to him like someone's insistent advice, and in the moment he realized a course of action.

He scooped the jacket up again and ran on, searching wildly for just the right location. He came to a small clearing—an oasis of sod and earth in the midst of thick woods. Just to the right of it lay a good size poplar tree. Rotted and weighed down by weather and wind, it was a victim of ice storms and vicious winter blizzards. The forest was filled with similar casualties. It was Nature's way of weeding out the weak and sickly. Sometimes, after a particularly bad winter, he recalled going into the forest and feeling as if he had wandered into a battlefield just after the fight had ended.

There wasn't a moment to lose now. He knew the man was only a short distance away.

He's enjoying this, Aaron thought. He probably could have killed me back where he shot Gary Lester, but deliberately had aimed directly at the earth before me to get me running. He wanted this chase and anyone who wanted it could probably bring it to an end at will. Aaron had to take an unexpected action. It was his only hope.

He went to the poplar tree and placed the jacket carefully behind it, permitting enough of it to show so it would look as though he was hiding behind it. The man would come into the small clearing and see the colors. It would catch his attention and hopefully, cause him to hesitate. Everything would hang on just how long he would pause and what he would do.

Aaron looked around quickly and spotted a particularly heavy bush to the left. It really wasn't sufficient cover for a good hiding place, but with his dark shirt and dark pants, perhaps he could blend in enough to remain unseen for the small amount of time he needed. It was a deadly gamble and he tried not to think of the odds or the consequences of failure. What he did know was if he continued to try to outrun him, he would lose.

As he crouched down and held his breath, it struck him how ironic it was that he was now using the strategy of a deer. He recalled a story his father had once told him.

"I remember your grandfather and I had chased this one buck for more'n a few miles when we came upon a doe and two fawn. 'Least we thought that's all there was. After they had fled, we paused near the spot they had been standing in. We were talkin' and smokin', just takin' a breather, you know, when all of a sudden Pa lets out a howl and points no more than ten yards away. There, submerged in the leaves was a fawn, probably only a day or two old at the most. Most men mighta walked right by it, honest to Pete. There it was, the tiniest little creature and it had somehow sensed protection in being still and merging with the landscape. Don't tell me about instinct," he said. "I seen instinct up close."

He heard the killer coming harder and faster now, and he realized that the killer's strategy had taken a new turn. He was no longer concerned about his being heard when Aaron stopped running. He had probably decided it was time for the kill. It was terrifying to think that another man had actually settled on taking his life, that another man was closing in with that intention.

As a boy when he was in fights, or even as a young man when he had occasion to defend himself, there was always that safety valve—that belief this would all stop before it actually became fatal. This chase had now gone past the fail safe point as far as his own life was concerned, and although so much of him fought to push that reality away, the visions of Lester's body sprawled on the forest floor, blood pouring forth freely, and the sight of naked Doc Fern running for his life served to bring it all home.

His heart pumped madly; his muscles tensed. Although he wore no coat, he was not cold nor did he once think of his own comfort as he squatted there in the cold wet earth. He listened with all his strength. He stared at the sound of cracking branches and crushed leaves and he waited. It was dusk now and when the man first appeared, he was cloaked in shadow. He wore the forest like a mask, but his silhouette was familiar.

This familiarity brought the sound of terror that rang in his head at an increasingly higher and higher pitch. He thought he would explode because of it. As the man drew closer to the clearing, he slowed his pace. When the killer stopped to listen, Aaron realized who it was, even though something about him had Aaron confused. He wasn't wearing his uniform, at least not his own uniform. He was wearing the uniform of a correction officer. He was wearing his father's old uniform. The realization came with the impact of a blow, shortening his breath.

Willie Brand stood no more than ten yards away. He was smiling madly as he held his rifle up around his waist and waited. It was an insane contest of silence and hearing. Aaron fought to keep thoughts and questions out of his mind. He needed to devote his full attention to remaining still and unheard. But why Willie Brand? What had made him into this maniac? Why was he wearing his father's clothes?

We always miss the obvious, Aaron thought. We had envisioned the killer to be a distorted figure from some horror movie. It made us blind. Willie was a weird sort of a guy. He lived alone, and without a family, his whole life seemed wrapped up in small town law enforcement. Aaron remembered once thinking that Willie Brand was married to his badge the way a nun was married to the church.

But there had to be more reason for all this. There had to be.

Brand took a few steps forward. As he drew closer to the small clearing, he turned his head slightly, almost like a wild animal tuning in sounds. It was chilling, eerie. There was truly something creature-like about him. His face was distorted, his mouth horribly twisted.

Aaron remained poised, but his calf muscles tightened so hard they ached him. Brand studied the clearing for a few moments and then smiled wider and relaxed.

He took larger steps, unconcerned about the noise now. He was heading for the fallen poplar tree. When he entered the clearing, Brand lifted his rifle to his chest and turned his whole body toward the downed tree.

Aaron didn't hesitate. He became an animal of brute instinct, raw and determined. To be otherwise would only detract from his effectiveness and slow down his reaction time. He sprang forward, leaping with all his strength toward Brand.

The crazed police chief turned in surprise just as Aaron drove himself into Brand's side. Brand lost grip on the rifle, and the two of them fell.

It became a struggle between two muscular giants. Brand's constant weight lifting and exercise had resulted in broad, thickly muscular shoulders. The sinewy lines in his neck strained as he twisted around to push off the grip Aaron still had around his lower chest.

But Aaron's arms were viselike. Rage and hysteria added intensity to his powerful body. Unable to break the hold, Brand reached out to dig his fingers into Aaron's face, trying to claw at his eyes.

Aaron pulled back and released him. He got to his feet first, and as Brand struggled to stand Aaron drove a hard, left kick just above Brand's Adam's apple, just below his chin. The blow was so painful and so quickly executed that Brand had no chance to defend himself or respond. His teeth slammed together, sending trickles of blood down his gums. He clutched at his neck and gagged, his eyes popping with the struggle to breathe.

Aaron hesitated for only a moment. He leaned forward and drove his malletlike right fist into the left side of Brand's jaw, and the police chief toppled unconscious.

Aaron froze at the sight of him and stared at the unconscious police chief, still finding it incredible that he had been hunted by him and done battle with him. Had all the world had gone mad? He had been dropped into a nightmare and nearly drowned by it. Had this really happened? He looked around to be sure he was still in the forest. Then he looked at Brand again. The man was as still as death. All distortion had left his face. It was difficult now to conceive of him as the mad killer of hunters, even with the incongruity of seeing him in his father's uniform.

Suddenly Aaron felt cold. The calmness that was creeping back over his body extinguished the fires of his passion and rage. He looked around and realized it had grown considerably darker. It was as if he had descended back into the world of reality and was noticing all of the obvious things usually taken for granted. He went for his coat and stopped on the way to pick up the rifle. It was a 308 and the safety was still on. Brand followed good hunting habits, even when he carried out his insanity.

After he put on his coat again, he knelt beside Brand. The police chief stirred slightly. Then he opened his eyes, blinking hard. He groaned and tried to lift his head. Aaron put the end of the rifle barrel against Brand's forehead and forced his head back to the ground. Brand stared up at him, a look of amazement on his face.

"Where's my brother?" Aaron demanded. "Where's Walker?"

"Walker?"

Brand's eyes grew smaller. Then a sensation of stinging pain ran up his face. It felt as though his jaw had been broken. He continued to taste his own blood. Aaron lifted the rifle away, but kept it pointing down at him.

"Why did you do it?" Aaron asked. "Why did you do all this?"

Brand made a feeble effort to get to his feet.

"Did you hurt my brother?"

Brand didn't respond. He was on one knee now and he turned and looked at Aaron. There was something childish about Brand's expression, something almost silly about it. His mouth was closed tightly, but his chin pulled downward. His eyes were small and the lines around his mouth and nose grew deeper and longer.

"Why . . ." Aaron began again, but he stopped as Brand's expression changed rapidly to one of great anger.

"Deer eyes," he whispered. "When I looked at his body, my father's eyes were like deer eyes."

"What? What the hell are you saying, Willie?"

Brand stood up and turned away. He held his left wrist against his stomach and began walking forward.

"I got to get home," he moaned. "My mother, got to tell my mother."

"You're not going home, Willie. We're going back to get Doc Fern," Aaron said quickly. "You better not have done anything to him. Just keep headin' in that direction."

Brand didn't respond. He continued on, staggering through the forest. Aaron followed, watching him and trying to reason out what had to be done now. Suddenly Brand picked up his pace.

"HOLD IT!" Aaron shouted, but Brand went on, almost into a run. Aaron kept after him. It was harder going because of the diminished sunlight, but Brand remained well outlined. As long as he was headed back, Aaron thought, it didn't matter how fast they went.

Suddenly Brand stopped and turned.

Aaron was astonished. The police chief had his pistol in his hand. He held it straight up.

Aaron dove forward. A moment after he landed, he heard the shot ring out. He lifted himself slowly and brought the rifle to his shoulder, but there was no one standing in front of him. He panicked for a moment and berated himself for being so careless as to let Brand walk off with a pistol in his holster. Now he was probably crouched behind a bush and with the increased darkness . . .

Another shot rang out but that didn't sound like a pistol shot, he thought. He hesitated and then stood completely and walked slowly forward. He could see him. Brand lay sprawled on his side. When he drew closer, he saw the streak of blood that had washed over the dead police chief's right eye and down his face. He stood there, staring at him and shaking his head in amazement. The crazed man had gone and shot himself. And right in the forehead, too!

Aaron caught his breath and gazed at the now considerably darkened woods.

"Walker. Doc Fern," he muttered to himself and rushed to get back.

Twelve

Doc Fern was sitting up but dazed when Aaron reached him.

He looked up at him, his clouded eyes beginning to focus. Before he asked anything, he turned sharply and looked back.

"We've to get out of here. Quickly," he said struggling to get to his feet.

Aaron put his jacket around him.

"Easy, Doc. He's gone."

"Gone?"

"Dead. Shot himself back there after I had stopped him. What's going on? Why was Willie Brand doing all this, and why was he dressed in his father's old uniform?"

Doctor Fern shook his head and closed his eyes.

Aaron looked down at the doc's feet. Both of

them were streaked with blood. Walking him back was going to be impossible. He realized it himself and slowly sank back to a sitting position on a dead log. Finding his clothing was just as difficult because he had no idea from what direction the doctor had been running or how long he had been running.

"I'll go get help," he said.

"Wait," Dr. Fern said, grabbing his hand to hold him from walking off. He looked out at the forest, his eyes still bloodshot with panic. "Are you sure he's dead?"

"I'm sure, Doc. I saw the bullet hole in his head. He's dead, believe me."

"Good. Good," he muttered.

Then they heard the gunshot and the shouting. Doctor Fern's eyes went wild again.

"It's a search party. Take it easy."

Aaron shot off Brand's rifle.

"We're over here!" he screamed.

There was another shot in response and then more shouting. He could hear them coming.

"Easy, Doc. We're all right. We'll get you out of here in a few minutes."

"Thank you," he said in a hoarse whisper.

"Why was he doing all this, Doc?"

The physician looked up at him.

"Like some dormant cancer, it came to life in his brain, I guess. I don't know what trigger it exactly.

Could have been anything from the sight of another dead man in the woods to something one of them said. It was wrong to make him beholden, dependent on the trustworthiness of others. I was just as much to blame, just as much a part of it."

"Part of what?"

"The cover-up. Willie Brand killed his own father. It was an accident, one of those horrible things. We were all out there in the hunting party. Willie was all of twelve and shouldn't have been, but his father insisted he come. Thought it would make him more of a man. He taught him how to use the rifle, but he had shot at a deer and forgotten to put it back on safety. He was the one tripped over a log. The gun went off and the bullet struck his father in the forehead, about right here," he said pointing to the center of his own. "He had been turning around to see why the kid shouted out. Boom and he was dead."

"It was Garth Allan's idea to say that Willie's father shot himself. His intention was only to ease the burden on the boy. What difference would it make to anyone? It had been an accident, pure and simple, but for a son to live in this community with everyone knowing . . . it just seemed sensible.

"I wrote the death certificate myself," he added.

"You mean every man who has been shot in the forest was in that hunting party?" Aaron asked.

"Skip Hewett died two ears ago, lung cancer. Smoked it into himself. Other than him, yes. I was the last one, and you know something, Aaron, I never put it together. How could Willie go off like that? He forced me into my wife's car and had me drive out here. This is about where it happened, you know. All the while I couldn't figure it out. Why? Then he made me go into the woods and, well, the rest you know. You should have seen him. It was like looking at a different person. It was like looking at his father. In the end I think that's who he thought he was, his father, returned to take vengeance on us all. That's probably what Willie believed he would do, or what he wanted done, and Willie lived to please that man. You had to see it in his face."

"I saw him."

"I don't think he consciously knew what he was doing himself. I think it's like that Oedipus story, he really was out there at times hunting for his father's killer, not realizing he was his father's killer, and when he did, he went crazy.

"I don't know how I missed it," he chanted, embracing and rocking his body. "The head wounds he inflicted."

"What about them?"

"They resembled the head wound his father suffered. It was a mad sort of vengeance. The guilt festered and festered inside him. I really believe he went into law enforcement as a strange way of balancing his conscience."

"Drop that rifle!" Aaron heard and turned to see Sheriff Winn, a deputy, two state policemen, and another game warden. Both state policemen had drawn out their revolvers. The sheriff's deputy crouched and held his pistol with his elbow braced on his knee.

"Don't shoot," Aaron cried. He realized they thought he was going to shoot the doctor.

"Just drop that rifle," one of the state policemen said. "Then walk forward slowly, with hands raised high."

He did so. As he walked forward the two deputies approached to stop and search him for another weapon.

"That's Aaron Kuhn," the sheriff said. "What's goin' on here?"

Dr. Fern stood up and shouted.

"It's all right. He saved my life. It's all right."

"You two get to Dr. Fern," Winn ordered his deputies. "Help him back. Get a blanket around him and whatever first aide you can give him. Call for an ambulance!" he screamed and they jumped.

"He can't walk on those feet," Aaron said. "They'll have to carry him back."

"Who shot Gary Lester back there?" the game warden demanded.

Aaron lowered his arms.

"Willie Brand, although, maybe not Willie. Maybe his father," he replied.

"What?" Winn said. "What the hell are you talking about? That sure looks like a 308 you dropped."

"It is," he said watching one of the state policemen retrieve it. "It was Willie's father's gun."

"I don't get it," Winn said.

"The doc can explain it better than I can," Aaron told him. "What about my brother?" he asked. "Has anyone found my brother?"

"Where's Willie Brand?" the sheriff demanded instead of replying.

"Brand's back there. He shot himself in the head with his pistol, a nine millimeter."

"Shot himself in the head!"

"We'll tell you everything," Aaron said, "but first, my brother. Gary Lester and I came up here looking for him."

"We know, the sheriff said. "They told us in town." Aaron looked at him and held his breath in anticipation. "Roger Murden here," the sheriff said pointing to the game warden, "saw him drive off as soon as he pulled up. The way he flew off set off alarms and we all converged on the spot. We haven't seen him, since. Why didn't he obey the moratorium?"

"He didn't know about it when he set out. His car was out there!"

"I told you he left. All that's out there," the sheriff said pointing back with his thumb, "is Lester's car and the doc's car. Brand must have come into the woods from another road or something."

"No, he drove the doc up here."

"Huh?"

"Thank God my brother got away," Aaron said thinking about Walker. "He must've circled and come out way up the highway and then walked down just as I had thought. Maybe he heard the shots and panicked."

"Maybe this, maybe that. Now what all this about Willie Brand and his father? I don't understand what you're telling us. He drove the doc up here?"

"I'm telling you in simple language," Aaron said, his eyes fixed on Winn, "that Willie Brand was your mad killer."

"Jeeze, that profiler was right. It was a law enforcement officer punishing hunting law violators."

"It was a lot more than that," Aaron said.

❦

They brought him in the darkness to his house and he was never so glad to see it. Walker's car was parked off to the right, and the porch light was burning. He had told as much of the story as he knew to the sheriff and then, with searchlights, he, and the law enforcement officers went back to find Willie Brand's body. By the time both Lester's and Brand's bodies had been carried out of the woods, the roadway was lined with cars—conservation department vehicles, state police, the BCI, and Steve Dickson.

Aaron was taken directly to Steve Dickson's car. He sat in the back seat and gave him all the details he knew. The state police kept the road blocked off. When it was done and they were taking him away, he was sure he saw Diana in the *Middletown Post* car.

"Don't talk to the press," Dickson told him. "Refer them to me. At least until we conclude this."

He nodded. He wasn't anywhere near the mood that would permit him to talk about it anyway. Before he went home, he went into the garage bathroom and did the best he could to wash off his scrapes and bruises and make them look less than they were. He brushed away as much of the mud and grime he could, fixed his hair and started for the house.

When he opened the front door and stepped into the hallway, his mother came out of the kitchen and stood looking at him. She didn't move toward him or make any gesture of relief, but he saw the look in her eyes.

"I called the police station and they told me where you had gone," she said. "You all right?"

He simply nodded.

"Why were all the police cars in town? There was another death?"

He just looked at her and nodded.

"Thank God you're home, she said. He walked toward her and she pulled him close. For a moment she just held him against her.

"Look at you," she said, released him and stood back.

"I'm all right, Mom," he assured her. "Really, I'm fine."

She nodded and looked at the kitchen.

"He's in there," she said. It was as if she were turning a juvenile delinquent over to the police. Aaron walked into the kitchen.

Walker sat at the table. He held a spoon in his hands and turned it over and over with his fingers while he stared down. Seeing him there like that—frightened and repentant cooled some of his anger. Actually, Aaron was relieved to see him, feeling as though Walker had been brought back from the dead.

"I didn't know about the moratorium," he said without turning. "I didn't expect you to come lookin' for me."

"You knew how she felt about it. You knew what it would do to her. Why was it so important?"

Walker didn't reply.

"I don't understand you."

"Look, I just thought I'd go up there and pop off a doe and come back. I didn't expect to strike out. I kept lookin'. We saw doe up there earlier this year."

"Thought they'd just be waitin' around for you, huh? Who were you tryin' to impress?"

"What'dya mean?"

"When the hell you goin' to grow up?"

"Look," Walker said standing.

"I nearly got killed because of you!" Aaron shouted at him.

All of the details, the struggle, the battle to survive came flooding back over him. His lips trembled. Walker had never seen him this close to hysteria, and the sight put a panic in his face. He looked at his mother for help and then back at Aaron.

Marilyn Kuhn brought her hand to her mouth and stepped back.

"What happened?" she asked. He didn't turn to her.

"Why'd you drive off when you saw the conservation car?" Aaron asked. He felt he needed to know every detail now. It would help bring things back to a logical perspective.

"Figured it was Smokey the Bear. He sat down

again. "Didn't want to hear no lecture from that idiot."

"That idiot's dead," Aaron said.

"Dead?"

"Tell us what happened, Aaron," his mother demanded. She sat down calmly at the table and looked up at him.

"Willie Brand shot him. He shot everybody. He tried to kill me too."

"Willie Brand? Oh dear God." She stared at Aaron, her eyes growing smaller. "You killed him, didn't you?" she asked with stoical acceptance.

Walker looked up expectantly.

"Didn't get the chance. He shot himself," Aaron said.

"After he tried to kill you?" his mother asked. She waited.

He nodded.

"Jesus!" Walker looked at the table and shook his head. "I heard some shooting, but I wasn't going to go back in the woods to see who it was. If I'd a known you were in there," he added turning quickly, "I wouldn't have left, Aaron. You know it."

"I know. Forget it, " he said realizing immediately how stupid a remark it was. "I'm goin' to shower and settle down some. Then I'll tell you all of it, or at least as much as I know."

He turned and walked to the doorway.

"Aaron." Walker stood up and approached him. "I'm. I'm sorry. I . . ."

Aaron nodded and looked over at his mother. She closed her eyes softly and opened them.

"Still got that special dinner?"

"Couldn't eat it all myself," she said. "C'mon, Walker, help with the mashed potatoes."

"Help with the mashed potatoes?"

Aaron laughed and turned to go out again just as the phone rang. All three of them looked at it without moving. The electricity in the air seemed to immobilize them.

"I'd better get it," Aaron said. He took a deep breath and lifted the receiver. "Hello."

"I just wanted to be sure you were all right," Diana said. The sound of her voice immediately relaxed him. It brought warmth back to his body, making him feel good to be alive.

"Can you see what I go through just to get you a good story?"

She laughed.

"I've just gotten bits and pieces, but that's enough to frighten the hell out of me."

"Where are you?"

"Down at the Centerville police station. The district attorney's having a press conference in a little while. Are they going to have you come down?"

"No. I told him I don't want to talk to anyone

about it right now. Let him do it all. It's his show. In the end, it's always their show. Politicians," he muttered.

"How's your mother?"

"She's all right. Now," he added looking at her. She was reheating things at the stove.

"And Walker?"

"Just really realizing what he did. It's striking home."

"I just can't believe it was you with all this."

"Did you eat yet?"

"Eat? I haven't even thought about it."

"Good. I'm about to take a shower. You think you could find your way up here by yourself? I don't want to go downtown just yet."

"Oh, I don't think I should . . ."

"What'ya talkin' about? We have a date. You wanna get the inside scoop, don'tcha?" he teased.

"Your mother might . . ."

"She's gets very annoyed if she makes a dinner and someone doesn't show."

"Okay, I'll be there."

"Good," he said. He held the phone for a moment without speaking and then said goodbye. His mother turned as soon as he hung up. "Diana. I told her she should come to dinner. Is that all right?"

"Of course."

He smiled at her resilience.

"Thanks," he said.

She looked at him and then at the table as if his father was sitting there.

"He'd be proud of you, Aaron. I know he would," she said.

He nodded and thought about it for a moment. Then shook his head.

"I have a date coming. I gotta get cleaned up," he said and rushed up the stairs.

Her laughter was more than just music to his ears. It was relief and it was hope.

❧

Steve Dickson looked as if he knew he had just gotten the nomination for president. The cameras clicked and the television equipment purred. The press conference had been moved to the Centerville community hall, right next door to the police station. It was packed with news people, police, politicians, and Centerville citizens who had learned some of the details and were still in shock.

Bill Douglas stood off to the left, smiling and shaking hands with everyone, taking special care to make comments to the reporters. He acted like a man running for office. Brian Donald talked quietly with the sheriff and Bob Foss.

Dickson turned to the crowd and indicated he

was about to begin. The place became quiet. He milked it, hesitating dramatically to look at some notes again. Then he smiled for the television camera to his left and began.

"We have just informed the governor that there is, in our confirmed opinion, no longer any danger to hunters in Sullivan County. The Maniac Hunter Murderer is dead. The governor will shortly announce the end to a moratorium on hunting in Sullivan County."

He paused and the reporters began.

"Is that true that a local law enforcement agent was the killer?"

"He was the Centerville chief of police. Yes."

There was a great murmur.

"Do you know why the chief of police was carrying out these executions?"

"We have some information, but before we provide a full explanation for what motivated these heinous acts, we want to have a more detailed discussion with our forensic psychiatrist, Doctor Paul Wheeler."

"But Brand's dead," someone said. "How do you evaluate a dead man psychologically?"

Dickson shook his head.

"We have someone who knows the history first-hand and can shed some light on this, but we all recognize our limitations. The public should understand we are doing the best we can under the circumstances. The main thing is we were able to bring it all to a conclusion and guarantee the safety of our visitors. I am proud of the people working with me."

"Wasn't another man killed today?" Diana asked. "Before you brought it to a conclusion?"

"That is true. We have notified his family. He was a conservation officer. A fine, dedicated man, I might add," Dickson said looking toward Brian Donald.

"How close were you to cracking this case before today's events?" Diana pursued.

All the other reporters were looking at her now, everyone wondering why she was driving at Dickson so hard and so sharply with her questions.

"We were right on it. Our investigative team, along with the state investigators, had narrowed things down considerably."

"Then it didn't come as any surprise that the chief of police was investigating murders he himself was committing?" she pursued.

Dickson's discomfort was obvious. He looked to Sheriff Winn for help.

"We didn't exactly pinpoint Willie Brand. We were, however, working under the theory that because all of the victims were violating one hunting law or another at the time of their deaths, it involved someone in law enforcement."

"But wouldn't that lead you to first suspect Gary Lester? His job was to enforce the hunting laws, wasn't it?"

"Gary Lester was a tragic victim today," Dickson shot back. "It behooves us not to add any blight to his fine record and the good memories his family, his children will have."

"The main thing," Bob Foss interjected, "is it's over. Our community is safe again."

"You don't think the governor acted too hastily in declaring a moratorium then?" the local television reporter asked, jumping in to take some of the stage away from Diana.

Steve Dickson looked down and then over at Bill Douglas who stared at him with a dumb smile frozen across his face. Bob Foss took a step closer.

"Well, I'm sure the governor acted out of what he considered to be the best interests of the people. Events happened so rapidly, as you all know. I recommended such a moratorium be put in effect almost immediately, but . . ." He smiled. "The powers that be had other considerations to consider."

"Political and economical?" Diana interjected.

"The main thing now is we have brought this disastrous situation to an end. Out of towners can feel safe coming here to hunt and recreate once again," Dickson practically whined.

Bill Douglas stopped smiling. Bob Foss crossed the room quickly and took him aside.

"There is increased talk about some form of stricter hunting controls," the television reporter said, stepping forward and having his camera man close in as well. "Do you think this is now necessary?"

"Well," Dickson began, looking directly into the camera. It felt good now. He was back into the rhythm of it. It was like campaigning again, being on the road, cameras clicking, people listening. There was forward movement. His train had paused, but it was roaring ahead now. "I don't think we have to go overboard with this. Most all our people who enjoy the sport of big game hunting are reliable, constructive citizens. They obey the rules we have on the books. They are concerned with safety. The point is our system worked. Our dedicated law enforcement agents were on the situation night and day. We have a great deal of which to be proud.

"However, if in the future . . ."

The recorders were on; the pictures being taken. Reporters scribbled quickly. In the back of the hall, citizens were mesmerized. Diana closed her notepad, glared at him with some disgust, and then marched out of the hall. Dickson saw her leave and breathed a sigh of relief.

Downtown the lights still burned at Sam's Luncheonette. Although he and his wife were exhausted from the day's business, they both figured on considerable spill off from the press conference, and the way finances were this time of the year, there was no excuse not to take advantage of every opportunity. It was part of the modern law of survival.

Just another instinct.

Epilogue

AARON HAD TALKED IT ALL OUT, finding relief in passing on the gruesome details.

Walker listened in fascination. His mother reluctantly gave it her full attention.

Diana sat so still it seemed as though she thought he would stop if she made the slightest move. When he was finished, Walker whistled and shook his head. Marilyn Kuhn went for more coffee, and Diana touched his hand. The gesture brought their eyes together and in the moment, he longed to be alone with her.

Afterward, they went for that ride up to the Neversink Dam. The dam served as a reservoir for the New York City Water Department. The area around the dam and most of the land adjacent to it was owned by the City of New York. At one point, however, the road passed nearly over the dam itself and a motorist could pull over and look out over the great lake. It was a beautiful sight at any time of the year.

Although there was no moon, the night sky was filled with stars, for the overcast that had cloaked the day in a dreary ceiling of dark grey had passed on. There was a gleam over the water and the tall trees surrounding the reservoir stood against the darkness, outlined in black draped shadows. They were the silent sentinels, making for a natural fortress. They kept the waters secure in the man-made lake and provided a buffer zone. It gave the reservoir area an untouched, primitive quality. The adjacent woods were fenced off and consequently, it was a reservation for nature. All forms of wildlife were here, especially various types of birds. There were even reports of eagle sightings.

"You were right," Diana said after they parked. "This is a beautiful sight."

"I've come here often by myself, just to sit and think."

"By yourself?" She asked with some skepticism, smiled and sat back.

"Well, in my younger days, I wasn't always alone, but ..."

"Thought so."

She was quiet for a moment and then snuggled

closer to him. They both looked out at the water.

He turned slowly to kiss her and she held onto him like she never wanted to let him go. He could actually feel her trembling in his arms.

"Hey," he said. "It's all right."

She sat back.

"It was really a frightening story you told. From the way you described him, it sounded as if he had reverted to being a child. He was truly out of control, no longer aware of who he was and what he was. As I sat there listening to you, I thought it sounds like *Psycho*, only instead of a Norman Bates becoming his mother, we had a grown man becoming his father out to get some sort of revenge."

"Yes."

"And then alternating between that and becoming a boy again before striking out at those who were threatening to him because of the horrible truth they knew and held over him."

Aaron nodded.

"The doc thought one of them might have triggered it with an inadvertent threat or something. Who knows? As far as he being a madman, I don't mind telling you, I was about as frightened as I've ever been when I saw his face. It was like rubber, changing, distorting, even his eyes."

"It's all right to be frightened, but you weren't just frightened, Aaron. You kept your cool and did what you had to do to survive. I don't know any man who could have done what you did," she added.

He felt his ego bloat, especially hearing these words from her.

"Sometimes, even liberated girls like me like to be in the arms of a real man," she kidded.

He laughed and then she shook her head.

"Talk about strength though. Your mother's so strong. Other women wouldn't have been able to listen or would have broken down and cried."

"Old stock."

"You really believe people have changed, don't you?"

"For the most part, yes. A lot of things have changed and have changed us."

"What about your concept of the hunt?" she challenged. He loved the sparkle in those eyes, a sparkle caught in the moonlight.

"That too. Hey," he said smiling, "this isn't one of your interviews, is it?"

"Never know until the morning paper comes out."

He laughed and she moved closer to him.

"You did promise me an exclusive report, you know," she said.

"It might take some time. This is a story that begins years and years ago."

"I don't care how long it takes," she said, her voice barely above a whisper now.

He leaned toward her and they kissed again. It was gentle at first; then he pulled her closer to him and they kissed harder and longer.

"Looks like I'm getting emotionally involved in my work," she said.

"That bad?"

"Not in this case." She leaned into his shoulder. "I suppose it will be a while before there is a real conclusion to all this."

"Frankly, I'll be glad to get back into the shop."

"The place will be a madhouse. You and Walker won't get much work done."

"Don't I know it?"

"Maybe it's time for a vacation."

"Not this time of the year. Too much work. After a while, this too shall pass, although for the moment, it's hard to believe it."

"You're a funny guy, Aaron Kuhn. I think it's going to take me a while to really understand you."

"Feel free to take your time. Schedule as many interviews as you like."

She laughed and they kissed again. Something caught her attention as she sat back.

"Look!"

She pointed out the window to the little incline that led down to the forest by the reservoir. A large doe stood quietly, peering in their direction. The moonlight was caught in her eyes."

"Deer Eyes," Aaron said.

"What do you mean?"

"Nothing," he said softly. He was surprised he had uttered the words. He certainly didn't want to tell her what Willie had said. He didn't want to tell anyone. It was something he would carry privately, and it was something that might make him hang up his rifle for a while, a long while.

"She's looking at us, isn't she?"

"She hears us," he said.

"Really? Even through the closed windows?"

"Sure."

"Standing there like that, she looks beautifully curious about us."

"And safe. There's no hunting permitted on the reservoir grounds."

"No hunting?"

"Absolutely not."

"I wish all the deer would come here then," she said. He laughed. "I mean it. I wish there was a safe place for everything and everyone."

There was something in the softness of her voice that made him yearn to keep her near him forever.

"You've got one right here," he said and held her tighter.

They sat there like that, looking back at the deer.

When it had its fill of them, it turned and went back to the darkness, leaving them alone with the water and stars.

And for a little while at least, it was truly as if they and the animal had found the peace and contentment of their own paradise.